P9-DOF-095

WORK SONG

WORK SONG

IVAN DOIG

RIVERHEAD BOOKS
a member of Penguin Group (USA) Inc.
New York
2010

RIVERHEAD BOOKS

Published by the Penguin Group

Penguin Group (USA) Inc., 375 Hudson Street, New York, New York 10014, USA ·
Penguin Group (Canada), 90 Eglinton Avenue East, Suite 700, Toronto,
Ontario M4P 2Y3, Canada (a division of Pearson Penguin Canada Inc.) ·
Penguin Books Ltd, 80 Strand, London WC2R 0RL, England · Penguin Ireland,
25 St Stephen's Green, Dublin 2, Ireland (a division of Penguin Books Ltd) ·
Penguin Group (Australia), 250 Camberwell Road, Camberwell,
Victoria 3124, Australia (a division of Pearson Australia Group Pty Ltd) ·
Penguin Books India Pvt Ltd, 11 Community Centre, Panchsheel Park,
New Delhi–110 017, India · Penguin Group (NZ), 67 Apollo Drive, Rosedale,
North Shore 0632, New Zealand (a division of Pearson New Zealand Ltd) ·
Penguin Books (South Africa) (Pty) Ltd, 24 Sturdee Avenue,
Rosebank, Johannesburg 2196, South Africa

Penguin Books Ltd, Registered Offices:
80 Strand, London WC2R 0RL, England

Library of Congress Cataloging-in-Publication Data

Doig, Ivan.
Work song / Ivan Doig.
p.   cm.
ISBN 978-1-59448-762-0
1. Single men—Fiction.   2. Miners—Fiction.   3. Butte (Mont.)—Fiction.
4. Mine rescue work—Fiction.   5. Montana—History—20th century—Fiction.
I. Title.
PS3604.O415W67   2010   2009042647
813'.6—dc22

Printed in the United States of America
1   3   5   7   9   10   8   6   4   2

BOOK DESIGN BY AMANDA DEWEY

This is a work of fiction. Names, characters, places, and incidents either are the product of the
author's imagination or are used fictitiously, and any resemblance to actual persons, living or dead,
businesses, companies, events, or locales is entirely coincidental.

While the author has made every effort to provide accurate telephone numbers and Internet
addresses at the time of publication, neither the publisher nor the author assumes any responsibility for errors, or for changes that occur after publication. Further, the publisher does not have any
control over and does not assume any responsibility for author or third-party websites or their
content.

To Carol Doig,
for all the harmony

WORK SONG

1

Morgan, did you say your name is? Funny things, names." The depot agent, an individual so slow I thought I might have to draw a line on the floor to see him move, was gradually commencing to hunt through the baggage room for my trunk, shipped ahead. "Any relation to old J.P., Mister Moneybags himself?"

I sighed as usual over that. His remark could hardly have been farther from the mark. Nonetheless, I couldn't resist dishing back some of the same.

"Cousins, thrice removed. Can't you tell by looking?"

The railway man laughed more than was necessary. "That's about as removed as it gets, I'd say." Poking into one last cluttered corner, he shook his head. "Well, I'll tell you, Mr. Third Cousin, that trunk of yours took a mind of its own somewhere between there and here. You could put in a claim, if you want."

So much for a storybook *Welcome back!* to the Treasure State, as Montana liked to call itself. While waiting for some sign of life in the agent, I already had been puzzling over the supposed treasure spot in plain view out the depot window—the dominant rise of land, scarred and heaped and gray as grit, which was referred to in everything that I had read as the Richest Hill on Earth, always grandly capitalized. Had I missed something in the printed version? As far as I could see, the fabled mining site appeared rightly christened in only one obvious respect. It was a butte, called Butte.

"You definitely have left me in want." I reacted to the agent's news with honest dismay, equipped with only the battered satchel that accompanied me everywhere. "The bulk of my worldly possessions are in that trunk."

Squinting at me, he tossed aside his agent's cap and donned a businesslike green visor. "Possessions like that do tend to bulk up when the claim form comes out, I'd say." He slipped the pertinent piece of paper onto the counter in front of me, and I filled it out as expected, generous to myself and not the railroad.

The most precipitous chapter of life always begins before we quite know it is under way. With no belongings to speak of, I gathered what was left of my resolve and stepped outside for my first full look at where I had arrived.

Everything about Butte made a person look twice. My train journey had brought me across the Montana everyone thinks of, mile upon hypnotic mile of rolling prairie with snowcapped peaks in the distance, and here, as sudden and surprising as a lost city of legendary times, was a metropolis of nowhere: nearly a hundred thousand people atop the earth's mineral crown, with nothing else around but the Rocky Mountains and the witnessing sky. The immediate neighborhood on the skirt of land out from the depot, as my gaze sorted it out, seemed to hold every manner of building from shanty to mansion, church to chicken coop, chop suey joint to mattress factory, all mixed together from one topsy-turvy block to the next. Butte stood more erect as the ground rose. In the city center, several blocks on up the slope, lofty buildings hovered here and there waiting for others to catch up, and the streets also took on elevation, climbing the blemished hill until workers' cottages mingled with mines and dump heaps along the top of the namesake butte. Up there, the long-legged black steel frameworks over the mineshafts populated the skyline like a legion of half-done miniatures of Eiffel's tower.

So, in some ways Butte appeared to me to be the industrial apotheosis of that proverbial city built upon a hill, and in other aspects the copper mining capital of the world showed no more pattern than a gypsy camp. I have to admit, I felt a catch at the heart at how different the whole thing was from the solitary homesteads and one-room school I had known the last time I tried my luck in this direction. Everything I knew how to part with I'd left behind in a prairie teacherage. But an urge can spin the points of a compass as strongly as the magnetism of ore, and in spite of all that happened back then, here I was once more in that western territory at the very edge of the map of imagination.

While I was busy gazing, a couple of bull-shouldered idlers in the shade of the depot eyed me with too much curiosity; somehow I doubted that they were sizing me up for any family resemblance to J. P. Morgan of Wall Street. With barely a glance their way, I squared my hat and hastened past as though I had an appointment. Which could be construed as the truth of the moment. The Richest Hill on Earth and I—and, if my hope was right, its riches—were about to become acquainted.

FIRST THINGS FIRST, though. I set out up the tilted city streets in search of lodging. In the business district ahead, proud brick buildings stood several stories above a forest of poles and electrical wires, another novelty I had not encountered in earlier Montana. But the world of 1919 was not that of a decade before in hardly any other way either; the Great War and four years of trenches filled with mud and blood had seen to that.

"Red-hot news, mister? Can't get any newer!" A boy with a newspaper bag as big as he was came darting to my side. I handed him a coin and he scampered off, leaving me with a freshly inked *Butte Daily Post.* The front page could barely hold all the calamitous items there were to post. ATT'Y GENERAL WARNS OF DOMESTIC BOLSHEVIKS . . . BUTTE BREWERY SHUTTERED BY 'DRY' LAW . . . WILSON CAUTIONS AGAINST 'WINNING THE WAR, LOSING THE PEACE' . . . BOSTON POLICE THREATEN TO STRIKE . . . America in that agitated time; not merely a nation, but something like a continental nervous condition.

There was little time left in my day for such thoughts: I needed a place for the night. The airy accommodations I could glimpse in the lofty blocks ahead were beyond the reach of my wallet. I dreaded the sort of fleabag hotel that I would have to resort to without my trunk—even the most suspicious hostelry, in my experience, unblinkingly provided a room if the luggage was prosperous enough. While I was studying the lay of the city and trying to divine my best approach, a sign in the bow window of a hillside house with a spacious yard caught my eye.

CUTLETS AND COVERLETS

OR, IF YOU'RE NOT WELSH:

BOARD AND ROOM

Intrigued, I headed directly to the blue-painted front door.

My knock was answered by a woman a good deal younger

than I expected a boardinghouse mistress to be. She was compact, in the manner of a dressmaker's form, shapely but with no excess. A substantial braid the color of flax tugged the upper lines of her pleasant face toward quizzical, as though she were being reined by some hand unseen. Whatever proportion of the world had knocked on this door, she seemed freshly inquisitive about a caller such as myself, well-dressed but not well-heeled. Her violet eyes met mine in mutual appraisal. "Madam," I began with a lift of my hat, "I feel the need—"

"I've heard that one before from half the men in Butte. I'm not a madam," she said, cool as custard, "and this is not a house of ill repute. For your information, that's on the next block over." The door began to shut in my face.

"Let me start again," I amended rapidly. "With night overtaking me in a city where I don't know a soul, I feel the need of warm quarters and a solid meal. Your sign appears to offer those."

"Ah, Griff's latest masterpiece. It caught your eye, did it." She peeped around the doorframe to consider the freshly painted words, a lilt coming into her voice. "He'd turn this into Cardiff West if he could. Step on in, please, Mr.—?"

"Morgan. Morris Morgan."

"Griff will approve, you sound as Welsh as a daffodil." She extended a slender but work-firmed hand, and I noted the less-than-gleaming wedding band on her other one. "Grace Faraday, myself." Appraising the newspaper under my arm and the satchel I was gripping, she paused. "Are those all of your belongings?"

"It's a long story," I said, as if that explained everything.

The upstairs room she showed me was neat and clean, with subdued wallpaper. On the bed was a coverlet of an old style with an embroidered dragon rampant; it would be like sleeping under a flag of Camelot. I can be picky, but I liked everything I had met up with under this roof so far.

As I toggled the switch to make sure the overhead electric bulb worked—another innovation—my landlady-to-be similarly checked me over. "Drummer, are you?"

It took me a moment to recall that the term meant a traveling salesman, one who drums up business. "No, life has given me other rhythms to march to, Mrs. Faraday. My family originally was in the glove trade, until circumstances did that in. I now do books."

"Poetry?" she asked narrowly.

"Ledgers."

"Then you'll appreciate my own bookkeeping, which starts with a week's rent in advance."

"Very wise," I said with composure, although coming up with the sum took nearly every bit I had. Now I really had to hope opportunity of some sort presented itself without delay.

"Welcome to Butte, Mr. Morgan," my new landlady said with a winning smile, complete with dimple, as she pocketed my cash. "Supper's at dark this time of year."

THE DINING TABLE WAS LAID for four when I came down a few minutes early to scout the premises. There was no wax fruit nor fussy display of doilies on the sideboard, a good sign. Instead, under the blaze of the modest but efficient electrical chandelier, a wedding photograph was propped in the spot of honor. Grace Faraday, even more fresh-faced than now, smiled out as capriciously as if the white of her bridal gown were a field of ermine, while beside her in a suit of approximate fit stood a foursquare fellow I took to be the prominently mentioned Griff. He at least had good taste in women and mustaches, as he wore a full-lipped Rudyard Kipling version not unlike my own.

Just then my hostess popped out of the kitchen with a bowl of boiled potatoes and nodded to where I was to sit, saying, "Make yourself to home, the other pair will be right along. Griff had to stoke the furnace and I told him to go wash up or eat in the street—ah, here's the thundering herd."

Through the doorway limped two scrawny half-bald figures that made me think I was seeing double. Both wore work overalls that showed no evidence of work, both held out knobby hands for a shake, and both were grinning at me like leprechauns, or whatever the Welsh equivalent might be.

The nearer one croaked out: "I'm Griff. Welcome to the best diggings in Butte."

"Same here," echoed the other. "I'm Hoop."

Was it humanly possible? I wondered, doing my best not to glance in the direction of the wedding photo during the handshake exchange with the wizened Griff. What manner of marriage could deplete a man from that to this?

With a twinkle, the lady of the house rescued me from my confusion. "These specimens are Wynford Griffith and Maynard Hooper, when no one is looking. They've been part of the furniture here since my husband passed on and I've had to take in boarders." As the duo took their places like old Vikings at a feast, she delivered the sufficient benediction: "We all three could be worse, I suppose."

"I'll try to fit in, Mrs. Faraday."

"Start by saving words and call me Grace, even though this pair of old Galahads refuses to."

"Wouldn't be right, Mrs. Faraday," Griff or Hoop said.

"Manners is manners," said Hoop or Griff.

"I go by Morrie." I dealt myself in, and formalities fell away in favor of knives and forks.

"Didn't I tell you, Hoop?" Griff said as he sawed at his meat. "That new sign works like a charm. What part of Wales do your people hail from, Morrie?"

"Chicago."

"Before they crossed the pond," he persisted.

"Griff, I am sorry to say, the exact family origins are lost in the mists of"—I searched the gazeteer of my mind—"Aberystwyth and Llangollen."

"The grand old names," he proclaimed, adding a spatter of un-intelligible syllables that could only have been Welsh. "'Tis the language of heaven."

"Why nobody talks it on earth," Hoop explained.

By then I was on about my third bite of the meat and ready to ask. "Venison?"

"Close," Grace allowed guardedly. "Antelope."

"Ah." I looked down at the delicate portion. "What a treat to be served cutlets." I emphasized the plural. "Are there seconds?"

She mulled that. "Tonight there are." Off she went to the kitchen stove.

While we awaited replenishment, the history of my tablemates came out. Now retired—"at least the tired part"—the pair had been miners, to hear them tell it, practically since the dawn of Butte. Which was to say, since copper became a gleam in the world's eye. The Hill, as they called it, held the earth's largest known deposit of the ore that wired everything electrical. Much of this I knew, but there was a tang to hearing them recite it with the names of mines such as Orphan

Girl and Moonlight and Badger. The crisscross of their conversation about life deep underground was such that I sometimes had to remind myself which was Griffith and which was Hooper. Although they looked enough alike to be brothers, I figured out that they had simply worked together so long in the mineshafts that the stoop of their bodies and other inclinations had made them grow together in resemblance as some old married couples do.

"So, Morrie, you've latched on in life as a bookkeeper, Mrs. Faraday says," Griff was holding forth as Grace appeared with the replenished meat platter, rosettes from the cookstove heat in her attractive cheeks. It was surprising how much more eye-catching she was as the Widow Faraday.

"Except when the books keep me." Both men bobbed quizzically and Grace sent me a glance. Offhand as my comment was, it admitted to more than I probably should have. With rare exceptions, my stints of employment had been eaten away by the acid of boredom, the drip-by-drip sameness of a job causing my mind to yawn and sneak off elsewhere. One boss said I spent more time in the clouds than the Wright brothers ever dreamt of. I had found, though, that I could work with sums while the remainder of my brain went and did what it wanted. "But, yes," I came around to Griff's remark about bookkeeping, "I have a way with numbers, and Butte by all accounts produces plentiful ones. First thing in the morning, I'll offer my services at the office of the mining company, what is its name—Anaconda?"

Forks dropped to plates.

"You're one of those," Grace flamed. Yanking my rent money from her apron pocket, she hurled it to the table, very nearly into the gravy boat. "Leave this house at once, Whoever-You-Are Morgan. I'll not have under my roof a man who wears the copper collar."

"The—?"

Hooper and Griffith glowered at me. "Anaconda is the right name for company men," Griff growled. "They're snakes."

"But believe me, I—"

"Lowest form of life," Hoop averred.

Enough was enough. Teetering back in my chair as far as I dared, I reached to the switch on the wall and shut off the chandelier, plunging the room into blackness and silence. After a few blank moments, I spoke into the void:

"We are all now in the dark. As I was, about this matter of the Anaconda Company. May we now talk in a manner which will shed some light on the situation?"

I put the chandelier back on, to the other three blinking like wakened owls.

Grace's braid swung as she turned sharply to me. "How on earth, you, can you land into Butte as innocent as a newborn?"

"I have been elsewhere for a number of years," I said patiently. "I knew nothing of this ogre you call Anaconda. To the contrary, I have only seen 'The Richest Hill on Earth' described in the kind of glowing terms the argonauts lavished on the California goldfields in 1849."

Hooper built up a sputter. "That, that's—"

"Hoop, house rules," Grace warned.

"—baloney. The company hogs the whole works. They've turned this town into rich, poor, and poorer."

Griffith furiously took his turn. "Anaconda men sit around up there in the Hennessy Building on their polished—"

"Griff, the rules," came Grace's warning again.

"—rumps, figuring out new ways to rob the workingman. They bust the union, and we build a new one. They bust that, and we try again. Accuse us of being Wobblies, and sic their goons on us."

I looked around the table for the definition. "Wobblies?"

"You really have been off the face of the earth, haven't you," Griff resumed crossly. "The Industrial Workers of the World. They're radical, see, and when they hit town, they tried to edge out our miners' union. The Wobs had their good points, but they riled things up to where the company squashed them and us both."

One chapter spilled over another as Hoop and Grace chorused in on Griff's recital of Butte's story. To hear them tell it, Anaconda was a devilish adversary. The company grudgingly paid good wages when unimaginable millions of dollars flowed in from its near-monopoly on copper, and slashed the miners' pay the instant those profits dipped. Across the past ten years the Hill and the city, I was told, had witnessed a cat's cradle of conflicts among the mineworkers' union, the Wobblies (they were called that, I learned, due to certain members' foreign accents that turned the *double u* sound of "IWW" into *wobble-u*), and the Wall Street–run company. There had been strikes and lockouts. Riots. Dynamitings. The Anaconda Copper Mining Company bringing in goon squads. A lynching, if I understood right, of a suspected IWW labor organizer. And even that was not the worst of the story.

"Then there was the fire." Grace's voice stumbled. "In the Speculator mine two years ago." She drew a breath. "One hundred sixty-four men were killed. My Arthur"—all the eyes in the room, including mine, darted to the wedding picture—"among them."

Griffith and Hooper moved uneasily in their chairs. "We was on the earlier shift," Hoop murmured, "or we'd be pushing up daisies with the rest of them."

In the pause that followed, I sat there before the jury of their faces.

There is something in me that attracts situations, I know there is.

Here I was, faced by three people with whom I had spent only forkfuls of time, asked to make one of those choices in life that can dwarf any other. I had to pick a side, right now, or else hit the chandelier switch again and bolt into the night.

I looked around once more at my expectant tablemates. Mentally asking their pardon for what might be called situational loyalty, I made a show of making up my mind.

"The Anaconda Copper Mining Company," I declared, "shall not have my services."

"Now you're talking!" Griff slapped the table resoundingly and Hoop nodded. Grace favored me with a dimple of approval.

"But what am I to do?" I turned out my hands, empty as they were. "I need work with decent pay to it. My funds have been delayed in the course of my journey." If you substituted *trunk* for *funds*, that was perfectly true. Grace's expression changed for the worse at this news.

Griffith looked the length of the table at Hooper.

"Creeping Pete," said Hoop. "Needs a cryer."

"Possible," said Griff. "Too sober?"

"Not for long."

"Righto. Got just the thing for you, Morrie."

2

The C. R. Peterson Modern Mortuary and Funeral Home admitted just enough daylight through leaded windows to let a few sunbeams wander among the casket display as if shopping from heaven. Otherwise, everything in the building was somber as a dead bouquet, and that included Peterson.

"Hmm." His back turned to me, he was leafing through a blackbound ledger that, with professional interest, I tried to peek at. All I could glimpse past his out-thrust elbows were column headings such as *Place of Death*, *Next of Kin*, and *Payment Due*. "Yes, yes, here they are, Griffith and Hooper, the both of them fully paid up on a 'Miner's Farewell' burial contract, our nicest. Candles and all." He clapped the ledger shut and turned around in creaky fashion. "Sound men, sound judgment. Generally." This last was accompanied by a lidded look that took me in from hat to shoetop.

"I give equal weight to their vouching for you as a possible employer, Mr. Peterson. Your establishment is very, ah, businesslike."

He seemed to brood on that. "Mr. Gorman—"

"Morgan."

"—what would you say recommends you to this line of work?" He swept a hand around the casket display.

You can't just say, *A strong stomach.* I glanced past him to the darkly furnished room that served as the funeral home's chapel, with its waiting bier and an antiquated organ that I could almost tell by looking would wail out notes fit for a Viking pyre. A thought struck me. "My funerary experience is not vast," I admitted, "yet I have been fortunate enough to be an observer at some historically solemn occasions. I happened to witness the funeral procession of Edvard Grieg, to name one."

"In Oslo?" He straightened up like a stork on the alert.

"There under the Scandinavian sky of heroes, with his own music resounding like the heartbeat of the fjords."

"What did they lay him away in?" he whispered.

"Rosewood," came to mind.

"The diamond of woods," Peterson uttered with reverence. "My golly, that casket must have been something pretty to see."

"Unforgettable."

"Hmm." He moved to his desk at such an unctuous pace that I saw where the nickname "Creeping Pete" came from. Picking up a list there, he read off: *"Dempsey, O'Connor, Harrigan—*and that's just this week's deceased. You're hired."

We dickered over the wage and, as we both knew we would, met in the middle. There was a further matter: my attire. Displaying a jacket sleeve nearly worn through at the elbow, I told him my tale of the missing trunk as if it were the loss of a royal wardrobe. "Surely if I am to uphold the name of this establishment, I should be better clothed than circumstances have left me, wouldn't you say?"

Not so much as a *hmm* met that; Peterson apparently took it as a matter of principle that anyone representing the funeral home should be at least as well-dressed as the corpse. He scrawled something on a pad and handed it to me. "Take this over to Gruber the tailor. He'll fix you up."

Tucking the note in my pocket, I turned to go, the vision of a new suit warming me inwardly. "Mr. Morgan," the sepulchral tone stopped me in the doorway. "You have been to Irish wakes before, haven't you?"

I was intimately acquainted with mourning; how many variations could there be? "Uncountable times."

"You start tonight."

"YOU'RE GAINFULLY EMPLOYED? That's not bad for a start." Standing on a chair, Grace took time from feather-dusting the chandelier to nod at me in general approval. "Even if it is when things go 'boo' in the night."

"I am not naturally nocturnal," I admitted, "but that seems to be when wakes take place."

"Just come in quiet, that's the rule of the house." She turned back to brushing at the chandelier with a practiced light touch, its crystals tinkling softly. Turbaned with a towel as she attacked these higher parts of the house, she looked exotic there on her perch, except for the familiarity of the violet gaze whenever she glanced around at me. I watched while she went at the chore, unexpectedly held by her stylish housekeeping. I had intended to go straight to my room and pass the time until lunch relaxing with a book, but the moment would not let loose of me. "You'll get to know the Hill"—Grace's words reached me as if across more distance than was between us—"like it or not."

Rousing myself, I began to say I could blame her prime boarders Hoop and Griff if the job didn't fit, when the floor shook under me, the chandelier crystals rattling as if trying to fly off.

"Jump!" I cried in alarm, my arms out to catch her.

Grace held to where she was, only flashing me a bemused smile. "My, how gallant. It's not an earthquake, if that's what you're thinking. Only dynamite."

Feeling foolish, I toed the floorboards, which seemed to have settled back into place. "What, they're mining here? Right under us?"

"Under every bit of Butte. There are miles and miles of tunnels— Arthur used to say it's like Swiss cheese down there." Her gaze at me had something like a jeweler's appraisal to it now. "Morrie? Do you have a minute?"

"Easily."

She allowed me to help her down from the chair. But as soon as we were settled at the kitchen table, where serious talk is most comfortable, Grace Faraday, landlady, took charge. "There's something you had better know, if you're going to be rooming here for a while." Contemplating me across the oilcloth, she tapped a finger on her cheek as if consulting the dimple. "Besides, you seem the sort who finds out anyway." She inclined her head to indicate the spacious yard that wrapped around the house, then again to include the room we sat in. "The mining company wants to get its hands on this," she confided. "Buy the boardinghouse, that is to say, and tear it down. They send someone around every so often, and I throw hot water at them."

I nearly swooned. "This house is sitting on a copper fortune?"

"Don't we all wish." She clasped her hands in a moment of mock prayer, then crumpled that. "No, it's quite the opposite," she sighed. "Anaconda wants to turn this into a glory hole."

I didn't even have to plead ignorance. Grace took one look at me and laid the matter out:

"A pit, really, but dug from below. If the ore vein they're drilling on happens to head for the surface, they follow it on up. When the ore plays out, it's cheaper for the company to bust through the ground and fence it off than to maintain an empty shaft." She made a wry face. "Glory holes aren't just any old where or we'd fall to China every time we go across town. The luck of the draw decides when and where Anaconda wants one, the company shysters try to tell me. That's the kind of luck I can do without." She ran her hands up and down her arms, shuddering as she did so. "At first it gave me hives, every time the house shook like that. Right away I'd break out as if I'd been rolling in the nettles." Seeing my reaction, she hurried to say, "Don't be upset, by now it takes more than a little dynamite to make me itch, and this house isn't going away if I can help it. The next time one of those copper collar monkeys comes calling . . ." The towel turban had been slipping toward her worked-up brow throughout this, and now she ripped it off as if it were one more nuisance.

"Grace, let me try to catch up here. Doesn't the mining company offer you a good price? Good heavens, you have what they want, this property. A classic case of supply and demand if I ever heard one, and—"

"That's not Anaconda's way," she set me straight. "They'll only pay the going price for a none-too-new boardinghouse, and that's next to nothing in these times. No, they'd rather set off their blasting every so often to get on my nerves and make me sell. They don't know my nerves," she said staunchly, hives evidently notwithstanding.

My own nerves still were feeling the quivers of the floor a few minutes before. "I am not an expert on cave-ins, but simply for the sake of speculation: What if they keep dynamiting and digging until a giant hole in the ground becomes a self-fulfilling prophecy, and this house falls in?"

Rather grandly, I thought, Grace shook that off. "The company bigwigs downtown won't let that happen. They don't want a lawsuit even Anaconda could lose."

"Let us hope not. I don't want to sleep in the bottom of a glory hole."

"This place will be as dusty as one if I don't get back to house-cleaning." She closed off my concern, only to give me another gauging look before she got up from the table. "I've spilled more to you than I intended to, Morrie. Why do you have that effect? Please, though, don't pass along any of this to Hoop and Griff, promise? I don't want them fretting about whether they're going to have a roof over their old fool heads the rest of their days."

"I shall be a sphinx," I assented.

"I figured you were capable," she said, the dimple adding emphasis.

THE BANTAM FIGURES of Hooper and Griffith, each talking into one of my ears, took me around town later that day. Downtown Butte, set into the lower slope of the Hill like the till in a cash register, was as busy as the streets could hold. One moment we had to dodge bowler-hatted Rotarians congregating for luncheon fellowship, and step aside for a covey of nuns the next. The bustling business district was only six or seven blocks long but made up for that size in other ways: amid the shops and stores were saloons (now speakeasies) as big as barns, and every block or so a grandiose hotel or office building stood out, as if bits of Chicago's State Street or New York's Fifth Avenue had been crated up and shipped west. Griff and Hoop took turns pointing out local landmarks: the restaurant where Teddy Roosevelt once ate a steak in plain sight, the theater bar frequented by Charlie Chaplin and other troupers in the prime of vaudeville, and around a corner from other commerce, the red-light district called Venus Alley, said to be the biggest in the West.

What aroused the passion of my tour guides, however, was the most dominant name in Butte. Passing the *Daily Post* building, where the faint whiff of newspaper ink hung in the air, Hoop spat and said, "Anaconda owns that rag." When I remarked on the architectural preference of brick over stone in so many of the tall office buildings, I was informed the Anaconda Company owned the brickworks. Not to mention—although Hoop and Griff assuredly did—the lumberyard, profiting off the woodframe neighborhoods where the mineworkers lived. Then our stroll brought us to the Hennessy Building, dressier than its neighbors in its terra-cotta trim and window mullions—if buildings could be said to be attired as we are, the Hennessy wore cuff links and a tie pin.

But the pertinent article was escaping my attention, Griff and Hoop had me know, as one or the other profanely attested that this grandest building was where the copper collar was fashioned: the headquarters of the Anaconda Company, up there on the top floor.

My curiosity was tickled. "The copper *collar*, though—why does just that phrase keep coming to your lips and Grace's?"

Hoop looked at Griff. "Might as well let it rip," he said.

"Think so?" said Griff. "Right here?"

"Where better?"

"Righto. Here goes."

There on the sidewalk, Griff squared himself up, took a stance amid the passersby like Caruso among the opera extras, and began to sing in a croaky baritone, to the tune of "The Old Oaken Bucket."

My old copper collar,
It makes my heart so proud.
When I wear the copper collar,
I fit right with the crowd.

No wedding band
Was ever so grand,
So it is always there to see,
The old copper collar,
That Anaconda fastened on me.

Griff finished on a sardonically sweet note that was very nearly a warble. Up in the top floor of the Hennessy Building, someone in a celluloid collar frowned down and the window was shut with a bang.

"The Butte spiritual." Hoop defined Griff's performance for me, and onward we went.

It was when the two of them tramped me up the streets to the other butte, the rising ground where those long-legged headframes spraddled atop the dozens of mineshafts and piles of tailings spilled down the hillside like gopher diggings, that the two of them truly came into their element. To me, the Hill seemed otherworldly, half mammoth factory, half fathomless wasteland; to my companions, it was home. Their bent backs straightened, and their gait became more spry. The ear-stinging screech of pulleys as ore loads were hoisted from the depths of the earth and elevator cages were let down seemed to reach them as the most melodious of sounds. In accompaniment, Hoop turned suddenly voluble. "We drilled in every corner of this hill, didn't we, Griff. In the Neversweat and the Glengarry and the Parrot and the Nipper and most of these other mines you see. One of us on the steel and the other on the hammer. We was a flash team, if I do say so myself. We'd make the hole in the rock in nothing flat, then set the dynamite, and blooey! Break loose a wall of ore that'd keep a mucking crew busy half a day." In all likelihood it was the effect of Hoop's words, but I thought I felt a tremor in the ground as he spoke. He paused, gazing around at the modern-day mining apparatus. "Now they drill with air." I took that to mean high-powered compressed-air drills, the throb of giant compressors a steady beat within the industrial medley around the mineshafts.

There is hardly any story more deeply engraved in human experience than a search for the Promised Land, a New Jerusalem where life can flourish and dreams run free. What a saga it was, then, that the barren rise of earth the three of us were standing atop had become such a place, to those unafraid to go into its depths. From what Hoop and Griff had told me the night before, I knew that the Hill's copper diggings, in the course of time and union persistence, had brought forth wages that workingmen anywhere else could only imagine. *Four and a half dollars a day!* my informants chorused with pride, at that time probably equaled only by Henry Ford's assembly line in Detroit. And no man who called himself a miner wanted to bolt fenders onto flivvers for a living. So, dust devils and dump heaps and discolored soil and everything else, the startling land I was gazing at was worshipped by hard-rock miners for its holy wage; in the pits and shafts of the world, the saying was, *"Don't even stop in America, just go to Butte."*

Griff, silent until now, had been watching the loaded ore cars trundle into view one after another at the Neversweat, a colossus of a mine with seven smokestacks rising from its buildings like a row of stark totems. "Got to hand it to Anaconda," he said grudgingly, "the buggers know how to get the ore out. Looky there, Hoop, they've busted up through the south shaft of the 'Sweat." An obviously fresh fence, its posts unweathered, enclosed a crater so gaping that it looked as if a meteor had struck and blazed on through to the core of the earth. Or at least so deep that anyone who fell in would go to glory, so to speak.

Brows all of a sudden furrowed with thought, my companions exchanged glances. "Morrie," said Hoop, "you maybe ought to know something—"

"—about the boardinghouse," said Griff, and then and there, they chorused the likelihood that in time to come Anaconda would have its greedy eye on Grace's property.

"Don't blab that to Mrs. Faraday," they anxiously cautioned me. "There's no sense worrying her head off beforehand."

"I won't be the bringer of that news," I pledged.

MY TOUR, to hear my guides tell it, now was about to really begin. For there, amid the gray polar wastes of that Richest Hill, were scattered the pockets of populace that I had glimpsed from the train station.

"Here's where the work of the world comes from," Griff pronounced, and Hoop bobbed agreement. Between them, they pointed out each neighborhood. Finntown, straggling below the colossal Neversweat. The Italians, it was stressed to me, occupied

Meaderville, not be confused with Centerville, where the Cornish congregated. Griff proudly singled out the smallish Welsh area of St. David's, christened for its church, near our boardinghouse; beyond that, the Serbians had their several blocks, elsewhere the Scandinavians had theirs, and below, at the edge of downtown, lay Chinatown, self-explanatory. My head was beginning to spin, and we had not even come to the sprawl of streets dead ahead, the Irish avalanche of small frame houses and overloaded clotheslines that constituted Dublin Gulch and beyond.

Wisely, Hoop hailed a mailman, and in a brogue that justified his assignment to the route, the postal carrier told me with great elaboration how to find the house of that night's wake.

That job done, Griff proclaimed: "You're all set, Morrie. The only thing to watch out for tonight is—"

Commotion blasted the last of his words away, so sudden and sharp my eardrums winced. The Hill had turned into a calliope, whistles shrieking at every mineshaft. "Change of shifts!" one or the other of my companions yipped as if school had let out.

Those next minutes will never leave me. Down from the mine mouths into the sloping streets cascaded hundreds of workworn men, turning into thousands as we stood watching. The Hill was black with this exodus. Here, on foot, the neighborhoods sluiced together as the miners trudged past, accented English of several kinds mingling with tongues my ear could not readily identify. It was as if Europe had been lifted by, say, the boot heel of Italy and shaken, every toiler from the hard-rock depths tumbling out here. Old habits had followed them across the ocean, husky Finns clustered with other Finns, the Cornishmen not mingling with the Italians, on across the map until each of the nations of Butte came to its own home street.

By now Griff and Hoop were wistfully calling out to fellow Welshmen going by. "Keep fighting for that lost dollar, boys! We're with you all the way, Jared!" This last, I could tell, was addressed to a lean, dark-featured individual at the front of the group, not nearly as far along in years as most of the other miners but plainly a leader. Striding along with a measured tread I identified as military, the younger man grinned through his grime and sent my companions a half wave, half salute.

"What, is there a wage dispute?" I asked in surprise, having heard the hosannas about the riches of the World's Richest Hill.

"There usually is," Griff grumped, Hoop nodding, "but this one's bad. The damn company just told the union it's lopping a whole dollar off the daily wage, can you imagine?" The calculating part of my brain certainly could; a twenty-two percent cut, a severe reversal of the Hill's holy standing. "That's a poke in the eye if there ever was one," Griff was fulminating further. "Jared there and his council are working on how to turn it around, you can bet."

"A strike?" I knew from their earlier recital of labor's struggles that the last time the union leadership called one, the strike had failed when Anaconda's hired thugs broke the spirit of the mineworkers.

"Nobody said that," Griff intoned secretively.

The last of the miners filed past, the next shift went deep underground into the catacombs of copper ore, and we three turned back down the hill toward the brick canyons of streets below. By contrast, the neighborhood I would be coming back to tonight looked made of matchboxes. More than ever I felt like a foreign traveler in the Constantinople of the Rockies. One particular question of the many crowding my mind made its way out first.

"Hoop, Griff, help me to understand something. Why does

Peterson, as Scandinavian as they come, pattern his business so strongly here to Dublin Gulch? Hiring me to stand in for him at wakes, for instance."

"Norwegians don't die enough for him to make a living," Hoop imparted. "The Irish, they're another matter."

3

Y ou're the cryer," simpered the woman, her own eyes red from weeping, who opened the door to me that evening. "I can tell by the cut of your clothes." Truly, I did feel quite distinguished in the olive-brown herringbone worsted suit, vest included, that the tailor had outfitted me with. The boardinghouse trio had assured me I looked freshly spit-shined.

"Ma'am," I began, having learned my lesson in Butte manners of address that first time with Grace, "at this sad time, I wish to convey the deepest sympathy for the loss of your husband, on behalf of the—"

"Ma!" she brayed over her shoulder. "It's the funeral-home fellow, dressed to the gills, come to pay his respects." She all but swept me into the house and steered me toward a tiny elderly woman, attired in the dignity of black and settled in a wicker armchair beside the open casket. "It's my rogue of a father, Lord save his soul, at rest there in the coffin," my escort instructed into my ear as she led me over. "Ma has been expecting you ever so much. Father O'Rourke sent word he can't come tonight, there's a fellow hurt bad at the Neversweat may be needing last rites. So we're awful glad to have a cryer to do the soothing."

This had me blinking. If I was expected to stand in for a priest, I hadn't negotiated wages with Creeping Pete nearly hard enough.

Approaching the shriveled woman perched there on the wicker, I carefully held my hat over the vicinity of my heart and started my recital over. I had made sure with Peterson: I was not expected to actually cry, but a mournful mien, complete with murmurs and respectful remarks toward the deceased, was the order of the night.

"—and you may be assured I speak for Mr. Peterson in offering fullest condolences, Mrs. Dempsey," I concluded the set piece I had memorized.

The widow gazed up at me in her crinkled way, nodded an inch, and broke into a crescendo of sobs.

"There, there, Ma," the daughter consoled but made no other move, "you just cry it out, that's the girl." To me, frozen there as if I had set off a burglar alarm, she hissed: "You'll want to circulate yourself, people will be coming for the next some while."

Shaken by the storm of wailing behind me, I headed for the refuge of the long table where angel food cakes and sliced bread and bologna and a plethora of pickles and preserves and a carnival-glass bowl of tame punch sat. There, I figured, the crowd as it gathered would find its way to me. The thought was the deed. In no time a strapping black-haired man of middle years detached himself from a hushed group that I took to be other Dempsey daughters and their uncomfortable husbands. He came at me like a wind around a corner. "Pat Quinlan," he provided, ready with a handshake. "That's what I like to see, someone with the good sense to wrap himself around the food."

In turn, I told him who I was as he fastened a keen gaze on me. He had the thrust of head I'd noticed in the miners at the change of shift, as if stooping under a mine timber. Facially, he showed the olive skin and conquistador cheekbones that affirmed the tale of Spanish Armada survivors washing up onto the coast of Ireland and contributing to the population.

"Morgan is your handle, is it," he seemed to taste my name. "Creeping Pete is maybe getting the knack. Last time he sent a scissorbill called George King. How much more English does it get, I ask you?"

"If he had dispatched King George to the occasion, perhaps."

"Sharp as a tack, are we. I like that." With a glint of his own, Quinlan asked, "What brings you to Butte?" His chin came up an inch in the enunciation of that last word, the local habit.

"Reputation." I began to invoke the Richest Hill on Earth, but he cut in with an all-too-knowing grin: "Yours or Butte's? Ah, well, this isn't the time or place to go into that." The widow's wail had settled into a kind of teary drone that still had me flinching, but Quinlan showed no sign it registered on him. Rocking restlessly on his heels, he critically observed the slow traffic of grievers across the room, the men bending a quick knee at the low coffin bench for a muttered Our Father, the women kneeling in earnest to recite Hail Mary. I felt like a heathen, or at least distinctly un-Irish, but my companion at the table clapped me conspiratorially on the shoulder. "Standing around without something that fits the hand, what kind of a wake is this?" Quinlan plucked two glasses from the table. "Here, hold these while I do the needful." Reaching into a pocket of his suitcoat evidently tailored for such an occasion, he brought out a whiskey bottle and began to pour, back and forth, with a heavy hand.

Hastily I asked, "Didn't I read that Montana voted itself dry?"

"'Dry' doesn't mean 'parched to imbecility.' You could look it up."

"Mr. Quinlan—"

"Quin," he insisted, still pouring.

"Quin, then. I do not normally partake."

"Nobody else does it normal at a wake either."

He corked the bottle and it vanished to its nesting place. "Upsy daisy." Quinlan drank as generously as he poured, while I took a small mouthful that left a sting all the way down. When my eyes cleared, I inquired into the source of the supposedly forbidden liquor. "Bootleg rye." He gestured northerly. "What else is Canada for?"

"You were a close friend of the deceased, Quin?" I asked, to give the whiskey time to settle.

"Scarcely knew him. But a miner stands by another miner, to the last six feet of earth." A moment of brooding came into his dark eyes. Catching me watching this, he resorted to the knowing grin again. "Drink up, Morgan my man." He set the example. "One swallow is a lonesome bird." As if remembering his manners, he hoisted his glass in salute toward the casket and its occupant. "Tim there knew what thirst is, he was healthy enough in that respect."

"He wore a mighty name," I mentioned, alluding to Jack Dempsey, the heavyweight boxing phenomenon.

"The name was the all. See for yourself—Tim was a shrimp. Add in the bouquets and he's still a lightweight."

"Featherweight, I'd say, the hundred-twenty-pound class." That drew a look from Quinlan. Just then another man with the tilt of a miner came up to us. Like all the others in the room except me, he was in what must have been his church clothes, a tight-fitting suit no doubt worn for both marrying and burying. "Mike McGlashan, meet Morgan, the new cryer," Quinlan did the honors with a flourish of his glass. "Join us in commemorating poor old Tim."

"Never, Quin." McGlashan wagged his head piously. "I'm on the wagon."

Quinlan's expression said he had heard that one before. He produced the bottle again, uncorking it like a magician. "Run that past your smeller and tell me if it's not the scent of heaven."

"Save me from myself, then," McGlashan sighed, covering his eyes and holding out a glass.

During this, the fiery rye splashed into my own glass, and on into me, as Quin and McGlashan gabbed and drank. Inevitably they came around to the lost dollar of wage. With morose acceptance, McGlashan said he and the men on his shift in the Orphan Girl were resigned to waiting it out until the price of copper went back up. That was typical foolishness, Quin said; his shift at the Neversweat favored a strike if that's what it took. The two argued in the manner of old friends going over customary territory while I took advantage of the food on the table. Conversation and alcohol flowed along in that way until another of those cloudy moments descended on Quin. Gesturing toward the Dublin Gulch neighbors trooping from one black-draped member of the Dempsey female clan to the next with long faces brought out for the occasion, he said in a commanding manner: "This is way too sad, you could cut the air in here like crepe." He reached in another pocket and came out with a small red book. It was about the size of a breviary, but if my eyes and the rye weren't misleading me, musical bars filled its pages. Yet it had none of the binding of a hymnal and I wondered aloud, "What manner of book is that?"

"What's it look like, boyo. It's the Little Red Songbook. Someone slipped it in my lunch bucket the other day, the scoundrels." Quin wetted a thumb and started turning pages. "They know their music, you have to hand them that."

McGlashan snickered. "Evans will think you're a Wob at heart." By then I could glimpse on the crimson cover a drawing of a muscular band of men, sleeves of their work shirts rolled up and arms linked in a chain of solidarity, and the words *Industrial Workers of the World*. The boardinghouse roundelay about Buttes's factions of miners returned to me, and I appraised Quin with fresh interest.

"It wouldn't hurt Jared to look over his shoulder now and then"—he turned aside McGlashan's remark and kept on thumbing through the little book—"but he's stubborn even for a Taffy." I had thought I was the only trace of Welsh amid the wall-to-wall Irish, but now I spotted across the room the soldierly figure whom Hooper and Griffith had called out to on the Hill. "Besides, he's only here with the union tribute." As I watched, the youthful but authoritative miner approached the widow, hat off, and bestowed on her an envelope which from the bulge of it contained a goodly amount of cash. "Are you going to stand there slandering me," Quin was chiding McGlashan now, "or sing? Tim there in the wooden overcoat would appreciate a tune about now, I bet. Ah, here's a nice one," he asserted, crimping open the crimson book to it. "Get Pooch Lampkin over here, he has a voice on him. And Micky O'Fallon, while you're at it."

I ducked away while the musical troops were organizing themselves, not sure my initial night as cryer should be spent in song. Peering over Quinlan's shoulder at the small songbook, the impromptu ensemble squared up and let loose:

> Oh Lord of all, of fowl and fish,
> Of feast of life, of ev'ry dish;
> Observe me on my bended legs,
> I'm asking You for ham and eggs.

"They're at it again!" a woman shrieked. "And Father O'Rourke not here to give them what for! Quick, the true music of the faith!"

Hastily the opposition vocal force formed up, a number of women in their darkest funereal best and a few older men pinched at the elbow by their wives and conscripted into the choir. Rigid as if they had been called to their feet in church, the bunch of them chorused out:

> O'er the sod of God,
> O'er the bogs of peat,
> Everlasting choirs
> Raise a concert sweet!

Undeterred, Quinlan and McGlashan and colleagues soared into their next verse.

> And if thou havest custard pies
> I'd like, dear Lord, the largest size.

Across the room the choir of the righteous responded in a roar:

> Heathendom shall go down,
> Though it be everywhere!
> God the Father's kingdom
> Fills heaven and earth and air!

Sweetly as boys, the Quinlan quartet warbled a last verse:

> Oh, hear my cry, almighty Host,
> I quite forgot the quail on toast.
> Let your kindly heart be stirred
> And stuff some oysters in that bird.

"Shame!" cried a particularly broad woman in black, charging across the room. "My poor uncle, Heaven forgive him, gone on beyond there in the plush box and you singing one of those Red songs. Pat Quinlan, you banshee. May God make your tongue fall out." Over by the door, I saw the young union man cast a rueful look at it all, put his hat on, and slip away from the proceedings.

Quinlan chortled. "Betty, you'd sell tickets to that, wouldn't you. Come have a glass with us, girl."

"I'll girl you, Quin." Nonetheless a glass appeared in her hand. "A taste, if you insist."

"Meet Morgan, the cryer," Quinlan thought to officiate. "He's new to Butte."

"Another pilgrim to the Richest Hill on Earth, have we here?" Betty turned her ample face to me. "Join the long line, Morgan my man." Luckily the bottle made its rounds just then, and while I hid into a gulp from my glass, I noticed that around the room the tone of the wake had lightened into loud conversation and laughter. Centered as I was in the commotion, I apprehensively looked over toward the casket, the item of business I supposedly was here to attend to. The widow seemed to be crying to herself in contentment.

I jumped slightly as Betty fingered the fabric of my lapel. "My, quite the glad rags Creeping Pete's put you in." With a critical cock of her head, she studied the rest of me. "You look awful learned to be among miners."

"One can never get enough of the school of life," I said with slightly slurred dignity. Tonight was certainly proving that. I had found out that Butte did not sprout shrinking violets.

As if I needed any more proof, Betty batted me on one shoulder and Quinlan on the other. "A man who knows his blarney," Quin commended. "I like that." He aimed his glass at me. "Morgan, a man as cultured as you can't help but have a tune stick to him along the way. Favor us with something, why don't you." The entire crowd around the table loudly seconded that.

"I regret to say, from what I've heard here tonight I'm not equal to the task."

Betty turned indignant. "You don't mean to tell us Creeping Pete's sent a man who can't sing a lick?"

"Really, I—"

"EVERYBODY!" Quinlan let out a shout. "The cryer's going to do us a number! Step on out, Morgan, and show us your tonsils."

I had no choice, and someone gave me a push toward the center of the room besides. The houseful of people suddenly loomed around me like a crowd at a bullring. Even the widow was wiping her eyes and watching me. My glass half full in one hand, I braced back with the other for some support and found I had put it on the foot of the casket. Inches away, the highly polished toes of the shoes of poor departed Dempsey pointed in the air. Swallowing deeply, I stayed propped there against the coffin wood as if this were the natural spot for the representative of the Peterson Modern Mortuary and Funeral Home, and tried desperately to think of any appropriate snatch of music. What issued forth was as much a surprise to me as to the audience.

> I cannot sing the old songs now.
> It is not that I deem them low.
> 'Tis that I can't remember how
> They go.

In the silence that met that, I bowed and retreated behind the casket. After long seconds, someone tittered and that loosed a chuckle in someone else, and then the whole crowd gave a collective belly laugh and people pressed in on me, a dozen at once making conversation and clapping me on the back and testifying what an enjoyable wake this was.

It was during this that I realized I was drunk as a gnat in a vat.

The rest of the evening became one long blur of relatives of the man who lay in state beside me and miners telling stories out of an endless supply and black-clad women wanting to know if they couldn't fetch me just a bite more of angel cake, while I concentrated on not tipping over into the casket.

At last everyone wore down, and after a groggy round of fare-wells and a final whap on the back from Quin, I stepped out into the street and began to make my unsteady way out of Dublin Gulch. The chill air of the Butte night collided with the alcohol in me. The stars were out but, I scolded them, too far to be any help to me. All too soon, I had to skirt the Neversweat glory hole. With the single-mindedness of the inebriated, I crept cautiously past, as if the yawning pit, darker than dark, might empty itself upward over me in an eruption of shadow. Luckily, things were marginally less inky after that. Such splotches of illumination as existed shone from mines that were being worked around the clock, and nearer to downtown I met up with occasional streetlights, so that my route as I wove my way toward the boardinghouse alternated between lit and dim. It fit my condition.

Here is where the mystery begins. I had the eerie sensation that the shadows were following me home from the Hill.

You would think a long walk in shivery weather ought to clear the head of such a phenomenon. The mysterious does not work like that. The more I tottered along, the worse the shivers. Out of the dapple of light and dark behind me, the shadows took shapes as warped as in a bad dream, sometimes huge and foglike, sometimes small and flitting. Like a steady cold breath on the back of the neck, I could feel the darkness changing form. Some small sane part of my mind kept telling me these specters were the distilled and bottled sort, but the corner of my eye was convinced otherwise. A time or two when I suddenly looked back, the shadows nearly became human, then faded into the other patterns of the night. If anyone was there, they were as uncatchable as cats.

Telling myself woozily this was what came of an evening spent in the company of a casket and its contents, I clattered into the boardinghouse and bed.

THE MORNING AFTER, Grace left on the stove a pot of coffee of a stoutness that would have brought the Light Brigade back to life.

Numb above my shoulders, I sat at the kitchen table and worked cup after cup into myself. I had missed breakfast. The household was well into its day, Hooper in the garden hoeing weeds at a stately pace and Griffith going down the hall with a monkey wrench in hand. Catching sight of me, Griff backtracked and stuck his head in the room.

"How's the crying game going?"

"I can still smell it on my breath."

"Didn't I tell you so?"

"Unfortunately, not quite." How I wished for that moment back, when he was warning me of the one thing to be watched out for at a Dublin Gulch wake and every whistle went off.

Griff waved away silly concern as he limped off. "You'll get used to the elbow-bending. It beats toadying for Anaconda."

I was debating that with myself when Grace bustled in with her shopping basket, fresh from dickering a bargain meat out of the butcher, no doubt.

"Morning, Morrie," she said pleasantly, "what's left of it."

"Short days and long nights are the career of a cryer, I foresee. The coffee was an act of mercy; thank you. Can I help you with those provisions?"

"You had better sit quiet and let your eyeballs heal, I'd say." Putting groceries away, she looked over her shoulder at me curiously. "I've had the good luck never to go to a wake. What was it like?"

I recounted to her what I could remember of the muddled evening. Mostly, the clink of glasses and the clash of singing voices came to mind. At the mention of Quinlan, she bobbed her head. "Quin was a friend of my Arthur, although they didn't see eye to eye on union matters."

"Then there was a Dempsey niece, a rather stout woman named Betty—"

"Betty the bootlegger." Grace had no trouble with the identification. "She knows the right people along the border. Prohibition is the making of her."

I sat wordless, more than ever a novice in the ways of Butte, dumbly considering a mourning occasion fueled with moonlight liquor that redounded to the profit of someone in the family. The C. R. Peterson Modern Mortuary and Funeral Home maybe was in the wrong end of the business.

"Morrie?" Grace closed the cupboard and joined me at the table, settling lightly. Her inquisitive look became pronounced. "I've had a fair number of boarders, besides the palace guard"—Griff could be heard banging in the basement—"but none of them blew in from nowhere quite like you. What was your last place of address, if I may ask?"

"Oh, that. Down Under, as they say."

"Under what?"

"I refer, Grace, to Australia."

"I was teasing. I'm not surprised you have an ocean or so behind you. You have that look."

"It's the mustache."

"My Arthur always said his was the brush hiding the picnic," she reported drily. "Women don't have that disguise."

"Spoken like a high priestess of the plain truth, Rose—I mean Grace."

Before my embarrassment could pool on the table, Grace gave my slip of the tongue the gentlest of treatment. "Whoever she was, was she as pretty as her name?"

"Every bit."

"Maybe it was worth some Down Under, then," she left me with, rising and reaching for her apron. "It's nearly noon, I have a meal to fix or the three of you will have to go in the yard and graze."

THOSE INITIAL WEEKS, the job of cryer was an introduction to Butte, definitely, although hardly the one I had sought. Life at the mortuary remained, well, creepy. First of all, there was usually someone dead on the premises, in one room or another. And the wage, while steady enough, was not one of the Hill's swiftest paths to riches; Creeping Pete's ledger was always going to be tipped in his favor, not mine.

What disquieted me more than either of those was that question of shadows. Was it a trick of the darkness and the bootleg rye? The occasional night when I managed to slip away from the convivial-ity of a Dublin Gulch coffin vigil long enough to dump my drink in the kitchen slop bucket, the shadows on the way home perhaps behaved less like lurking black furies; but they never quite vanished. Something quivers in a person at such times, like a tuning fork set off by phantom touch. You look back along a darkened street that is suddenly limitless and whatever is there keeps eyeing you hungrily. Watching over my shoulder as I zigzagged to the boardinghouse after each wake, I had to wonder whether an old loss was catching up with me. Every footfall, it seemed, brought the thought of my brother and the cold lake waters that took him.

Not all haunting is mere superstition. I'd noticed a certain look in Grace's eyes whenever Griffith and Hooper got going on the evils of Anaconda and the Speculator fire and its perished miners; at such moments Arthur Faraday left his matrimonial picture frame and came to her side, I would have wagered.

One of those suppertimes, as Griff and Hoop hobbled off to their own pursuits, I spoke up as she somberly cleared away the dishes.

"May I be of help?"

She took so long to answer, I wondered if she considered the question hypothetical. But then she looked over with a flicker of interest and said, "You can dry, if you don't have dropsy."

Following her into the kitchen, I took up a dish towel. "As Marco Polo said, I know my way around china. I did dishes at the Palmer House between school terms."

"It seems there is no end to your talents," Grace said with exaggerated wonder, making room for me at the sink. It had been a long while since I settled in side by side with a woman to such a chore. With her braid tucked back and her sleeves rolled up, she was an aproned vision of efficiency at her dishpan task. Still, I could tell something troubled her. I asked, "Have the glory hole grabbers been giving you a bad time again?"

She shook her head. "No, it's not that. It's our anniversary. Arthur's and mine." Slowly washing a plate, she went on: "Seven years ago today we were married. I don't know why this year bothers me so much." She looked cross with herself. "I'm sorry, Morrie, I didn't mean to mope."

"Grief sometimes goes by numbers," I suggested gently. "Seven, that's the copper anniversary."

"I might have known you'd have the answer, you schoolbook." She flicked a few drops of dishwater at me. "I'll simmer down, I promise." By now I was well aware she could also simmer up faster than the law of heat transfer ever predicated, but I was learning to weather that. It seemed worth it for the glimpses of the woman behind the landlady veneer. When something serious was not on her mind, she had the best smile, bright and teasing. That came out again now as she glanced at me and the dimple did sly work. "Let's fish around in you, for a change. Off on a toot again tonight, are you?"

"Grace, it is my job. I seem to recall you being all for it."

"Anyone who runs a boardinghouse needs to be in favor of whatever a lodger does to come up with the rent." That canny glance again. "Within reason."

I smoothed my mustache while I thought that over. I had to admit, presenting myself at a wake most every night made me feel uncomfortably like one of those mechanical statuettes of Death that clank out of a guildhall clock tower at the appointed hour and chase the merrymakers around the cupola. Grace had a point about the reasonableness of that as a lasting occupation. "Life as cryer does have its drawbacks," I conceded to her. "A main one is that I wake up each morning feeling as if my brain were being pickled, gray cell by gray cell."

She prompted: "And while you still have a few to spare?"

"Tomorrow," I said with sudden decision, "I shall find the public library and consult Polk."

Grace paused in her sudsy grapple with the meat platter, puzzled. "Poke who?"

"The Polk city directory." I smiled. "The treasure map to where ledgers are kept."

4

There is an old story that any Londoners with a madman in the family would drop him off at the library of the British Museum for the day. I was given a searching look as if I might be the Butte version when I presented myself at the desk of the public library that next morning and requested both the *R. L. Polk & Co. City Directory* and Julius Caesar's *Gallic Wars* in the original Latin.

The stout woman I took to be the head librarian—she had eyeglasses enchained around her neck commandingly enough for it—scrutinized me some moments more, then marched off into the maze of shelves while I found a seat at a broad oaken table. Everything was substantial, the brass-banistered stairway up to the mezzanine of books in tall rows, the green-shaded electrical lights hanging down from the high ceiling like watch fobs of the gods. I have always felt at home among books, so when the woman from the desk plopped my requested two in front of me, they seemed like old friends dropping by.

Aware that I should get down to business, I nonetheless drew the *Gallic Wars* to me first, unable to resist. I had ordered it up by habit, as a test. To me, a repository of books is not a library without that volume in the mother of languages, but merely a storehouse for worn copies of H. Rider Haggard's jungle thrillers and the syrupy novels of Mrs. Mary V. Terhune. No, Caesar's prose that reads like poetry—*Gallia est omnis divisa in partes tres*—is essential in a collection of knowledge, a siren call from Roman words to ours. Handling the book fondly as I was, I became aware of its own touch: tanned leather, not the more common calfskin cover put on for show. I examined the binding: sewn rather than glued. On the pages, lovely to finger, the sentences practically rose from the paper in a strong clear Caslon typeface. What I was holding was an exceptionally fine copy, so much better than my own that had gone astray with my missing trunk that I momentarily found myself envious of the Butte Public Library.

Just then a drove of schoolchildren came pattering through, herded toward the downstairs by their shushing teacher, evidently to a story hour. Second-graders, I judged, that unhushable age when whispering is as natural as breathing. I felt a pang as the class passed through like a murmur in church. The distance of ten years evaporated, and I swear, for some moments I was back at the Marias Coulee one-room school, my stairstep eight grades there in front of me as intricate and intriguing as a daily circus. And after school, the mental workout of Latin lessons with the keenest pupil a teacher ever had, Paul Milliron. Sitting there, watching this motherly teacher shoo her boys and girls along as they descended the library stairs a whisper at a time, I envied her the job but knew it was too late in the school year for me to even think of such an application. Besides, my credentials were not exactly the standard ones.

Sighing, I patted Caesar and closed him away. Opening the city directory, I began to work my way through the idiom of Polk. There they were as ever, the abbreviated citizens found throughout America, *brklyr, carp, messr, repr,* et cetera. The skills of bricklayers, carpenters, messengers, and repairers were not my own. Nor on subsequent pages could I see myself employed in feather dying, felt mattress manufacture, or fish salting. Dutifully I paged on through, searching for where ledgers that fit my talents might be found. Butte, I discerned, had a modest number of banks for a city of its size; a plenitude of funeral homes; an uninspiring variety of mercantile enterprises; and one Gibraltar of assets, the Anaconda Copper Mining Company. I can't deny, it was tantalizing, that financial colossus which surely needed *bkprs*—bookkeepers—of a certain talent to sluice the riches of the Hill into Anaconda coffers.

Temptation had to vie with distraction, however. Something about the *Gallic Wars* at my elbow kept diverting me. Even when they are closed, some books do not shut up. Why was this beautifully sewn leather edition, a collector's item if I had ever seen one, spending its existence on a public shelf in a none too fastidious mining town? Once more I peered at those tiers on the mezzanine, and if I was not severely mistaken, many other handsome volumes sat there, beckoning, in bindings of royal reds and greens and blues and buffs. Curiosity got the better of me. Up the stairwell I went.

And found myself in a book lover's paradise.

As though some printerly version of Midas had browsed through the shelves, priceless editions of Flaubert and Keats and Tolstoy and Goethe and Melville and Longfellow and countless other luminaries mingled on the shelves with more standard library holdings. I could not resist running my fingers along the handsomely bound spines and tooled letters of the titles. What on earth was the matron at the desk thinking, in scattering these treasures out in the open? Yet the more I looked, the more I met up with the complete works of authors, surely deliberately collected and displayed. Mystified, I was stroking the rare vellum of a Jane Austen title when a loud voice made me jump.

"You look like a bookworm on a spree."

I am of medium height, but when I turned around, I was seeing straight into a white cloud of beard. Considerably above that, a snowy cowlick brushed against furrows of the forehead. In a suit that had gone out of fashion when the last century did, the man frowning down at me had considerable girth at the waist and narrowed at the chest and shoulders; like the terrain around us, he sloped.

Caught by surprise, I had no idea what to make of this apparition confronting me amid the books. The beard was as full as that of Santa Claus, but there was no twinkle of Christmas nor any other spirit of giving in those glacial blue eyes.

Keeping my own voice low, I responded: "Butte is rich in its library holdings, as I assume we both have discovered?"

"Finest collection west of Chicago. Too bad the town doesn't have the brains to match the books," he drawled at full volume. "Quite a reader, are you? Who do you like?"

Appropriately or not, my gaze caught on a lovely marbled copy of *Great Expectations.* "Dickens," I began a whispered confession that could have gone on through legions of names. "There's a person who could think up characters."

"Hah." My partner in conversation reached farther along in the shelves of fiction. "I'll stick with Stevenson, myself." He fondled along the gilt-titled set of volumes from boyish adventure to phantasmagoria of shape-shifting souls. "It takes a Scotchman to know the sides of life." Abruptly he swung around, towering over me again, and demanded loudly: "You like Kipling, or don't you?"

Oh, was I tempted to recite: *What reader's relief is in store / When the Rudyards cease from kipling / And the Haggards ride no more.'* Instead I put a thumb up and then down, meanwhile murmuring, "His stories are splendid sleight of hand, the poetry is all thumbs."

"Not short of opinion, are you." He fixed a look on me as if he had shrewdly caught me at something. "Saw you down there, pawing at Caesar. English isn't good enough for you?"

"Lux ex libris," I tried to put this absolute stranger in his place, "whatever the language on the page."

"If light comes from books," he drawled back, "how come Woodrow Wilson isn't brighter than he is?"

That stopped me. Was I really expected to debate the intellect of the president of the United States within hearing of everyone in the building?

Just then a couple of elderly ladies entered the Reading Room below, still chattering softly from the street. Frowning so hard the beard seemed to bristle, my companion leaned over the mezzanine railing. "Quiet!" he bellowed.

That legendary pairing, madman and library, seemed to be coming true as I watched. All heads now were turned up toward us, the woman at the desk whipping her eyeglasses on and glowering in our direction. I envisioned arrest for disturbing the literary peace, even if I was barely an accomplice. "Perhaps," I whispered urgently, "we should adjourn to a less public spot, lest the librarian take steps—"

"Ignoramus, I am the librarian." Straightening himself to new white heights of cowlick, he frowned fiercely down at me. "Do you genuinely not know who the hell you're talking to?"

"I remember no introduction," I said coolly.

He waved that off. "Samuel S. Sandison. Come on into my office before you cause any more ruckus, I want to talk to you."

I hesitated before following, but the ravishing books were too much of a lure. Edging through the doorway of his overflowing office at the back of the mezzanine, I made sure that the nameplate on the desk matched what he had told me. Sandison sandwiched himself behind the desk and wordlessly pointed me to a book-stacked chair. I cleared away the pile and gingerly sat. "Mr. Sandison, the books you have here . . ." I hardly had the words. "They're works of art in every way."

"They ought to be." He stroked his beard, as if petting a cat. "A good many of them are mine."

"Yours?"

"Hell yes. From the ranch."

"Ah. The ranch. You were a livestock entrepreneur, I take it? Sheep?"

"Cattle." He delivered me a look that made me want to duck. Well, how was I to know? From the train, Montana expanses appeared to me to be as populous with fleeces as the heavens are with clouds.

Sandison leaned across the mess of his desk as though I might be hard of hearing as well as dim of intellect. "You mean you have never heard of the Triple S ranch?"

"I confess I have not, but I have been in town only a short time."

"It's gone now," he growled. "That's why I'm here. It was the biggest spread in the state; everybody and his brother knew the SSS brand."

"Mmm. By 'brand,' do you mean the practice of searing a mark onto the animal?"

"That's what branding is. It's the Latin and Greek of the prairie."

That startled me. "Intriguing. And so SSS would translate to—?"

He laughed harshly. "Saddle up, sit tight, and shut up, my riders called it. Most of them stuck with me anyway." An odd glint came to him. "I had an army of them, you know."

"I regret to say, I am not seer enough myself to know the intricacies of reading burnt cowhide." It fell flat with him. "But I am eager to grasp the principle behind alphabetizing one's cows—"

"It's not alphabetical, fool. Brandabetical."

"—excellent word! The brandabetical concept, then. Do you start with the full lingual entity, in this case 'saddle up, sit tight, and shut up,' and condense from there?"

"Hell no," he let out, and immediately after that, "but you're right in a way. SSS stood for Seymour-Stanwood-Sandison. I had to have backers in the ranch operation. Money men." Those last two words he practically spat. Eyeing me as though I were guilty by association, he drawled: "I saw you with your nose stuck in Polk. I suppose you're another refined hobo who heard about the Hill and came here to make a killing."

"A living, I had in mind."

"Hah. You packing around any education worth the description?"

"The Oxford variety."

He looked at me skeptically.

"I bootstrapped my way through."

"Another shoeleather philosopher," he grumbled. "The Wobblies were full of them; they must empty out the bughouse into Butte every so often."

"I see my little joke did not catch on. Actually, I did work my way through an institution of higher learning—the University of Chicago."

He tugged at his beard. "In other words," he said as if it might be my epitaph, "all you know anything about comes from books."

I bridled. "That is hardly a fair assessment of—"

"Never mind. You're hired."

"You are mistaken, I haven't even made up my mind where to—here?"

"Here is where the books are, ninny."

5

Sam Sandison? He's meaner than the devil's half brother. If you're gonna be around him, you better watch your sweet—"

"The rules, Griff."

"—step, is all I was gonna say, Mrs. Faraday." Griffith speared a potato and passed the dish onward to me, along with a gimlet gaze. "You must have hit him when he was hard up for help, Morrie. He don't hire just anybody."

"I was as taken by surprise as the rest of you appear to be." Announcement of my sudden employment at the library had set my suppermates back in their chairs, for some reason that I could not decipher. "What can you tell me of my new lord and master? None of you were so bashful about the business practices of the Anaconda Company." The gravy boat came my way, but nothing else of substance from any of the threesome. "For a start, Griff, what exactly is the meaning of 'meaner than the devil's half brother' in regard to Samuel Sandison?"

"He's one of the old bucks of the country, tougher than"— cutting strenuously at the piece of meat on his plate, Griff glanced in Grace's direction and hedged off—"rawhide. Had a ranch they say you couldn't see to the end of. I don't just know where. You, Hoop?"

Hooper gestured vaguely west. "Someplace out there in scatteration."

"Employing, he told me, a veritable army of cowboys—but I would imagine any livestock enterprise of that size needed a rugged crew and a firm hand?"

"You're lucky he's only bossing books around anymore," was the only answer from Griff. Vigorously chewing, he turned toward the head of the table. "Heck of a meal, Mrs. Faraday."

I sampled the stringy meat and sent an inquiring look. "Not chicken."

Grace shook her head.

"Rabbit, then."

"My, you do know your way around food," she remarked, a compliment or not I couldn't tell. It occurred to me how much I was going to miss the tablefuls at wakes.

TAKING LEAVE of the C. R. Peterson Modern Mortuary and Funeral Home took some doing.

"As I have been trying to say, Mr. Peterson, I am sorry—"

"But you're the most popular cryer I've had in ages." He himself appeared ready to weep.

"—to have to give notice, but another opportunity has presented itself."

He cast a mournful look at the ledger. "One of our busiest times since St. Patrick's Day."

"I am sure an equally qualified cryer will be called forth by the need."

"There'll always be an opening here for you," he said feelingly, the lids of the caskets standing at attention behind him.

THAT WAS THE END of being chased every night by shadows. Yet something lurked from that experience, the sensation of being trailed through life by things less than visible. I tried telling myself Butte after dark simply was feverishly restless, what with the thirst of thousands of miners built up in the hot underground tunnels being assuaged in speakeasies, and desire of another kind busily paying its dues in Venus Alley—practically nightly, Grace turned away some lit-up Lothario seeking a house of the other sort. In that city of thin air and deep disquiets, wasn't it to be expected that even shadows would have the fidgets? It is surprising how persuasive you can be when talking into your own ear.

So, I set out from the boardinghouse that first morning with a sense of hope singing in me as always at the start of a new venture. Samuel Sandison had instructed me to present myself at the library before it opened at nine, and I knew he did not mean a minute later. When I approached the rather fanciful gray granite Gothic building on the central street called Broadway—modesty seemed to have no place in Butte—I saw a cluster of people outside the front door and was heartened by this sight of an eager citizenry lined up to get at the literary holdings.

In their midst, however, loomed Sandison, and bringing up the rear was unmistakably the Reading Room matron, looking sour. The group proved to be the entire library staff, all the way to janitor. Sandison was counting heads before letting anyone through the arched doorway—the same mode of management, I was to learn, he had used on his cowboys each morning at the horse corral.

He took notice of my presence with a vague gesture. "This is Morgan, everybody. He'll be puttering around the place from now on."

I filed in with the rest of the staff, happily conscious of the palatial grandeur, the Tuscan red wainscoting, the dark oaken beams set against the ceiling panels of white and gold, the all-seeing portrait of Shakespeare above the Reading Room doorway. And beyond, the regal reds and greens and gilts of those books of Sandison's collection, the best of their kind anywhere.

But no sooner were we in the building than he cut me out of the herd, and, just as adroitly, the matron of the Reading Room. "Miss Runyon will show you the ropes," Sandison provided with another of those gestures that might mean anything. "Come on up when she's had her fill of you," he dismissed us and mounted the stairs to his office.

Miss Runyon and I considered each other.

"What foolishness has he put you in charge of?" she demanded, as though she had caught me trespassing.

"That seems yet to be determined."

"That man." Her voice had a startling deep timbre, as if the words resounded in her second chin. "He runs this place to suit himself. The trustees would never have named him librarian but for those precious books of his." Clapping her chained eyeglasses onto her formidable nose, she directed: "Come along, you had better know the catalogue system."

Miss Runyon kept me in tow as we circumnavigated the Reading Room, her realm and her orb, her temple and her fortress, she let me know in every manner possible. I took note of the goodly assortment of dictionaries and cyclopedias, and the respectable selection of magazines and the newspapers racked on spine sticks, all of it recited to me as if I were a blind man in a museum. One oddity, though, she paid no attention to; conspicuously paid it no heed, if I was not mistaken. It was a display case, glassed over, taking up one corner of the room. My mild inquiry about it brought:

"Pfft, that. The boys' dollhouse."

Naturally that increased my curiosity and I went over to it, Miss Runyon clopping after me. Encased there, with plentiful nose smudges and handprints on the glass testifying to the popularity of its viewing, sat an entire miniature mine. It looked so amazingly complete, I half expected it to bring up teaspoonfuls of earth from under the library. Headframe, machine house, elevator shafts, tunnels, tiny tracks and ore cars, the entirety was a Lilliputian working model. With disdain Miss Runyon told me the diorama had been built for a court case over a mining claim and afterward donated to the library. "He"—her eyes swept upward toward Sandison's office—"insists it sit here in the way. It's a nuisance to keep clean."

"Wonders often are," I murmured, still taken with the remarkable model of the workings of the Hill.

"Now, then," Miss Runyon said haughtily, "is that enough of an initiation into librarianship for you?"

"The most thorough, Miss Runyon, since my introduction to the Reading Room of the British Museum."

I seemed to have invoked the Vatican to a Mother Superior. "You, you have actually been—?"

"Under that great domed ceiling, with its delicate blue and accents of gold, with every word ever written in English at one's beck and call," I dreamily sketched aloud, "yes, I confess I have. And would you believe, Miss Runyon, the very day I walked in, my reader's ticket in my hand, the seat of destiny was vacant."

"The seat of—?"

"Seat number three, right there in the first great semicircle of desks." I leaned confidingly close to her. "Where Karl Marx sat, those years when he was writing *Das Kapital*. I will tell you, Miss Runyon, sitting in that seat, I could feel the collective knowledge, like music under the skin, of all libraries from Alexandria onward."

With a last blink at me, Miss Runyon retreated to her desk and duty.

WHEN I WENT UP to Sandison's office, I found him standing at its cathedral-like window, trying to peek out at the weather through an eyelet of whorled clear glass. "Damned stained glass," he grumbled. "What do the nitwits think a window is for?" He rotated around to me. His old-fashioned black suit was as mussed as if he had flung it on in the dark, and instead of shoes he wore scuffed cowboy boots that added still more inches to his height. "The downstairs dragon show you every mouse hole, did she?"

"Quite an educational tour. What I am wondering, Mr. Sandison—"

"Hold it right there." He held up a rough hand as he moved to his oversize desk chair and deposited himself in it heavily. "When somebody calls me that, I feel like I'm around a banker or lawyer or some other pickpocket."

To escape that category, I asked, "Then what form of address am I to use?"

He looked across his desk at me conspiratorially. "I'll tell you what. Call me Sandy. The only other person I let do that is my wife." He chortled like a boy pleased with a new prank. "It'll drive that old bat Runyon loco."

"Sandy, then," I tried it on for size, none too comfortably. "What I need to know is the scope of my job."

"I suppose." Rubbing his beard, he gazed around the cluttered room as if some task for me might be hiding behind one of the piles of books. "Morgan"—there was a dip of doubt in his tone as he spoke it—"how are you at juggling?"

"Three balls in the air at once is a skill that persists from boyhood," I answered cautiously, "but when it comes to ninepins—"

"No, no—the calendar, oaf, the calendar." Irritably he pawed around in the pieces of paper that carpeted his desk and finally came up with that item. "People always want to use this damn place, they need a room to hold this meeting or that, you'd think a library was a big beehive. Myself, I don't see why they can't just check out a couple of books and go home and read. But no, they bunch up and want to cram in here and talk the ears off one another half the night." He squinted as if drawing a bead on the offenders penciled in on various dates. "The Shakespeare Society. The Theosophists. The Ladies' and Gentlemen's Literary and Social Circle. The League of Nations Advocates. The Jabberwockians. The Gilbert and Sullivan Libretto Study Group. And that's hardly the half of them, wanting some damn night of their own to come in here and take up space. They've all got to be juggled."

"I think I can tend to that, Mr.—"

He shot me a warning glance.

"—Sandy."

There may have been a cunning smile within the beard. The librarian of Butte, for everything that entailed, settled more deeply into his chair. "I figured if you're a man who knows his books, you can deal with the literary types who come out when the moon is full." He passed the much-scrawled-upon calendar to me. "They're all yours now, Morgan," said Samuel Sandison with that intonation I came to know so well.

Looking back, that exchange set a telling pattern. You would think, with two persons in one cloistered office, for he had me clear a work space for myself in a corner, that he might sooner or later call me Morrie. Yet that familiar form of address never passed his lips. Each time and every time, he would either preface or conclude what passed for conversation between us with a drawled *Morgan?* even when it wasn't a question. As if it were my first name.

As if he knew.

MORGAN LLEWELLYN. That is my rightful name. Yes, *that* famous breed of Llewellyn. I know I carry only a minor share of its renown in the world, but reflected glory is still glory of a sort. It was my brother, Casper, who reigned as lightweight boxing champion of the world, "Capper" Llewellyn in the inch-high headlines every time he won by another knockout. And I was his "genius" of a manager.

Even yet he causes me to lie awake, when the mind tussles with itself before sleep comes, thinking of how life paired us so peculiarly. Casper was magical, if confidence and prowess count as magic. Even as a boy, he had the cocky outlook that nothing was out of the reach of a good left hook, and my role as older brother often amounted to fishing him out of trouble. Which perhaps made it inevitable, when he was matriculating as a boxer in Chicago's West Side fight clubs and I was graduating from the university, that he insisted I become his manager. He did not possess my brains and I did not have his brawn, he pointed out all too accurately, so we had better join onto one another as if we were Siamese, in his words. Casper could be exasperating, but in the ring he was a thing of beauty, a Parthenon statue of a perfect athlete sprung to life, and I have to say, I felt somewhat wizardly in fashioning his boxing career for him. Carefully I chose opponents who would build his record, alternating his bouts between the easy fighters called "cousins" and the tougher ones we stropped Casper's skills on. It became only a matter of time until the name Casper Llewellyn would be on the card of a title fight.

Now the other tussle in the mind's nightly shadows. Rose, delightful maddening Rose.

Along the way, he and she met, a wink served its purpose, and they fell for each other like the proverbial ton of bricks. Brother-in-law was added to my responsibilities. At first I was wary of Rose as an adventuress—why don't I just say it: a gold digger—but soon enough saw that she and my brother were a genuine matching of hearts. Pert and attractive, whimsical and ever whistling, she was a sunny addition to the Llewellyn name. Luck seemed to have found us, as Casper's purses for winning grew and grew, and when he became the lightweight champion, we felt we had truly hit the jackpot. The three of us grew accustomed to high living. Somewhat too high. Rose never saw a satin dress and a saucy hat to go with it that did not appeal to her, while Casper threw money around as if it were going out of style. And I have to admit, money does not stick to me, either. That's why a large supply seemed such a good idea.

It was one of those situations you know you ought not to get into, but do: the pugilistic science, the fight game, the glove trade, boxing in all its guises was uncommonly good to us, yet income did not nearly keep up with outgo. So, it was Casper's brainstorm to throw the fight with the challenger, Ned Wolger. Rose and I might not have listened to him but for the odds on his side—he was a three-to-one favorite to wallop Wolger. That walloping could simply be postponed, as he put it, until the inevitable rematch. In the meantime, all we had to do was put our money on Wolger, spreading those bets around out of town so as not to attract suspicion. Rose and I saw to that, and in the last round of the title match, Casper, shall we say, resigned from the fight. And we collected hand over fist. Too much so. The Chicago gambling mob turned murderous about the amount it had lost on an apparent sure thing.

That part haunts me to this minute: Lake Michigan, blue as sword steel beside the city, and the gamblers seizing Casper and making an example of him, in the infamous fate called "a walk off the dock."

Before they could lay hands on us, Rose and I fled together. Not with the money, alas, which was consigned forever to a biscuit tin wherever Casper had stashed it; he never did trust banks. Left on our own, with the gambling mob ever on our mind if not on our trail, she and I took shelter in Minneapolis, where she had been in household service. Minneapolis was still too close to Chicago for comfort. Then a propitious ad we had placed in Montana newspapers brought Rose a job as housekeeper for a widower and his three sons, and like so many seekers of a new life, we boarded a train for the homestead country of the West. Events took their own willful course after that. We posed as brother and sister, but in the aloneness of prairie lodgings the two of us became man and woman in the flesh, so to speak.

Only for a season, it turned out. I lost her, fair and square, to the widower, Oliver Milliron, a good man and friend. His eldest son, Paul, was astute in other matters besides Latin, and it was he who drew from me the pledge to mean it when I gave away Rose at the wedding and to never return to Marias Coulee, and the vicinity of temptation. It has not been easily kept. No day since have I not thought of Rose.

———

"Morrie? Morrie, anyone home between your ears? I asked: How was your day at the library?"

"Sorry, Grace. My thoughts were elsewhere."

"Miles away, I'd say. White meat or dark?" She was majestically carving off slice after slice of turkey, a surprise feast to the other three of us at the supper table. "I hope it's not as hard on the nerves as standing over a corpse every night. Wakes would give me the willies."

"Oddly enough, the library is somewhat more solemn, in a way. May I ask what the occasion is, with this festive bird?"

"The price is down, always to be celebrated." Dishing out judicious servings of turkey, she returned to that other topic: "Just what is it you do all day there in Sandison's stronghold, besides keep the books company?"

An apt question, not easily answered. Day by day, besides my juggling act with the meetings schedule, it had been gruffly suggested to me that I organize the disorganized subscription list of magazines and newspapers, find someone to fix the drinking fountain, deal with Miss Runyon's complaints about squeaky wheels on book carts passing through her sanctum, respond to a stack of letters from people with the kinds of questions only a library can answer—in short, I was tasked with anything Sandison did not want to do, which was very nearly everything.

"This, that, and the other," I replied to Grace honestly enough. "If the library can be thought of as the kitchen of knowledge, I seem to be the short-order cook."

Griff and Hoop were saying nothing. She gave them an exasperated look and sat down at her place. Almost immediately, Griff gasped and straightened up sharply. I had the impression Grace's foot may have given his shin a tap. More than a tap. "I was about to say," he rushed the words, "you getting along hunky-dory with Sandison?"

"We are on"—first-name basis did not quite cover the situation— "what might be called familiar terms. I call him Sandy."

"Heard him called a lot, but never that."

This seemed to bring a sense of relief around the table. Hoop came to life. "Might have plenty of library customers pretty soon, Morrie. Mornings anyway. There's strike talk. We was at the union meeting last night—"

"I could tell," Grace inserted. "I heard you come in." As I unavoidably had, too.

Griff stiffened again, apparently of his own accord this time. "Refreshments are in order after a business session," he maintained, prim as if the pair of them hadn't reeled in around midnight, bumping the furniture and misjudging the stairs.

"Anyhow," Hoop sped past the spree after the meeting, "there's talk that the union might go out if the snakes won't give on the lost dollar." Even I knew that would be something like a declaration of war.

"And bring in more goons and strikebreakers," Grace underscored that, "like the last several times?"

"Those yellow-bellied buggers got on everybody's nerves a little too much the last time," Griff said, wielding a fork as if fending off such invaders. "The other unions didn't like the way we was treated, they might be next. Evans and his council have made the rounds, they're not as hot in the head as the last fellows were, and they've got most everybody ready to side with us. Even the streetcar drivers.

Shut down the whole town this time, we could, if the mine strike gets called." He summed up magisterially, "Things could work out just fine, if them others don't stick their noses in and make trouble."

Grace, I noticed, looked as if strike talk was the kind of thing that gave her hives. Trying to keep up with the nuances of Butte, I asked, "Those others are . . . ?"

"The Wobblies," said Hoop. "Who else?"

"They'd just love to see a strike get out of hand," Griff laid it out for me. "The more blood in the streets, the better they figure it is for them. The Wobs would turn this into Russia if they could." All at once the crimson cover of the jolly Little Red Songbook made more sense to me.

"They aren't the only ones who can play it cute, though." Griff still was wound up, his fork punctuating his words. "Thanks to them, Evans has got Anaconda looking at its hole card in the negotiations about getting the dollar back. It'd rather deal with him than the IWW any day."

"The meek shall inherit, if they are clever enough about it," I mused aloud.

"That sounds like something that shook out of a library book."

"I was merely complimenting the union's strategy at the table, Griff. I am not taking sides on the issue of a strike."

Grace was. She reached to the turkey platter and plucked up the wishbone. "See this, you pair of busybodies?" *Snap*, and she brandished the wish-fulfilling piece of the bone at the supposedly retired miners. "There, now, I've asked that you not get your old fool heads broken on a picket line."

"Aw, Mrs. Faraday, it maybe won't come to that." Griff sounded as if he was trying to convince himself along with her.

Something Hoop had said stuck with me, and I turned to him. "If the men do go on strike, why would any of them frequent the library just mornings?"

"Speakeasies don't open until noon."

IN MYTHOLOGY, Atlas alone has the world on his shoulders, but in real life the globe of concerns rests on each of us at any given time. After that suppertime discussion, what weighed on me when I settled into bed as usual with a lovingly done book from the library— *The Education of Henry Adams*, in this instance—was the gravity of the times. The immeasurable shadow of the 1914–1918 war still lay over the affairs of nations; Europe's old jealously held boundaries were being torn up and rewritten, for better or worse, at the Paris peace conference. Russia already had shaken the political firmament by doing away with the Czar and yielding to the new fist of the Bolsheviks. America's habit of throwing a fit to ward off contagion was at high pitch; activists with a leftist tinge were being hounded by government agents, even jailed or deported. Alongside that, the laboring class started at a deep disadvantage whenever it challenged the masters of capital. Strikes were its only effective tool, the way things were, but the powers that be resisted those with force if necessary. It added up to a jittery period of history, did it not? I knew enough of life to understand that every era has a set of afflictions, yet 1919 seemed to be a double dose. The pages in front of me, stylishly written, did little to dispel such heavy thoughts. Henry Adams, descendant of two presidents and with as much blue blood in his veins as there is in America, confessed at length in his autobiographical *Education* to a life contradictorily adrift on oceans of ignorance. Adams had not lived to see the turbulent aftermath of the Great

War, but even so he professed little hope of ever finding "a world that sensitive and timid natures could regard without a shudder."

I closed the book on that sentence. There was no point in reading about timid natures in Butte.

THE EDUCATION OF MORRIS MORGAN had a new chapter waiting the next day. It began in the Reading Room, where I was poring over the subscription list with Smithers, the young librarian on the periodicals desk, to see how we might squeeze more magazines into the budget we had. I felt a tap on the shoulder and turned around to an angular woman dressed in old-fashioned style, gray and gaunt as a duchess in a Goya etching. "You are the person," she enunciated to me so loudly and clearly that every head in the room snapped up from reading, "in charge of evening groups, I believe? I wish to speak with you."

I looked hopefully toward the mezzanine, but for once, Sandison was not on hand to roar "Quiet!" at the offender. Peculiar characters are drawn to a library like bees to a flower garden, so I turned to this one with the most authoritative air I could, and, indicating I was nearly finished with what I was at, murmured, "If you'll wait in the foyer, ma'am, I'll be with you in just a minute."

"Hsst!" The warning hiss from Smithers came a little late. In an ingratiating tone, he was saying: "How are you today, Mrs. Sandison?"

"Ah. Actually, we can finish this later," I told Smithers, and quickly ushered the visiting personage into the mineralogy section, the nearest room not in use.

Now that we had privacy, Dora Sandison paused to study me, which did not take her long. Even her eyes were gray, and they were the sort that did not miss a trick. She was as tall as her husband, and acted taller. I had heard the library staff refer to the Sandisons as the grandee and the grandora, and could understand why. "I regret taking you away from your other task," she said, her expression indicating nothing of the sort. "However, the evening group of which I am a member has a most pressing need."

"I'm sorry to hear that," I responded warily, trying to imagine which of the clubs that met in the basement auditorium would attract such a personality. The Theosophists, to unravel the mysteries of the Divinity? The League of Nations supporters, to correct the habits of governments?

She surprised me with a conspiratorial smile. "We require music stands."

"Music—?"

"The Gilbert and Sullivan Libretto Study Group is not provided with music stands, if you can believe that."

"I see." A sense of caution grew in me. "Surely this is the kind of request that your husband has dealt with, up until now?"

"Oh, horsefeathers," she brushed away my concern. "You know how Sandy is about such things."

Now I really did see. I could just about recite what Sandison's response to a request solely on behalf of Gilbert and Sullivan aficionados would have been. *"Don't they have hands? Holding a piece of sheet music in front of their noses shouldn't strain them too much."*

"My husband, bless his soul," she went on in a confiding tone, "sometimes carries matters too far. He takes the ridiculous view that answering the needs of a group I coincidentally am a member of would constitute preferential treatment, can you imagine?"

I chuckled nervously. "There is the point, Mrs. Sandison, that no other group has seen the need for such, um, equipment."

She snorted, very much like Sandison himself. "That is their failing rather than ours, then," she instructed me with a glint in her eye that wouldn't be argued with. "We sorely lack such equipment, as you call it, to hold our libretto sheets when the member whose turn it is takes our group through the intricacies of the lyrics of the chosen operetta..For example, '*Strike the concertina's melancholy string! Blow the spirit-stirring harp like anything! Let the piano's martial blast rouse the echoes of the past!*'" During this demonstration she waved her arms in my face as vigorously as a semaphore flagger.

She paused and caught her breath. "You can surely understand," she said as if I'd better, "the presenter needs to be free to gesture, or the spirit of Gilbert and Sullivan is lost."

Sometimes it is wise to bend before the gale. "I'll see what can be done about music stands."

She smiled slyly again. "I'm so glad Sandy put a reasonable person in charge of such matters."

With that, Dora Sandison departed in as grand a fashion as she had arrived, and I was left with the equipment problem. I searched the building high and low, but the marvelous holdings of the Butte Public Library did not include music stands. Somehow a purchase would have to be made, and I groaned at what was ahead of me, knowing how tight Sandison was with a dollar when the purchase of anything other than a book was involved.

"Sandy? If I could have a minute of your time?" Grumpily he left off reading a rare books catalogue and creaked around in his desk chair to face me. "Spit it out, Morgan."

"We have a request from an evening group for some freestanding smallish reading racks to hold the sheets of paper they work from, and—"

"Hah. You've been hearing from the Giblet and Mulligan Society about those damn music stands. My wife is in that group, and I've told her the same thing I'll tell you: the library can't show favoritism to any one bunch."

"Naturally not. But those rather modest implements would be of use to other groups as well."

"What for? Don't they have—"

"—they do have hands, but there are occasions when they would welcome some kind of device to hold certain items." I groped for some sort of example. "The Ladies' and Gentlemen's Literary and Social Circle, for instance, when they wish to have photo displays to go with their discussion of the works of Robert Louis Stevenson. The mystical castle in Edinburgh." My fingers conjured that citadel in the air. "The sinister backstreets of London where Jekyll transmogrifies into Hyde." I turned my hands into claws and made a grotesque face.

Sandison watched my little performance incredulously. "That's what goes on with that la-de-da bunch? Dry-goods clerks and young women afraid they'll be old maids sit there and actually follow Stevenson's stories from scene to scene?"

"Stranger things have happened," I said, true as far as it went.

He smacked a hand to his desktop, a sound like a shot. "That's genius for you. What a writer." I was given the kind of look a cowboy probably received for coming late to the corral. "Why didn't you tell me this before, Morgan? Go on over to Simonetti's music store and buy the things." He jerked open his bottom drawer, dug into the small strongbox that held petty cash, and handed me some money. I waited for him to jot down the sum or have me sign for it or however he handled a disbursement, but he simply waved me out of his sight and went back to pawing through the list of books he craved.

Out on the street in the freshness of the day, and having survived both Sandisons, I sauntered along with snatches of song in me; Gilbert and Sullivan can do that to you. The Montana weather for once was as perfect as could be, sunshine slanting between the tall buildings, checkerboarding the busy street, passersby in their downtown clothes brightening or dimming according to warmth or shade. The street tableau of shoppers and strollers seemed removed from talk of a strike, even though the Hill and its clashes were never far off. The day was so fine I tried to put such thoughts away and simply enjoy being out on my errand.

Emerging from the music store with my arms full of music stands I felt like an itinerant choirmaster, but Butte apparently saw stranger sights every day and no one paid me much attention. I was passing a haberdashery when my own eye was caught by the window display. An Arrow collar mannequin was admiring itself in a mirror; I could do without the collar, but draped on the mannequin torso was an exemplary suit—blue serge, librarianly. I stopped to admire the cut and material, smiling to myself as I thought of something Casper would say when about to commit an extravagance: *"How's a guy ever going to be rich if he doesn't practice at it?"* Riches were still eluding me—I needed to do something about that at some point—but my library wages were adding up a trifle, and that suit beckoned, come payday.

Turning to go, I glimpsed past the mannequin into the mirror and froze in my tracks. In the reflection, I could see across the street, half a block down, to where two bulky figures were assiduously studying the plate-glass display of a pet store. They were not the type to be in the market for parakeets.

Window men.

I would know the species anywhere, but in Chicago they had been rife enough to be a civic nuisance. Private detectives spying on lovers

who happened to be married to other people. Pinkerton operatives
lurking on some mission. Plainclothes policemen trying to keep an
eye on the mob, or mobsters trying to get something on the police.
Sometimes it seemed every Chicagoan was trailed by another, half a
block behind. And whenever the one in front paused to tie a shoelace
or buy a newspaper, the one trailing had to evince sudden interest in
the nearest store window. The duo in the mirror—why should I rate
two?—still were rapt over pets.

As I committed their sizable outlines to memory, another mental
image was jostled: these two together were a near fit to the worst of
those shadows that had followed me from wakes. But that was too
much imagination. Wasn't it?

Casually as I could manage, I walked back to the library, the music
stands feeling like an armful of lightning rods with a storm on the
horizon. When I reached the big front door, I opened it slowly so
that I could see behind me in the glass. The window men were gone,
naturally.

THAT EVENING AFTER SUPPER, I knocked on Griffith's door.

The shuffle of carpet slippers, then the door flung open and Griff
stood there in his long underwear and workpants, like a watchman
roused by an out-of-place noise in the night. "What's up, Morrie?"
Down at his side, in his right hand, something sharp glinted. "Need a
new notch in your belt?"

For the second time that day, my feet felt planted in quicksand. "I
didn't mean to intrude, I'll come back another—"

"Naw, step on in." The pointed instrument cut a circle in the air
as he indicated a table and chair crammed into the far corner of the
room. "Fixing Grace's purse strap for her." Ushering me in, he went

on over and put down the awl he was holding, atop the leatherwork. "Guest gets the chair." He perched on the edge of his bed, toes of his slippers barely reaching the floor. "What's on your mind? You look spooked."

"This will sound silly, but I think I'm being followed around town."

Griff perused me, his wrinkles wrinkling even more. "Let's get Hoop in on this." He banged the heel of his fist on the wall, and shortly Hooper came in, bringing his own chair.

I described to them that morning's experience, and the unlikelihood that the two idlers were pet fanciers. "Keep this to yourselves, please. I don't wish to worry Grace about this."

"Or have her kick you out of here on your can," Hoop said.

"Well put."

Griff hopped off the bed, went to the window, and pulled down the blind. "Tell me this," he intoned, turning to me. "When you lit down from the train, was there a couple of bruisers hanging around?"

"Big and bigger," Hoop specified.

"Beefier than ordinary, yes, now that you say so, there was such a pair at the depot."

"That's them," Griff said. "Anaconda's goons. The one big enough to eat soup off the top of your head is Typhoon Tolliver."

I felt as if the seat of my chair had just pinched me.

Hoop was saying, "Jim Jeffries flattened him—"

"—in the second round of the title bout, right hook to the jaw," I finished for him. "What on earth is he doing in Butte?"

"Beating people up," Griff had no trouble answering that. "The Anaconda Company don't play pattycake."

"But—" Some questions scare off words. Why was I a candidate for a beating from an ex-heavyweight pug?

Hooper answered that without it being asked. "That bunch in the Hennessy Building sics the goons on any union organizers who come in from the outside." He and Griff looked at me critically.

I shook my head.

"Especially anybody working for the Wobblies," Griff prompted.

I shook my head harder.

"Somebody who'd lay low until the right time," said Hoop.

"Then stir things up like poking a hornets' nest," said Griff.

"Anaconda don't like that kind of thing," Hoop added.

Another shake of my head, as much to clear it as anything else. "I am not any kind of an organizer, believe me. I simply came here to get ri— to find decent work." Both old men watched me mutely. "The goons, as you call them, are wasting their time on me."

One or the other of my listeners, like ancients who had heard it all before, spoke up. "You better hope they get tired of it."

THE NEXT DAY WAS SUNDAY, day of rest for the library, but not for the boardinghouse. Scarcely was I seated for breakfast, wondering where the others were, when Grace forged out of the kitchen all but wrapped in a tie-around apron over a nice dark dress. Along with my plate of sidepork and eggs, she delivered with a flourish:

"I wondered if you might like to go to church."

"Church." I hadn't meant for it to come out quite like that, but it sounded as though I was trying to identify the concept.

Hooper came through the doorway, also dressed in surprising Sunday best and smelling of musky cologne. "What this is, Griff's filling in with the choir. They're hard up."

"Ah. And bringing his own audience, insofar as it can be conscripted?"

"He'll be in much better voice if he sees us there, he happened to mention," Grace coaxed with a nice example of a Sunday smile.

"He can stand all that kind of help he can get," Hoop chipped in.

I put up my hands. "I know when I'm outnumbered." Obligation takes strange shapes. Back in Casper's earliest bouts, I had mastered the tactic myself of "papering the house," as it was called, by giving away tickets by the handful if necessary to fill the seats of the arena. If Griffith dreamed of a sellout crowd for his star turn with the choir, I understood intrinsically.

THE SNUG REDBRICK CHURCH with its peaked hat of cupola looked as if it had been smuggled in from a vale in Wales, and no sooner had Grace and I and Hooper slid into seats at the back of the congregation than the creased little minister, peering over half-moon eyeglasses like a veteran counter of crowds, nodded to himself and launched into prayer. In Welsh. Evidently Grace had not anticipated this any more than I had, both of us trying to keep a straight face at not understanding a word of what plainly was going to be an hour of many hundreds of words. Actually, some time into the minister's spate my ear figured out the repeated invoking of "Iesu Grist," and I sat there caught up in the wayward notion of Christ as grist, the mills of faith grinding fine the belief in a clear-eyed savior at that moment across half the world. Sunday certainties, which left only the rest of the week.

The praying rolled on like thunder until the minister reached a final crescendo of syllables that sounded like *tragwyddoldeb!*

"Eternity!" Hoop translated to the other two of us in a hoarse whisper, and that was definitively that.

"Welcome, all ye, the accustomed and the new faces." The surprise

lilt of English from the minister sent Grace and me melting toward
each other in relief. Not much taller than his pulpit, the elderly man
of faith again peered around the church as if counting the house,
this time shook his head instead of nodding, and declared: "A suf-
ficiency will be heard from me soon enough. Let us get on with the
singing." With that, the male choir filed up, all in severe black suits
and blinding starched white shirts, two dozen strong, Griff at one
end, proud as a parrot. Church or not, he sought out the three of us
with a broad wink, welcoming us to the occasion he plainly saw as
the Welsh Miners' Choir of Butte, starring Wynford Griffith.

The choir director, burliest of the bunch, stepped from the ranks,
gave a steady bass hum, which was picked up by the others in a com-
munal drone that seemed to vibrate the building. Then, as if in one
glorious voice the size of an ocean's surf, they swept into hymn after
hymn. I sat there enchanted, Grace swaying gently next to me. Music
makes me almost willing to believe in heaven.

Then, though, came a chorus I could have done without.

> Were I to cherish earthly riches,
> They are swift and fleet of wing;
> A heart pure and virtuous,
> Riches and eternal gain will bring.

There is that about the Welsh: they can sing their way under your
skin, to the bones of your being. I needed no reminding that riches,
in what pursuit I had given them, had proved to be elusively swift
and winged. Yet why did a Richest Hill on Earth and its supposed
opportunities exist, if not to be tapped? Was I really supposed to
count my gains in life only afterward, in the time of *tragwyddoldeb*?

Eternity did not seem much of a payoff if you had to scrimp to get there.

My spell of brooding broke off when the old minister, frail as a leaf after the gusts of the choir, ascended to the pulpit once more.

"'Tis no sense to maunder about, when but one thing is on every mind." He gazed severely over the settled moons of his glasses. "There is talk of a strike in the mines, is there not?" The rustle of the congregation answered that.

"I have had my say any number of times before," the ministerial voice sounded weary, "on the stopping of work and the negotiating of wages. The two seem as bound together in this town as the two sides of a coin." Aha! Not even the man of the cloth could set aside the propensity for earthly gain. Perhaps I was imagining, but his own choir seemed to be looking at him as though he had just caught up with a main fact of life. "The shepherd does not leave his flock, even when it may have wool over its eyes," he went on drily. "If the mines do shut down, the church shall again have a strike committee. We'll again gather food and clothing for the families left bereft. Depend on that." He paused, drawing on the silence. "A word of caution, however. If you men do go out"—he looked out over the stooped miners' shoulders that filled half the church—"or you women march in their support"—a similar gaze to the upturned faces of the wives—"as you have been known to do, walk the line of the law very carefully. The times are not good. The sedition laws that came with the war are not fine-grained as to whether a person is the Kaiser in disguise or a Bolshevik with a bomb under his coattails or an honest miner seeking honest pay. Some of you had a taste of that last time, when I had to go down to the jail and bail you out for the hitherto unknown crime of 'unlawful assembly.'" Reaching in over his glasses, he pinched the bridge of his nose as if to shut off that memory. "The church coffer is no longer sufficient for bail," the words came slowly now, "nor can we keep contributing to legal defense funds. This time around, it will all be up to your union. You can help its cause and your own by being mindful of that pernicious statute until wiser heads can change it. Otherwise, Butte's finest, to call them that"—it was well known that Butte policemen were Irish, and not the Dublin Gulch ore-shoveling type—"will pick you off like ripe apples. For now," his voice rose, "render therefore unto Caesar the things which are Caesar's."

I squirmed at that. I perfectly well knew it to be a biblical parable, but it was not Caesar up there in the Hennessy Building, pulling strings attached to the police department.

The minister took off his spectacles, folded them, and seemed to shake his head at himself. "Let us return to the singing."

As we walked out after the service, Grace pursed a look at me as if to see what I thought. "My Arthur used to say there are those who make a scarecrow of the law." I thought it best not to say Arthur had read some Shakespeare along the way. Directly ahead of us, Hoop and Griff were stumping along, sleeve cuffs flying as they dissected the sermon. Watching them, Grace said soberly: "The union is going to have its hands full, isn't it."

THERE WAS NO KNOWING how these things come about, but somehow that Sunday spate of Welsh sermonizing and song rinsed away the window men. The way was clear, to and from the library, the next day and the next and those after that, and while I habitually peeked over my shoulder for figures lurking half a block behind, they were notable only for their absence. It was as I indeed hoped, I could tell myself: the goons or their bosses saw me for what I was, a glorified library clerk sauntering meek and mild to church, and were wasting no further time on me.

Which was a lucky thing, because I was falling in love with the Butte Public Library. Walking up to it each fresh morning, its Gothic turret like the drawbridge tower into the castle, I warmed to the treasures within those softly gray granite walls. Sandison standing there at the top of the steps counting us off as if checking his herd came to seem patriarchal rather than high-handed. The staff softened toward me—with the exception of Miss Runyon—as I picked up stray tasks that they wanted to dodge. The nooks and crannies and grandiosities of the old building intrigued me, like an ancient mansion labyrinth leading back to Gutenberg's printing press and the start of everything, and always, always, there were the lovely classic books tucked away here and there for stolen snatches of reading. Down any aisle, Stendhal or Blake or Wharton or Cather or Shakespeare or Homer or any of the Russians waited to share words with me, their classic sentences in richly inked typefaces as if rising from the paper. I suppose the best way to say it is that the library's book collection, courtesy of that snowtopped figure with the Triple S initials, was the kind I would have had myself if I were rich.

In short, work of this sort fit me from head to toe. I could even put up with sharing office space with Sandison, as his chain-lightning moods kept a person alert. The old saying had his name on it: he may have been hard to get along with, but harder to get along without.

The library ran on one principle: Samuel S. Sandison was next to God. Whether above or below, opinions varied. His style of administration was as effective as it was unpredictable. For hours on end he would stay holed up in the office, apparently oblivious to anything happening elsewhere in the building. Then without warning he

would barge out of his lair and prowl from floor to floor, wearing the
expression of a man who took pleasure in kicking puppies. The result
was an amazing library: the staff was on its toes every second, and its
offerings were, of course, first-rate. I have to say, the man responsible
for all this was not exactly an officemate easy on the nerves. The only
mirth Sandison showed was when he spotted a bargain book in some
catalogue of rarities and he would let out a *"Heh!"* and smile beneath
his wreath of beard. Mostly, being around him was like having the
Grand Inquisitor grading one's homework.

"Goldsmith," he characteristically would snap over his shoulder
from where he was enthroned in his desk chair, and I had mere seconds to figure out whether he meant for me to trot across town to the
dealer in fine metals or commence a conversation about the poet of
England's peasantry.

Guessing, I recited: *"'Ill fares the land, to hastening ills a prey /
Where wealth accumulates, and men decay.'* Rather daring for his day,
wouldn't you say, Sandy?"

"Romantic twaddle about how nice it was to live in huts, I'd call
those elegies of his."

"That's too dry a reading of him," I protested. "He had a wicked
wit. Who else would have said of Garrick that onstage he was won-
derfully simple and natural, it was only when he was off that he was
acting?"

That brought a snort. "Doesn't mean old Goldilocks could tell
a hoe from a hole in the ground. Robert Louis Stevenson, now,
he knew his stuff about how life really is." And with that, Oliver
Goldsmith, or whomever, would be consigned to the vast second
rank and remain unbought.

"Morgan?" The dubious drawl that met me this particular day told
me I was in for another assignment of the Sandison sort. "You started

something with those music stands. Now Miss Runyon claims she can't function unless she has a corkboard on a tripod to pin pictures on for the kids' story hour. Go down there and see what you can rig up."

As I was passing his desk, he looked askance at me over one of the catalogues of rare books that were perpetually open in front of him. "Oxford flannel?"

"Serge." I brushed a bit of lint off the new blue suit. "Like it?"

"You look like an undertaker."

Down the stairs I went, past Miss Runyon's cold eye, to the spacious meeting room all the way in the basement. The basement had originally been intended as an armory, and its thick walls made it a fine auditorium, no sounds escaping to the outside. You could about hear the spirited echoes of the Shakespeareans and the philosophical ones of the Theosophists lingering amid the pale plaster foliage of the scrollwork around the top of the walls. A curtained stage presided across one end of the room, and at the other stood a spacious supply cabinet. I was rooting around in the cabinet for anything resembling corkboard and a tripod when I heard the entry door swish closed in back of me.

I glanced over my shoulder and there the two of them were, big and bigger.

"Look at him, Ty." The one who was merely big had a pointed face with eyes that bulged like those of an eel, probably from so much time spent planted in front of store windows peering sideways. "In that prissy suit, you'd almost think he's the real item, wouldn't you."

The response from the figure half a head taller than him clip-clopped in at a heavy pace: "If we wasn't smart enough to know he's up to something, yeah."

The lesser goon was alarming enough, but Typhoon Tolliver I knew to be made of muscle, gristle, and menace. In the boxing ring

his roundhouse blows stirred a breeze in the first rows of seats—
hence his nickname—and had he been quicker in either the feet
or the head, he might have become an earlier Jack Dempsey. As it
was, his career of pounding and being pounded made him no more
than a punching bag that other heavyweights needed to get past on
the way to a championship bout. His flattened features and oxlike
blink were the kind of thing I had been afraid would happen to
Casper, another reason behind cashing in on our fixed fight and
the intention to steer the ring career of Capper Llewellyn into early
retirement after he regained the title. Trying not to stare at Tolliver
and his ponderous bulk, I brushed my hands of my cabinet task and
managed to utter:

"The business of the library is conducted upstairs, gentlemen. If
you would follow me—"

My break for the door was cut off by Eel Eyes, barring my way
with a coarse left hand that justified the Latin *sinister.* "We like it
down here," he said lazily. "Nice and private, we can have a talk." He
sized me up with a tilt of his head. "Let's start with what brings a
fancy number like you to Butte. You slipped into town real easy, didn't
you, no baggage or nothing."

That threw me. "Just because the railroad lost my—"

"You're pretty slick," Eel Eyes gave me credit I did not want. "But
you can't pull the wool over Ty and me. We get paid good dough to
be on the lookout for wise guys like you. Some gold-plated talker
who just shows up out of nowhere," his tone was mocking, "if you
know the sort. And sure enough, you no sooner hit town and that
Red songbook starts doing its stuff at those burying parties. Then
you latch on at this joint, where all kinds of crackpots come out at
night. It all adds up to one thing, don't you think, chum?"

This was a nightmare. "I can explain every one of those—"

"I bet you can, fancy-pants." He leered at me. "After what happened to the last organizer for that Red pack of Wobblies, you have
to come sneaking into town all innocent-like, don't you. You can
maybe fool those stupid miners up on the Hill, but Ty and me got you
pegged."

"One of them outside infiltrators, yeah." Tolliver's belated utterance unnerved me a great deal more than anything from the other
goon. His conversation came off the top of his head and out his
mouth seemingly without passing through his brain. It was as if
he had speaking apparatus on the outside of his head, like English
plumbing.

"I am a denomination of one," I protested hotly, "employed by no
one but this library, whose gainful work you are keeping me from.
Now if you will accompany me upstairs, I can lead you to someone
who will set you straight about—"

Typhoon Tolliver took a flatfooted step and planted himself in
front of me. "You look like somebody, under that face spinach. Ain't
we met somewhere?"

"Surely I would recall such a mishap."

"Don't get smart on us." He loomed in on me. "You been somewhere I been, I just know it. Chicago, how about?"

Here was where family resemblance was a danger. I looked like
my brother, whose face had appeared on boxing posters on every
brick wall in that city. Maximum as my mustache was, it amounted
to thin disguise if someone concentrated hard enough on the countenance underneath to come up with the name Llewellyn. Goons do
business with other goons, and this pair would not waste a minute
in transacting me to the Chicago gambling mob. Which meant I
was a goner, if Tolliver's slow mental gears managed to produce the
recognition he was working at.

I snapped my fingers. "Aha! The World's Fair, of course! The African native village and the big-eyed boys that we were." Wiggling my eyebrows suggestively, I took a chance and leaned right into the meaty face. "The bare-breasted women of the tribe, remember?"

Tolliver blushed furiously. "Every kid in Chi was there looking."

"We know of two, don't we, although the passage of the years has dimmed my recollection of you more than yours of me."

"Yeah, well, sure, what do you expect, a mug like yours—"

"Knock it off, both of you." The one with those aquarium eyes moved in on me. "Let's try another angle on what kind of four-flusher you really are. What did you do in the war?"

"I was elsewhere."

"Like where?"

"Tasmania."

"Say it in English when you're talking to us," Tolliver warned.

"It's in Australia, stupe," the other one rasped. "And you weren't in any rush to come back and enlist, is that it? You look like a quitter if I ever saw one. No wonder this country is full up with pinkoes and—"

"Infiltrators," Tolliver recited mechanically.

"—and stray cats from half the world and—" The lesser thug's yammering broke off and he eyed me suspiciously. "What're you cocking your head like that for?"

"Just listening for the clink of your own medals."

You find concern for reputation in strange places. The pointy face reddened to the same tint Tolliver's had. "I kept the peace here at home."

"I can imagine."

"Hey, punk, a smart aleck like you can end up in a glory hole if you don't watch your—"

Swish, and then *bang!* All three of us jumped.

Samuel Sandison towered in the doorway, the flung-open door still quivering on its hinges behind him. "What's this? The idlers' club in session?"

All at once there was more breathing room around me, both goons stepping back from the perimeter of authority Sandison seemed to bring with him. What was I seeing? He was twice their age, and though of a size with Tolliver, no physical match. Yet the two burly interlopers now looked very much like spooked schoolboys. Why the white-faced wariness all of a sudden?

Sandison's ice-blue gaze swept over them and onto me, and I blinked innocently back. "We're only here because this helper of yours is up to something," the pointy-faced one was saying, not quite stammering, "and the people we work for need to know what he's—"

"Quiet!" Sandison boomed, the word resounding in the enclosed room. "You tell them on the top floor of the Hennessy Building that they maybe run everything else in town, but not this library. Clear out of here, and I mean now."

The pair cleared out, but not without glares over their beefy shoulders at me.

Now all I faced was the stormcloud of beard. Sandison inspected me as if having missed some major feature until then. "Miss Runyon told me you were taking an unconscionably long time down here. Morgan? Are you up to something?"

"Sandy, I swear to you, I am an utter stranger to the battles of Butte." That left Chicago out of it.

He shook his head. "If you weren't such a bookman, I wouldn't have you on the payroll for more than a minute." Turning to go, he said, as if he was ordering me to head off a stampede: "Get the damn corkboard rigged up so we don't have to hear any more from that old heifer Runyon about it."

I PICKED AT MY FOOD that suppertime, drawing a look of concern from Grace. "More turkey, Morrie? It's not like you to be off your feed."

Down the table, two sets of bushy gray eyebrows squinched in similar regard of me. Neither Hoop nor Griff asked anything about my disturbing day, however, in respect of our pact not to bother Grace's head about the goons' interest in me. Pushing away my plate, I alibied: "A touch of stomach disorder, is all. Nothing a restful evening in my room can't fix, I'm sure."

Upstairs, flat on my back atop the dragon coverlet while I stared at the ceiling and waited for inspiration of some sort to show up, I never felt less sure of fixing anything. The zigzags of life were more puzzling than ever. There I lay, in the most comfortable circumstances I had known for a long while, with work that nicely employed my mind, and the goons of the world were sure I was a secret operative for the most radical wing of the laboring class. It was dizzying. If America was a melting pot, Butte seemed to be its boiling point. The Richest Hill was turning out to be also a Cemetery Ridge of copper to be fought over, and some trick of fate had dumped Morris Morgan—all right, Morgan Llewellyn—right in the middle of it. Not the spot I thought I was choosing when I stepped down from that train.

A train runs in both directions, the ceiling reminded me, as boardinghouse ceilings tend to do. Lying there looking up at the map of plaster imaginings, I felt an old restlessness. It was a lamplit evening in the Marias Coulee teacherage, when I knew I was losing Rose, that a faint stain in the beaverboard ceiling seemed to suggest the outline of Australia. Even here in Grace Faraday's well-maintained accommodations, did that swirl in the plasterer's finishwork over by the window resemble South America?

Fate comes looking for us, often when we are most alone. Stealthily the conclusion I was waiting for crept down from the ceiling and took shape in the corner of the room. My gaze followed it to my satchel, shabby reliable companion in a portable life.

I swore softly to myself. Ordinarily I do not use profanity, but that was the least of what had been fanned up in me by the bluster from Eel Eyes and Typhoon Tolliver. Bouncing off the bed, in a hurry of resolve now, I crossed to where the satchel waited. Grappled it open wide. Dug to the bottom of it, past spare socks and the poetry of Matthew Arnold, to where they lay.

Brass knuckles. The "Chicago pinky ring," weapon of choice for the streetwise combatant facing an unfair fight.

It had been years since I needed to resort to these, but they never aged. As I tried them on now, they fit across the backs of my hands cold and secure. Even the most vicious street fighter had to hesitate at the dark sheen of armor on a fist, the set of nubs that could gouge into skin like a can opener. Of course, knuckles of metal did you any good only within striking range of an opponent. But I had sparred enough as a warm-up partner for Casper in training camp; I knew at least as much footwork as that lummox Tolliver. And unless I had lost the knack of sizing up an adversary, the more mouthy goon was the type who would blink hard at the sight of brass knuckles. He would not rush to have that well-shaven pointy face marred to the bone.

Quitter, he'd called me. We'd see.

WOULDN'T YOU KNOW, no sooner was I prepared to put my fortified knuckles on the line against Anaconda's lurkers than they ceased lurking. Even when I deliberately dawdled on downtown streets, passing the time of day with the blind newspaper seller or picking up the latest gossip from the hack driver at the nearby hotel, I could not draw the goons out. As the days lengthened, their cloak of shadow shrank, further discouraging any encounters. Fondling the brass knuckles in my suitcoat pocket as I went to and from the library, it was as if I were rubbing amulets that kept away evil spirits. Although I knew the real force that had stopped the goons cold in their tracks was Samuel Sandison, whatever that was about.

As for me, the lord and master of the books kept me hopping. It was a mystery how the Butte Public Library had managed to operate before I was there to catch all the tasks delegated from that kingly desk of his to mine.

This particular Friday had started as usual, with Sandison drawling, "You know what needs doing, or at least should," and disappearing off to somewhere undisclosed, while I faced tabulating the week's checkout slips sent up from the issue desk. He was a demon promoter of the library and wanted the list of current favorite books unfailingly in the newspaper at the end of each week. It was not an inspiring task, as the most popular book of the past seven days invariably turned out to be Mrs. Mary V. Terhune's *My Little Love*, and I sometimes had to adjust the arithmetic to get Thomas Hardy and Edith Wharton onto the list at all; Proust of course was hopeless. So, by the time I fiddled with the citizenry's literary taste to more or less satisfaction, the messenger would be there waiting to rush my compilation to the *Daily Post*. Messengers raced across Butte, jumping on and off the trolleys and trotting the edge of the sidewalks as they carried typed instructions back and forth between the downtown headquarters and the mine offices, workers' cashed paychecks from stores to banks, small goods from the department store to the wealthier homes, and so on. Our stretch of street was served by a gnomelike courier named Skinner. Old enough to be thoroughly bald, Skinner nonetheless had the pared build of a jockey and was never motionless, on one foot and then the other as he waited to be handed whatever was to be delivered. I had learned to let him jitter there in the doorway; the man apparently was not constructed to sit in a chair.

I was nearly done typing up that week's list from Miss Runyon's checkout slips when Skinner, waiting restlessly as usual, blurted:

"Where you from, pal?"

"Mmm? Chicago."

"Small world. Me, too." I stiffened. "Maxwell Street and Halsted, know it?" he said from the side of his mouth, sending a deeper chill through me. The toughest neighborhood of the toughest section of that hardknuckled city. Was this going to be a repeat of Tolliver and Eel Eyes? Another message of the threatening sort from the Anaconda Company? Panic began to set in as I realized I was in my shirtsleeves, with my suitcoat—and its protective cargo of brass knuckles—on a hanger across the room. A disturbing look on him, the wiry man now bounced toward me on fleet feet as I grabbed for an inkwell, anything, in self-defense. Practically atop my desk as he leaned in face-to-face with me, Skinner demanded:

"Cubs or White Sox?"

I relaxed somewhat; baseball rivalry was not necessarily lethal. But it is surprising how an old grudge can hold up. In a ring constructed over the infield of the White Sox stadium, Comiskey Park, Casper on a cool clear Columbus Day had defeated Kid Agnelli—knockout, third round—before twenty-five thousand paying customers, and the owner of the White Sox and the ballpark, Charles Comiskey, had shorted us on the purse. Not for nothing was he known in Chicago sporting circles as Cheap Charlie. I would root against him and his team if they were the last baseball nine on earth. "My allegiance is to the Cubs," I put it more temperately to Skinner. "I once saw Tinker to Evers to Chance produce four double plays in one game. Masterful."

Skinner hooted. "The Cubs ain't what they used to be. The Sox got the real players these days, they're going to the Series, you watch."

"I shall." Sealing the book list in a gummed envelope, I handed it to him indicatively. "Now, do you suppose this missive could possibly find its way to the *Daily Post*?"

No sooner had the messenger scampered off than Sandison filled the doorway. Bypassing his desk, he lumbered over to the stained-glass window and peered out through one of the whorls like a boy at a knothole, a sign that something was on his mind. Something on his desk that he did not want to face.

"Sandy, you seem perturbed," I said diplomatically.

"I've just been with the trustees. They raked me over the coals about the library budget. Wanted to know where every damn penny goes." Turning from the window, he shook his head, the wool of his beard quivering. "They have a reason, I suppose. Few months ago, the city treasurer took off with everything he could lay his hands on."

"Bad?"

"Enough that the elected fools downtown see an embezzler under every bed now. Damn it, I thought it was hard to keep track of a few thousand cows—that was nothing compared to running this outfit." He passed a hefty hand over his cowlick as if trying to clear his head from there on in. "Spending that much time on numbers drives me up the wall. I don't see why the idiot trustees can't just trust a man."

I remember it exactly. Opportunity was in the air of that office, distinct as ozone. Idly piling paperwork from here to there, I said as though his bookkeeping burden were merely something I could add to the other stacks on my desk: "Thank heaven you have an arithmetical person on hand."

"Who?" Sandison eyed me. "You? You mean you can handle books that don't have mile-long words in them?"

"Assuredly."

"Are you telling me you're a certified accountant?"

"Mmm, *certified* perhaps is too confining a term. As you might imagine, standards are different from here to there. But along the way in life, I've had considerable experience with ledgers."

Sandison dropped into his desk chair, his weight sending it wheeling toward me. "Morgan? You just said you're not an accountant. What the hell then do you do with these ledgers you're talking about?"

"Oh, mend them. From the inside out." From his furrowed look, I could tell Sandison was not satisfied with that reply. "Let me put it this way, Sandy. Numbers are simply a language I happen to understand—Latin, numeracy, both have certain principles, fundamental in themselves. Surely you know the story of the bookkeeper and the desk drawer? No? Allow me. Every morning, a certain bookkeeper would come into the office of the firm, hang up his hat and coat, seat himself at his desk, pull out a drawer and look in it for a few seconds, shut it, and only then turn to his work. For forty years this went on—the same drawer, opened and shut, every morning. Finally came the day he retired, and the minute he left the office for the last time, the rest of the office staff crowded around his desk and one of them slowly opened that drawer. In it was a single sheet of paper. On it was written: 'Debits go on the left, credits on the right.'"

Sandison did not find my little tale as entertaining as I had hoped.

"The long and short of it is," came his rumble, "you claim you know how to balance the books."

I nodded. "To the last penny, if it comes to that."

He sat there and frowned for some time. He could be intent as a fiend when he was mulling a matter. "All right," he grudgingly granted at last, "you probably can't make any more mess of the arithmetic than I have. You're in charge of the damn bookkeeping. Come over here and start getting acquainted with the ledgers."

I walked on air back to the boardinghouse at the end of that day. The one fundamental principle of bookkeeping that had always stood out to me was that if you know how and where the money flows, you are hard to get rid of.

6

Live it up while you can, Mister Man About Town,
Because what you gonna do when the rent comes roun'?

Whistling it softly to myself, I contradicted the catchy popular tune by counting out my rent money as usual, that subsequent week, as I came down a few minutes early for supper. Grace was not there to take it. The table was not yet set. This was a new experience; generally the Faraday Boarding House ran like a seven-day clock.

I peeked in the kitchen, to find supper uncooked but Grace steaming.

"Make yourself useful, please," she said testily, bent low to the opened oven. "Yell up to the others that supper will be a while yet. This bird refuses to get done."

In double defiance—pale and dry—the latest turkey lay there in the roaster, and after calling upstairs to Hoop and Griff to hold on to their appetites, I returned to the kitchen, rolling up my sleeves. "If I might suggest, it is time to baste the beast."

"Baste," Grace said, with a fry cook's doubtfulness.

"Allow me." Crouching where she had been, I spooned the turkey's drippings over the breast and drumsticks, then stoked up the kitchen stove with a couple of pitchy sticks of wood. "There, now, the meal has no choice but to cook."

No sooner had I said so than the floor did a little dance. Silverware jingled, and Grace steadied a cream pitcher. After a moment, she dismissed the latest shake of everything. "That could have been worse."

"Grace," I let out along with my breath, "I will gladly take your word for that." I doubted I could ever get used to dynamite going off beneath the house.

Pushing a rather fetching flaxen wisp of hair off her forehead, she studied me as if I was the newest distraction. "Sit down for a minute, star boarder. There's something we need to talk about."

I went still. Was I in for another grilling about whether I was an IWW secret operative? What was I supposed to do, march around Butte wearing a sandwich board that read I AM NOT A WOBBLY?

"If it's about an unfortunate event in the library a while back," I fended as I settled across the kitchen table from her, "that was sheerly a case of mistaken—"

"It's church," she announced, rolling her eyes. "There's talk. About us. 'Ye and me,'" and she did not a bad imitation of the wee Welsh preacher. Griff had been asked to fill in with the choir a few more times, and the two of us and Hoop duly had made command performances as audience. What was wrong with that? Answering my inquiring look, Grace fanned with a hand as if brushing away pests. "What some of the nosy ones around the neighborhood are saying is"—she reddened at the exact words—"I'm taking up with a boarder. The old biddies."

Gossip, forever the whisper in the wind. "Mmm," I met Grace's report with uncertainty.

"Morrie?" Her violet eyes took in mine, a test that wouldn't go away. "Do you feel, um, taken up with?"

"I am about to fork over my week's rent," I said, unsure of how much honesty beyond that was a good idea just then. "That tends to put matters in a certain perspective."

Carefully folding my money away into her apron pocket, she allowed: "It does, doesn't it." Still hesitant, she went on: "There's the matter of appearances, though. A boardinghouse has to be extra careful not to be lumped in with—" She gestured off toward the fleshly neighborhood of Venus Alley.

Now Grace looked at me, but not quite straight at me. "So you know what this means. I'm sorry, but—"

I waited, dreading the prospect of trying to find any other lodging in Butte as cozy as this.

"—you'll have to go to church just with Hoop," she finished off her decree. Then bounced up to take out the perfectly roasted turkey.

REPRIEVED AT THE BOARDINGHOUSE, I could now busy myself learning the ins and outs of the library's finances. Sandison's style of bookkeeping had been what might be called extemporaneous, with occasional casual entries of *Miscellaneous book purchases* followed by sums that might well make a library trustee gulp. Trying to untangle his method, if that's what it was, I finally spotted in the ledger pages of staff wages and hours his hole card, so to speak. Me. Counting up, I could see there was not quite as much staff as was budgeted for— always a position or two short—and he covered those gaps in service, and doubtless put what would have been the wages into that bland

expenditure on books, by shuttling employees from job to job during the course of a day. That works until, say, the board of trustees'
president's wife is kept waiting at the temporarily vacant genealogy
desk. My arrival plugged a lot of slots. Shunting me from task to task
as Sandison did took those burdens off the other staffers; on a ranch
I believe I would have been called the choreboy. I didn't mind; variety has always been more to my taste than its opposite. I even was
growing fond of the diverse evening groups, catching the end of the·
discussion those nights when it fell to me to go back to the library and
close up, enjoying the verbal volleying about Hamlet's nervous condition or Wilson's strategy at the Paris peace conference. (However, I
prudently waited for the Gilbert and Sullivan clan to vacate entirely
before I tended to the music stands, lest Dora Sandison pounce on me
with some other demand.) And on a more daily basis, when needed
at a desk, I happily stepped into that role of librarian as bartender of
information. Presiding over shelves of intoxicating items, dispensing
whatever brand of knowledge was ordered up, I am sure I poured
generously. At least Sandison must have thought so, the morning he
told me to get downstairs and fill in for Miss Runyon at the Reading Room main desk as she made her grand descent to prepare for
story hour.

Elevated there at the high desk, I was coping with patrons' questions when commotion broke out in the foyer.

"*Don't,* pigface."

"Can't take it, huh, bag ears?"

"Jack and Molly, quit that or I'll have your hides."

The purr of threat in the teacherly voice settled things down,
at least momentarily, and in trooped as rough and tough a crowd,
male and female, as I had seen yet in Butte. On the other hand,
they were twelve-year-olds and a freckle epidemic was loose among

them. In flat caps and pigtails, hand-me-down britches and mended pinafores, plainly these were children from one of the neighborhoods on the Hill, spruced up for the library visit, but the sprucing could go only so far. Watching casually as edgy girls and pushing boys milled down the stairwell to the auditorium, I took a bit of guilty pleasure in the thought that Miss Runyon would have her hands full with this mob.

"Mr. Morgan." The purr was close at my side. "Your mustache is back."

I turned and was nearly startled off my sitting place.

"Rabrab!" I blurted, drawing nasty looks and one severe *shhh* from the Reading Room patrons.

A knowing laugh arrived with the same throatiness as the purr. "You remember. But you would, wouldn't you. Did you know the whole school used to call you the Walking Encyclopedia?"

I had last seen Barbara Rellis as a sixth-grader, a dark-eyed willow of a girl on the lookout for intrigue. Foremost in my memory was my first day of teaching at the Marias Coulee one-room school, when she ever so innocently raised her hand during roll call and asked if for the sake of keeping up with certain contrary stunts of the boys she couldn't turn her name around, most of it at least, just on the schoolground where name-calling ran every direction anyway? I found an appealing flavor of logic in that and let her. The Rabrab of then had filled out into a fashionably bobbed young woman, still slender but with a substantial bodice, and those eyes that so often held mischief like a flash of struck flint now had authority to them as well. She called over to the tail of the brigade dragging its feet in the stairwell. "Margie, mind them, please, give them a swat if you have to. Tell the story lady they're all hers, she can start. I'll be there in a minute." An older schoolgirl, obviously conscripted for the outing, took charge and the last of the children were hustled down the stairs.

Rabrab's—Barbara's—attention swung back to me. "I see that little smile," she said with one of her own, "don't try to hide it. You caused this, you know, my ending up a teacher. A number of us have. Paul Milliron is already a county superintendent, had you heard?" She was studying me, from my mustache on in, a faint wrinkle of puzzle-ment at the side of her eyes. "At first I didn't think it could be you, perched here like the head canary. In Butte, of all places. We were told you'd gone to—where was it? Transylvania?"

"Never mind. In the here and now, I—"

"Have you been back to Marias Coulee, since?"

"Not in person. I mean, no. Rab—Barbara, that is—"

This time her smile was the sly schoolgirlish one I remembered so well, as though she had something sweet tucked in her cheek. "You can call me that. It would make two of you who do. That's rather nice."

We were conversing in spirited whispers, not the best etiquette for the Reading Room, and I summoned Smithers from periodicals to sit in for me. Hurriedly escorting Rab out into the foyer, where there was only Shakespeare to overhear us, I began trying to contain the situation.

"About Marias Coulee. I must take you into my confidence, Rab." It worked. The racehorse keenness she had always shown at any prospect of conspiracy was immediately there to see. "It is best if no one in our old neighborhood knows I am back in Montana," I went on, "because of—well, possible hard feelings, you'll understand." I paused for what I hoped was drama's sake. "Rose and I had a falling out. A family matter."

She swooped on that. "It happens over and over, doesn't it. A brother and a sister, you'd think they were built to get along, but no, they find every way there is to get crosswise with each other. I see it all the time in my pupils. So I'm not surprised—those of us at school thought you and Rose were born in different phases of the moon, as the saying goes. And you won't go back now because you don't want to stir up old trouble—that is so like you, Mr. Morgan."

"I could not have put it better myself."

Rab leaned closer, back to whispering. "Now I'll let you in on a secret. It just happened, the other night. I'm betrothed. E-n-g-a-g-e-d," she rattled off as if in one of Marias Coulee's spelling bees. She wrinkled her nose, turning in an instant into the perfect facsimile of a pretty and mischievous bride.

There was no hiding my smile this time. "The lucky man is getting more than he bargained for."

"But keep the news to yourself for now," she added anxiously. "My pupils can be such awful teases, and I want to wait until the school year is over to—"

As if the word *pupil* had triggered open a gate at the head of the hall, here toward us came one of the schoolgirls, mostly knees and pigtails. Undoubtedly she had put up her hand in that urgent way that allowed her to go to the lavatory, but she marched right past it until she was practically at the hem of Rab's smock.

"Just so you know, Miss Rellis, Russian Famine snuck off."

"Not with you around, Peggy, I'm sure. Now do your business and scoot back downstairs." The class tattler flounced happily into the lavatory, and Rab spun to me. "Is there another staircase?"

I took her down the hallway toward the set of stairs at the back of the stacks. "Rab," I questioned as we quickstepped along, "isn't your class somewhat advanced for story hour? They look very much like—"

"Sixth-graders," she sighed. "Don't you dare laugh, Mr. Morgan." She herself had been a ringleader—it was the kind of class that had many—in the populous sixth grade that had been my biggest handful in the Marias Coulee schoolroom.

"I won't bother to say justice is served," I told her archly. "But story hour at that level—what sort of story?"

"First aid."

It was always hard to tell with Rabrab whether she was pulling your leg. She shook her head as I scrutinized her. "It's the school board's big idea." Her expression sharpened. "Most of the boys will be in the mines in just a few years, and most of the girls will be hatching other children, up on the Hill. The thinking is, it might spare the public treasury in the future if they learn some first aid before what is going to happen to some of them happens. In theory, I suppose I can't argue with that." Another sigh. "In any case, your Miss Runyon here is looked upon as the apostle of first aid. I'm told she was greatly disappointed that she was too far up in years to boss the nurses in France during the war."

"I can imagine. Here we are." I unlocked the delivery door to the stacks, and we stepped in.

To be met with sounds such as I had never heard put together before: a shoeleather *chuff-chuff-chuff* spaced what seemed a dance step apart, followed by a drawn-out soft whizzing like a very long zipper being drawn down.

"That'll be him," Rab said under her breath. "See?"

Beyond the bookshelves sheltering us, a boy as spindly as any I had ever seen was racing up the long staircase to the floors above. As if built on springs he bounded up the stairsteps three at a time, on the brink of trying for four, and when his leaps carried him to the top, the race against gravity, against himself, momentarily over, he in one swift mounting move jockeyed his legs over the banister and slid back down. There was a heart-stopping pneumatic grace, a fireman's fearless ride down a twisting pole, in the way he shot to the bottom. The instant he touched the floor again, he was back into motion, *chuff-chuff-chuff*, trio after trio of stairs flown over by the broomstick legs.

"He does it at school whenever he can," Rab's murmur was close to my ear. "You should see him on the fire escape." Just watching him here was mesmerizing enough; I felt as the audience must have when Nijinsky first flew out of the wings onto a ballet stage, and human ability would never be seen the same again. This pint-size dervish seemed determined to spring at the steep staircase until he could sail up it in one weightless jump.

"Wladislaw, that's enough," Rab called to him. I could have told her a teacherly tone was not effective in cases of extremity; it took something more.

Oblivious, the boy launched off on another waterbug skim up the cascade of stairsteps. Rab cupped her hands to her mouth and let out a shout that would have cut fog: "Russian Famine, do you hear me?"

"Yes'm. Can't not."

Strawy hair flopping, he slowly glided off the banister and dropped on the balls of his feet in front of us. He did not appear guilty, simply caught. I could see how his classmates came up with the nickname, brutal as it was. Gaunt as an unfed greyhound, the hollow-cheeked boy did resemble a living ghost from starvation times on some distant steppe. He met our gaze with a bleak one. "I was just fooling around a little."

"While you are supposed to be in class learning about first aid," Rab chided, combing his hair out of his eyes with her fingers. "Come, say hello to Mr. Morgan—the library couldn't run without him."

The boy's reluctant handshake was like squeezing a puppy's paw. As quick as seemed decent, he rubbed his hand on a hip pocket and cast an appeal to his teacher. "Can't I skip that aid junk, Miss Rellis? Pretty please? All it's gonna be is rags and sticks," he maintained, with a certain degree of clairvoyance. "I seen them bring that Bohunk mucker up the other day at the Neversweat, wrapped up like a mummy and just as dead anyhow. The roof comes down on them in the mine and they're goners. How's rags and sticks gonna help that?"

Wisely not debating the point, Rab instructed with firmness: "You're going to be a goner of another kind—after school until the seat of your pants wears out—if you don't get down there in that room with the rest of them, right now."

"Yes'm. Pretty please don't do no good with you." The spring was gone from him as he hunched off to class.

We watched him trail away, Rab making sure he went down to the auditorium rather than out the front door. "He's an acrobatic marvel," I remarked, "especially since he's so thin you can see through him."

"Wladislaw has been given the thin edge of life in every way," she filled in the story for me. "His parents and a baby sister died in the flu last year. He's being brought up, if you can call it that, by an old uncle. The man has a peddler cart, he sharpens knives around town." She shook her head somberly. "What they live on is anybody's guess." As if having taken a cue from her rubber-legged pupil, she pirouetted to leave. "I'd better go or your Miss Runyon will be sending out a search party. We still have catching up to do, though." She peered at me quizzically, schoolteacher and schoolgirl merged into a single soul of curiosity. "Such as, why *does* that mustache come and go?"

I had my answer ready, along with a slight smile. "We all have our disguises in the masquerade party of life, don't we, Rabrab?"

She took that with a laugh and another crinkle of her nose. "That sounds just like you. But I'm not letting you get away that easily. You have to meet my Jared. Tomorrow night? Join us for supper at the Purity."

THE PURITY CAFETERIA, I found, prided itself on its snowy table-cloths, the forest of tables and chairs that could hold a couple of hundred customers at a time, and, the dubious piece of progress that demarcated it from a café, a total absence of waiters. NO WAITING! YOUR FOOD AWAITS YOU! proclaimed a large sign in red, and across the rear of the ballroom-size dining area stood a line of counters with the menu's offerings, condiments, cutlery, glassware, and so forth. "A new customer! They must be cleaning out heaven!" I was greeted by a plump bow-tied individual, evidently the owner, presiding over the cash register. "Sir, I can tell from here, your belt buckle is hitting your backbone. Skip right in and fill on up."

Smiling thinly at that gust of Butte bonhomie, I cast around for Rab and her fiancé amid the eating crowd. I spied him first, with a prickle of inevitability up my backbone.

Rabrab had been leaning in, tasting something off his plate, as lovers will, and as her bobbed head came up into view, she spotted me and waved.

Mindful of his manners, the young man stood and turned to me with a soldierly correctness that I could have predicted. He'd had that same deportment while tendering the union's envelope of benefit to the widow Dempsey, and in marching like a Roman at the head of the miners in shift change on the Hill. Rabrab gazed up at him as if she'd had him made to order.

"The men in my life," she announced fondly. "Jared Evans, this is Morris Morgan."

"Morrie," I amended over the handshake, to put us on familiar terms.

"Jared," he said, perhaps humorously, perhaps not.

As soon as chairs were under us, he sat back and regarded me through dark deep Welsh eyes that reminded me of Casper's, only more reflective. Beyond that, he and Rab together were like matched cutouts in charcoal paper by a scissor portraitist, his slicked-back hair black as hers. Any children of these two would be ravens. Yet there was something even more striking about this lean chiseled man, and it took me a second to single it out. His ears were different sizes; the left one was missing its earlobe, clean as a surgery. Together with the fathoms in that gaze, it gave him the look of a reformed pirate. I tried not to stare at the foreshortened ear, which of course only creates another level of attention.

Still examining me with those grave eyes, Jared spoke as if I were a question brought before the podium. "You're the cryer. You get around."

"A temporary appointment," I brushed away my career of wakes. "The best kind to have where a coffin is involved."

Rab rippled a laugh. "Now he's the resident genius of the library, aren't you, Mr. Morgan? Have you read every book in it by now? I remember when you knew everything there was to know about comets, and that was just the start of—"

"Flattery does not have to be laid on more than an inch thick, Rab," I waved that to a halt. Basking in her words more than I should have, I shared to Jared: "You must know how she is by now—when her enthusiasm gets going, she'll talk your ear off."

Immediately I wanted to crawl under the table. Jared's dark brows drew down as he leaned in and pointed a cocked thumb and finger at me like a pistol, and I wildly wondered what I was in for. Then, of all things, he winked.

"A German bullet took care of that for me. I got off lucky—they didn't call that sector Dead Man's Hill for nothing. A medical corpsman slapped a patch on me and I went right back into the thick of it." Fingering what was left of the ear, he dispatched a droll half of a smile to the rapt Rab and around to me. "I have to watch out not to be too proud of it—the earmark none of the rest of the herd has."

As when Sandison plunged off into livestock terminology, I chuckled uselessly.

Rab came to my rescue. "Mr. Morgan, you need to hunt up some food. We had to start, Jared has a meeting. He usually does."

"To dicker the lost dollar out of the Anaconda lords and masters?" my natural interest in wages prompted me to ask.

The question was flicked right back to me. "How is it that you know we're in there dickering?" Over a deliberative sip of his coffee, the union leader held me in that compelling gaze again. What was it about the Richest Hill on Earth, that I seemed to be a suspect of some kind no matter which way I turned?

"My usual dining partners," I alibied hastily, "are Griffith and Hooper at the boardinghouse. They discuss matters."

Jared's look softened somewhat. "If that's who you're hanging around with, you probably know more about anything and everything in town than I do."

In the time soon to come, I would learn that Jared Evans had been thrust from the thick of one war into that of another. The combat between the hierarchies of Europe had at last reached a mortal end, while the struggle he came home to on the Hill showed no sign of abating as long as there was corporate capital and there was unionized labor. Flint and gunpowder had the same relationship. Put simply, although Hoop and Griff in their telling of it to me seldom did, the Great War had crippled the once-mighty Butte miners' union; its bargaining power had been hampered by government decrees, rivalry from the IWW, and Anaconda's imperious determination to fatten profits at the expense of wages and workers' lives. Jared alit back into the middle of all this, chosen for that sense of capability he carried as naturally as the set of his shoulders. The better I came to know and observe him, I could not help thinking of Rab's beau as a paradoxical version of Lucius Quinctius Cincinnatus, the Roman soldier who fought his battle and returned to his plow; Jared had been summoned from the battlefield to plow the ungiving ground of Butte's conflicts.

"You two," Rab broke in now, her napkin a flick of white flag between us, "would rather talk than eat, I know, but'that's not me." She was onto her feet, poised in the direction of the dessert counter. "Rhubarb pie. I can't resist. Jared, sweet, can I bring you some?"

He leaned back in his chair and stretched mightily, a man with much on his mind and a long night of negotiating ahead of him. "Just some more java, thanks, if you have enough hands."

"Back in a jiffy," she promised. She sailed off, spiffy as a Riviera princess in the shorter style of dress that was coming into fashion; you could actually see she had legs.

"I had better follow Rab's example," I said, starting to get up to find a meal for myself. Only to be stopped in mid-rise by Jared's thumb pinning the sleeve of my suitcoat to the table. It was a very substantial thumb.

"How does it come to be"—unmistakably the words were those of a stern young fiancé—"that you call her 'Rab'?"

"I, ah, officiated on that name."

That didn't seem to help. "Officiated how?"

Rapidly I told the story of Barbara's verbal somersault into Rabrab in my classroom. The thumb grudgingly lifted from the fabric of my sleeve. "All right," he granted, "it makes two of us who call her that. That's a great plenty."

With a measure of relief I moved off toward wherever the food waited. "You're lagging," Rab scolded as she passed me, bearing a tray with her slice of pie and Jared's cup of coffee. "Only until I can track down the breaded veal," I assured her. Grace had many virtues as a landlady, but it had been a considerable time since I had seen a cutlet.

Cafeteria dining, Butte style, evidently meant that half the clientele was fetching mounds of food for itself at any given moment, and so I had to work my way through the crowd to the counter where the meat dishes were listed, past a huge mahogany breakfront stacked with glassware and coffee cups and saucers. Squeezing around that furniture, I popped into an opening in the meal line, nearly bumping into the larger-than-life figure piling a plate with liver and onions.

Typhoon Tolliver and I stared at each other.

"The rumor is wrong, then, Typhoon. You don't eat hay."

"You," he said thickly. Beside his tray, I saw his fists ball up.

Something about the way I thrust my hands into the side pockets of my coat halted any further movement from him. I had decided that if it came to blows, I would try to hit him on the left fist with my brass knuckles, in the hope of putting his best punch out of action. But I did not particularly want to test that tactic, and from his slow, perplexed blinks, Typhoon seemed not sure he wanted to initiate anything either. Before he could think it over too much, I rushed to say: "The crowd in here is not going to be entertained by you beating me up in public—this isn't the boxing ring."

"No, it ain't," he agreed with that.

"Where's"—I cast a hasty glance around for the telltale set of side-ways eyes—"your partner in crime?"

"Who, Roland? He goes for that Chinee stuff." Typhoon swiped a dismissive paw in the direction of Chinatown and its bill of fare. "Noodles and chicken feet or something. I can't stomach it myself." Independence seemed to be linked to appetite somewhere in that big thick head. "He and me ain't joined at the rib cage."

"Then he doesn't need to know we're showing the good sense not to whale into each other in front of two hundred witnesses and get ourselves arrested, does he."

"I guess maybe not." The mention of witnesses caused the flat-faced pug to look around nervously, peeking over the top of the breakfront for anyone watching our impromptu meeting. I did the same, around a corner of it. We both had more than enough reason to be jittery. It was perilous for me to be seen talking to a prime Anaconda goon, and just as detrimental on his side of things to be caught conversing with me, possible Wobbly that I might be. Luckily, back at the table, Jared's attention centered on Rabrab, and Typhoon's jerky scan around the room evidently did not pick up any watchers either. Rolling his big shoulders, he huffed to me:

"There'll be another time, punk."

"Until then, I'd be careful if I were you," I responded in a con-cerned tone. "You see the union bug there?" I inclined my head toward the small but significant Federation of Labor emblem in the bottom corner of the wall-hung certificate attesting that the establishment proudly employed members of the Cooks and Dishwashers Brother-hood. "I hear that if the crew in the kitchen knows you wear the cop-per collar, they slip ground glass in the onions."

I left him staring down at his plate.

"What, did the calf have to be butchered first?" Rab bantered when I returned to the table with my cutlet.

"Something like that." No sooner had I sat down than Jared leaned my way and spoke in a low tone. "Morrie," he tried the name out, "I maybe jumped on you a little too hard there at first, about union matters. Rab worked me over and says you can be trusted." His face said, *We'll see.* "Keep this under your hat, but there might be a work action, sometime soon. I'll make sure Hoop and Griff stay out of it. I'm telling you now so you don't have to worry about the old devils, all right?"

"I'll try not to. From what they've told me, though, doesn't Butte turn into a hornets' nest during a strike?"

"I didn't say 'strike,' did I?"

"We went through enough of that, last time," Rab said as if instructing both of us. "Anaconda's squads of bullies in our streets. You'd think we weren't Americans."

"That smarted," Jared admitted, his brow creased. He looked over at me. "A year ago I was getting shot at in a trench in France, and I come home to the mines, and next thing I know, a bunch of muscle-heads who never even got overseas are ambushing me on the picket line. We're going to try to get around that this time."

Rab traced a chevron on his shoulder. "My sergeant."

Covering Rab's hand with his own, he made a wry face, again in my direction. "You tell me, is it a promotion or a demotion to head up the union council when Anaconda is trying to make us eat dirt?" The question lingered in those agate-dark eyes. "When the company goons broke the strike last time, the men kicked out the council leaders." He spoke the next very levelly, as if sharing it between Rab and me. "The same way they'll kick me out if I don't deliver the lost dollar."

"Can't not, as Russian Famine would say," Rab said confidently. "You have to budge Anaconda somehow, so you will. I'll bet on it."

For their sake and Butte's, I hoped she was right. Jared got up, saying he had to get to his meeting, and Rab moaned that there was a school board session she had to attend, while I had to make sure there were enough chairs for the Shakespeare Society's Merry Wives' Night back at the library; and I imagined Typhoon and Eel Eyes would be flexing their shoeleather and muscles somewhere in the night, too.

7

Sometime soon, in the vocabulary of Jared Evans, turned out to mean the very next morning. As I rounded the corner to the library, I saw that the usual line of staff and a few patrons at the door had grown mightily and fanned out like a peacock's tail, the entire street filled with new faces. For a moment my soul lifted at this surge of literary interest from the citizenry of Butte. Then it dawned on me that the atmosphere of the city had changed overnight. The Hill's normal throb of labor was not to be heard: no ore trains were running, the seven smokestacks of the Neversweat were empty pipes in the air, the headframes stood as stark and still as gallows. And the mass of fidgeting men here in the light of day ordinarily would have been at work in the everlasting night of the mines. Whatever Jared's definition of a "work action" was, it closely resembled a wildcat strike.

A crowd is a temperamental thing. I could tell at once that as watchfully quiet as this one was, it would not take much to make it growl.

The minute I arrived, Sandison—grim as thunder—beckoned me

up. The library staff nervously held its place at the closed door as he and I stepped to one side and conferred.

"What are these lunkheads doing here, Morgan, instead of out on a picket line somewhere?"

"Sandy, I know no more about this gathering than you do."

"Some help you are. What are we supposed to do about all this mob?"

"Put out more chairs? There are stacks downstairs from when the Shakespeareans—"

He cut me off with a look. "Let them in and make them at home, are you telling me? Hell, man, the Butte Public Library isn't supposed to take sides in some damn dogfight of this kind." Then the oddest thing. There on the topmost step, Sandison turned and gazed out at that sea of workingmen's faces, much the way a pharaoh might have looked down from a pyramid. In that suspended moment, he seemed to draw something known only to himself from those so many eyes. Then he gave a laugh that made his belly heave.

Shaking his head, he climbed onto the base of one of the doorway pillars. I feared he might fall, but he clambered up as if he did this all the time. The sight of him perched there, with the white aureole of his beard and cowlick against the grave Gothic stone of the building, made the crowd fall silent; once more, I could feel that strange mixed mood of apprehension and fascination that followed Samuel Sandison like the shadow at his heels.

"It looks as if the library has some new visitors today," his voice rang off the building across the street, "and I have one thing to say to all of you. It pertains to behavior that will not be tolerated in this public institution." Throughout the crowd I saw faces darken, the phalanx of idled miners readying for yet another warning against "unlawful assembly" even here. "You maybe do it out of habit up there on the Hill or down in the shafts," Sandison blazed, hands on his hips, "but this is not the place for that kind of thing, understand? I am only telling you once." He glowered down at some of the hardest men in Butte as if they were schoolboys playing hooky. "No spitting."

With that, although I would not have thought it possible, his voice rose to another level. "Let us in, Morgan."

ONCE INSIDE, I made straight for the cashbox Sandison kept in his desk, grabbed a fistful of money, and sent someone scurrying to the newsstand down the street to buy all available reading material. I would worry later about a ledger entry for *Miscellaneous diversionary matter.* Next, several of us lugged chairs from the auditorium to the Reading Room, the mezzanine, even the foyer. Meanwhile the miners circulated, speaking in hushed tones if at all, as they got the feel of the grand paneled rooms and the tiers of the world's writings. With the arrival of the newsstand supplement of newspapers and such, so many men settled at tables and in corners with newsprint spread wide that the Reading Room took on the look of a schooner under sail. The library staff, originally taken aback as I had been, caught a fever of enthusiasm at having constant customers, cap in hand, requesting guidance; librarians do not ordinarily receive such worship. I detected a warm gleam of triumph even from Miss Runyon when a stooped miner asked in a thick Italian accent for *L'avventura di Cristoforo Colombo* and she was able to produce a pristine Florentine edition from the mezzanine treasure house.

One thing I particularly noticed: the display case in the far corner drew onlookers as though it were magnetized. Man after man crouched to contemplate the mine model, so complete from tip of headframe to deepest dungeon of tunnel, the compressed vision of the mines standing empty on the Hill this day. It was as if the glass of the case was a smudged crystal ball, with hints of what lay ahead if one could only make them out.

BUSY WITH EVERYTHING, I was hastening down the hallway and past the drinking fountain when a familiar voice caught up with me. "Just a suggestion, but the flavor of the water in this place would be improved by piping in some rye."

"Quin!" The Irish conquistador face looked more solemn in this circumstance than it had at wakes. "I had no idea you were the library-going type."

"Funny, boyo." Quinlan winked and indicated toward the horde in the Reading Room. "A lot of us feel the call of culture today. In about a hundred percent of those cases, the wife told us to get out of the house."

"Why not on a picket line, showing solidarity?"

He arched an eyebrow, amused or the opposite. "Tsk, Morgan, for a sighted man you're deep in the dark, aren't you. There's no picket line. No negotiating session. No anything whatsoever. Jared Evans just made some kind of safety excuse and pulled us out at the start of morning shift like that"—he snapped his fingers—"and is letting Anaconda stew about it." He hardened as I watched. "Whether it gets us our fair wage or we need to try stronger persuasion—" The shoulders of his coat lifted, and I was aware that the Little Red Songbook, in some pocket or other, could find an adherent in more than musical ways. "We'll see if the lop-eared Taffy knows what he's doing." Quinlan's expression suggested it would not be easy to prove to Dublin Gulch.

At the end of the day, I had to resort again to the higher powers to uncloud the bafflements of Butte for me.

Hooper was several rungs up, against the weather side of the house, industriously slapping on paint while Griffith held the ladder. "Everything still standing, downtown?" Griff called out upon sight of me.

"Every brick in place, when I left. Why weren't the pair of you in the middle of things today?"

Hoop dipped his brush and stroked a comet of paint onto the siding. "Told not to."

"Saving us for when we're really needed, Jared says," Griff reported. He wagged his head in general acknowledgment. "Caught Anaconda with its pants down today, he sure did. Put a Welshman in charge and you start to get somewhere. Look at Lloyd George." He gestured as if the prime minister of Great Britain might materialize to set things straight in Butte.

"Yes, but—"

"Your turn," Hoop called down.

I waited while the two of them traded places, like two aged sailors scrambling in the rigging. "But why this so-called *work action* instead of a genuine strike?"

"No strike, no strikebreakers." Holding the ladder with both gnarled hands, Hoop looked around at me as if deciding how much more tutoring I was worth. "Besides catching that other gang—"

"—with its pants down," Griff contributed, along with an emphatic swipe of his paintbrush.

I must have looked blank. Top and bottom of the ladder, both of them eyed me. The silence grew until at last Hoop spelled out:

"The Wobblies. They'd cut in on a strike, try to take it over if they knew it was coming."

"Send in infiltrators." To hear Griff echo Typhoon Tolliver was an unnerving experience. I drew myself up.

"As a mere bystander"—it was hard to tell if that registered on those walnut faces—"it appears to me the union council won the day, as you say. But what happens tomorrow?"

The last word was Hoop's. "Things go back to their normal confusion."

TRUDGING UPSTAIRS to my room to wash up before supper, I reflected again on that zigzag pattern of life. There I was, simply a hopeful empty-pocketed climber of the Richest Hill on the planet, and suspected of something more by nearly everyone except Rabrab, who usually saw connivance behind every mustache. At least, I told myself with a grim smile, tonight I could look forward to a meal not garnished with a goon.

But when I opened the door, my room looked as if it had been visited by a typhoon.

The bedding lay in a heap on the floor, the pillows flung onto the dresser top. The truly alarming thing, though, was the mattress, standing on its side and teetering toward me like a falling wall, while someone grunted in exertion behind it.

"You thugs!" I cried, wildly fishing in my pockets for the brass knuckles, expecting the pointy-faced Anaconda man to burst from the closet while the bigger one mashed me with the mattress. "Get out of here or I'll—"

The mattress stopped its waggle. Around an edge, Grace's face came into view. "Morrie!" She appeared as startled as I was. "Is it that time of day already?"

"Room devastation time, you mean?" The brass knuckles swiftly pocketed out of her sight, I stepped toward the disarranged bed.

"I'm glad you're here, you can help me turn this mattress," she said reasonably. "I do this every so often, so you don't have to sleep on lumps." I took an end and we flopped the mattress into place. As she unfolded fresh sheets she looked across at me curiously. "You came in sounding like you were declaring war. What were you so worked up about?"

"Oh, that. Everything upset as it was, I thought I'd caught Hoop and Griff playing a prank on me," I alibied. "Tossing the room—all boys do it, and aren't they that at heart?"

"They're supposed to be painting the bad side of the house."

"I must have come around the other way."

Grace cocked an eyebrow. "'Thugs'?"

"The word comes from *thuggee*, Hindu for someone who sneaks around and, ah, does mischief to you."

She shook her head, making her braid dance. "I always learn something around you."

I made no answer. A fresh apprehension was coursing through me. Over in the corner of the disheveled room, my satchel was missing.

Busily fluffing a pillow, Grace took a few moments to catch up to my alarmed gaze. "Oh. I had to move your bag out of the way. It's in the closet."

Undisturbed or gone through? I nearly asked. Suspicion was the contagion of Butte; now I was the one catching it. For once I was glad my trunk was not there, to disclose any of its secrets.

My landlady, dimpled with either innocence or guile, by now was done with the freshened bedding, the room miraculously back in order, and she announced she had better see to supper. "Grace?" I halted her before she could swish out the door. "You've been through the war of nerves between the men and the mining company before. What's your sense of this one?"

She bundled her hands in her apron as she considered my question. "My Arthur," she invoked somberly, "used to say taking on Anaconda is like wrestling a carnival bear. You have to hope its muzzle doesn't come off."

THE SPEED OF SOUND is slightly less than that of a shock wave, and so the tremor in the dark of that night shook my bed, and every other in the city, a few instants before the noise of the blast arrived.

Even foggy with sleep, I knew this was no usual detonation, no dynamiting at the depth of a glory hole. I stumbled to the hallway. Half-dressed, Hooper struggled from his room, yanking into the remainder of his clothes, while Griffith already was putting on coat and hat. At the head of the hall, Grace clutched her bedgown around her throat as she witnessed the exodus, then sent me an agonized look.

She did not even have to deliver my marching orders aloud. I dressed hastily and set off with the limping pair of old boarders to the Hill.

UP THERE, in the ghostly light of the headframes, a murmuring crowd was clustered around a mineshaft called the Flying Dutchman. When people gather from the nooks of a mining town to the surface of a disaster, they bring every degree of dread, and as the three of us edged through the throng I could feel the mood of apprehension, the air was sticky with it. Each arriving set of eyes, mine included, expected the sight of bodies laid out on the hard ground. But Griff and Hoop, pointing and muttering, saw at once this was no mineshaft accident, no explosion and flash of deadly flame deep in a tunnel. Instead, over near the machine house, beneath a now askew sign reading PROPERTY OF THE ANACONDA COPPER MINING COMPANY, the mine's pay office stood open to the night, its front wall blown out.

Blue-uniformed policemen were chiding the crowd to stay back, while burly civilian types who could only have been plainclothesmen prowled the blast site. Reporters were clamoring out questions and receiving no answers. Flash powder kept going off, the hollowed-out pay office in rinses of light that would put it on front pages all across the state.

My companions were not impressed. "Mighty poor job of setting the dynamite," either Hooper or Griffith appraised there in the deep shadows of the Hill.

"Could've done that much with firecrackers, couldn't we?" said the other.

To me, the building looked devastated enough, the huge ragged hole in its front displaying broken bricks like snaggled teeth. I moved closer to the skeptical experts. "Do I hear that this blast wasn't up to your standards?"

"The stupid pay office is still standing, isn't it?"

"Well, yes."

"That's no kind of a result, if you're gonna blow something up."

"Waste of a good fuse and a match."

"But," I wasn't able to budge from the evidence of my eyes, "the front of the building is by and large gone."

"So what? They'll get bricklayers in here in the morning and have it fixed back up before you can say boo."

"Spell this out for me, then," I gave in. "How would someone who was an old hand at blowing things up have done it?"

"All it would have taken," Hoop explained patiently, "was to set the dynamite at the corner of the building."

"It'd slump over like a dropped cake," Griff mused, practically smacking his lips as he envisioned it.

By now the cloud of reporters and chain lightning of photography flashes were concentrated around one small circle of men next to the Flying Dutchman's headframe. Even though I had expected something of the sort, my heart sank. As flash powder flared again, I saw in the glare the strong but strained features of Jared Evans in the midst of his beleaguered union officials. Although I had nothing to lend but moral support, I headed over.

An arm slipped authoritatively through mine, nearly scaring the life out of me. "I just knew you'd show up, Mr. Morgan," Rab's warm voice was next to my ear. In stylish scarf and jumper, she cut an unlikely figure there in the industrial spoils of the Hill. With perfect prepossession, she assessed the cordon of newspapermen surrounding Jared and the other union men. "Look at the mob of them. They're like pecking birds."

As the two of us sorted our way there in the semidark, we could hear the volley of questioning. Peppered from all sides as he was, Jared raised a hand for quiet.

"We're told no one was hurt," he chose what to deal with and what not to. "Given that someone is killed in the working conditions in these mines every week of the year, in this nasty incident only bricks suffered any harm, for a change."

"Anaconda says provocation like this will make it take 'all necessary measures' to deal with a strike," called out a newspaperman in a better topcoat than the others, which marked him as working for the *Daily Post*, the mining company's mouthpiece. "What's the union think of that?"

"There is no strike," Jared deliberately raised his voice above the clanks and clatters of the night shift in the other mines around. "When the miners of this hill go out, there's never any mistaking it— you can hear the grass grow, up here. That's it, gentlemen, no more chitchat, thanks." To his council members: "I'll catch up with you at the union hall. We're in for a late night." Jared's expression had lifted measurably when he spotted Rabrab, and she and I skirted the pack of reporters to join him. As we did so, Rab "accidentally" tripped the *Post* man, sending him stumbling into an oily puddle and cursing at the splatter on that spiffy coat.

Smiling tiredly, Jared chucked his feisty fiancée under the chin. "You'll get us a big headline."

"They'll smear you no matter what," Rab predicted, "in that waste of ink they call a newspaper." Making a face at the mangled pay office, she went on: "So the sneaks resorted to this. I suppose they think they're clever."

"They're not far from it," Jared let out a slow breath of judgment. "They've put us in a hole about the size of that, for now."

By then I felt reasonably sure that in the company of Jared and his union followers, I was not in with dynamiters—even inept dynamiters. To catch up with the conversation, I contributed in a confidential tone: "The Wobblies, you mean. It's in their interest to stir up all the trouble they can, so they did it with a bang, hmm?"

Jared and Rab looked at me as though I were speaking in tongues.

He shook his head. "If the Wobs wanted into this, they'd more likely blow up a machine house. Something that would really cripple this mine."

I was back to bafflement. "Then who?"

"Mr. Morgan, put your thinking cap on," said Rab. "It's so obvious."

Weary as he was, Jared took pity on me. "Anaconda. Their goons. To blame it on the union."

THERE ARE MOMENTS in a lifetime when you can taste history as it is happening. When the flavor of time, from one hour to the next, somehow is not quite the same as any day before. So it was, at the start of the intense summer of 1919, as the miners of Butte and the mining corporation cooked up strategies against each other. Dickens should have been living in this hour to tell the tale of the two cities, the one of the neighborhoods of the Hill, and the other of the tall offices downtown, in the double-numbered year.

The morning after the bombing of the pay office, along with breakfast Grace delivered a firm suggestion. "This might be a good day for everybody to stay in."

"How come, Mrs. Faraday?" Griff could have taught innocence to a cherub. "Nice weather, it'd be a shame not to take a little walk downtown."

Hoop went to the point: "We wouldn't want to miss anything."

"And I suppose you," Grace turned to me in exasperation, "are going to say the library will curl up and wither away if you're not there."

"Not at all," I said from behind my coffee cup. "But my job might, if I don't show up as usual."

Off the three of us went, into the tense center of things. There is an atmospheric condition known as earthquake weather, a blanket stillness that forecasts a shaking-up; this day was like that. Hoop and Griff and I hiked up the Hill to that vantage spot of my first day in town and waited. With the city braced, with squads of policemen at the ready, we held our breath as it came time for the morning shift of miners to appear. They did so in eerie silence, the long files of men spilling into the streets of Meaderville and Centerville and Finntown and Dublin Gulch as if forming a somber parade. They marched toward the police lines with barely a murmur. And then turned in at the gates of the mines and went to work as if all was normal.

AT SUPPER, Griff and Hoop were downcast and Grace was not serving up sympathy. "No blood in the streets, how disappointing. Jared Evans must be more sane than some I could mention."

"He'd better have something up his sleeve," Griff said.

THREE MORNINGS LATER, I rounded the corner of the library into a teeming streetful of miners and Sandison frowning down at them.

I worked my way through the crowd, dropping questions as I went. Sandison met me at the top of the steps, looking even more disgruntled than usual. He drew me aside behind a pillar, while the library staff and the miners gawked back and forth. "What do the knotheads say?" he pumped me without preliminary. "Have they quit fooling around and actually gone on strike this time?"

"Not as such," I reported. "It's another work action—just the morning shift, they told me."

"How many more times is this going to happen?" he demanded, as if I were in charge of that.

Knowing Jared Evans, I put up my hands helplessly. "Doubtless as many as it takes. Wouldn't you say it's a tactic that goes back to Roman history, Sandy? You will recall the great delayer, Fabius Cunctator, who outgeneraled his foes with skirmishes that put off the climactic battle time after time. It appears to me that the union similarly is using these stoppages to wear on Anaconda's nerves and—".

"They're practicing on mine, I can tell you that much," he disposed of my discourse. "Are we running a library or a union hall?" Scowling at his own question, he heaved himself around for another look at the packed street. I barely caught the words in his gust of exhalation: "Oh, hell, let them in, Morgan."

FULL AS A CHURCH on Christmas, the library brimmed with activity, much of it mine as I sped from task to task. Sandison commanded from the mezzanine, on the lookout for anyone forgetful enough to spit on the sacred floor, and things seemed to be going well until midway through the morning, when he flagged me down with the news:

"Miss Runyon has gone home in a nervous fit, the excitement has been too much for her. You'll have to take over the story hour."

"Now? How? Whatever short notice is, this is less."

"The tykes are on their way," he overrode my protest. "You wouldn't want to break their young hearts, would you?" Did the man actually have a sense of humor? I would have had to part that beard of his like a curtain to be sure. "Get yourself down there," he ordered.

I raced to the basement, hoping against hope that the auditorium's supply cabinet held some storybook that Miss Runyon had in reserve for emergencies such as this. Rummaging frantically, I came up with a dog-eared *Mother Goose Tales*. Well, it wasn't Aesop, but it would have to do. I breathed easier; from my experience in the one-room school, even jaded fifth-graders eavesdropped keenly enough when those old nursery tales were read to the younger children.

Then I heard the thumps and scuffles on the stairs.

By the time the freckled heathens of the sixth grade spilled into the room, with Rab riding herd behind them in a harried way, I had given up on Mother Goose. More like a rough-dressed horde than a class, boys and girls alike threw themselves into chairs and looked me over. *Who's this gink?* I heard the loud whispers. *How come so much of him is mustache? Where's Old Lady Bunion?*

"Everyone, shush, or else," Rab recited as if by rote, meanwhile shooing the final straggler in from the hallway. Pale as a chalk figure, Russian Famine slouched past her, sending me a prisoner's gaze as he took the farthest seat of the last row.

His classmates ignored him but not one another, pinching, poking, prodding, and generally provoking disorder. How well I remembered it all. Grade six somehow transforms obedient school-children into creatures with the bravado of bandits and the restlessness of overage Sunday schoolers. Rabrab herself had turned into a schoolyard Cleopatra at that time of life; the Marias Coulee sixth-grade boys went dizzy in her presence. Now I watched her brightly approaching me, while behind her a pugnosed boy and a redheaded girl swatted each other over the issue of elbow room. If Rab, with her battlefield experience, couldn't command best behavior from this bunch, what chance did I have? The dismaying thought occurred to me that, in Butte, perhaps this *was* best behavior.

"Mr. Morgan, what a treat," her velvet murmur greeted me as we stepped aside to confer. "My pupils don't know how lucky they are."

"I can see that. I was hoping for a second-grade choir of angels."

Rab wrinkled her nose at her squirming tribe. "They're somewhat worked up today."

"I wonder why."

"The Hill is a little excitable this morning," she hedged, "but Jared is only doing what he thinks is necessary."

"Maybe so. The question is, what am I to do with this mob of yours, Rab?"

"Anything you like, as long as it teaches first aid," she said contradictorily. "That's a must—we don't want the school board on our necks." She thought to add: "Nor, I imagine, Sam Sandison."

I had forgotten the medical aspect. Seeing my blank look, Rab prompted: "Your Miss Runyon starts off with Florence Nightingale as a nurse in, oh, say the Crimean War, with shot and and shell whizzing everywhere, and somehow jumps from there to strapping one of the pupils up in bandages. Then, next story hour it is Florence Nightingale happening upon some awful accident in London, and—"

"I get the picture."

There was nothing to be done but square myself up and advance to the stage of the auditorium. Restive in the seats below, the class eyed me like cub lions in the arena waiting for a Christian meal. So be it; I took off my suitcoat and tossed it to a surprised Rab, then rolled up my sleeves as if for a fight.

"Blood," I said in a tone practically dripping with it.

The word did its work, for the moment at least. Two dozen sulky faces showed flickers of interest.

"Blood is red as fire, and thicker than rain," I did not let up. "Blood percolates secretly all through us, from finger to toe. It outlines our family, whom we speak of as our own flesh and blood. When we are afraid, we feel our blood run cold, and when we are angry, we are hot-blooded. No other substance carries the magic of life so tirelessly." As I talked on, I pressed a set of fingers to my wrist. "The heart beats in its mysterious way, day and night, so blood never sleeps." I finished taking my pulse. "While I have been speaking, my heart has pumped blood sixty times. If it had stopped doing so, back there when I rolled up my sleeves to test it, by now I would stand before you dead."

Several more heartbeats went by as my audience caught up with that. A litany of gasps, a lesser peal of nervous laughs. One girl crossed herself.

Before such attention wore off, I swept my listeners through the Greek suppositions of Hippocrates and Galen—that blood simply sloshed in us like water in a jug—to William Harvey's discovery that the substance in fact goes around and around. "The circulatory system, as it is called, sends this miraculous fluid circling through us." There is a glaze that comes over a class if too much of a topic is pressed on them at one time, and I could tell from a first few restless feet and territorial elbows that I was reaching that limit.

Folding my arms on my chest in thinking mode, I paced the stage. "Roll up your sleeves, everyone." This was a gamble. Hardboiled boys and pouty girls among the group showed no inclination to do so. But Rab got on the job, patroling mercilessly, and soon enough I had a forest of naked arms in front of me.

"There is a superstition that your life can be read in the palm of your hand," I began, "but really, it is written there on the underside of your wrist." I bustled them through taking their own pulse, emphasizing that the underskin rhythm was actually the contractions of arteries as blood was pushed through by the pumping of the heart. As intended, even the most heedless twelve-year-old could not ignore the message of existence there just beneath a surface barely thicker than paper. "And," I rounded off the arm lesson, "the blood that keeps us going has to find its way back to the heart to be pumped again. See the blue tracings between your wrist and elbow? Each of those is a vein. A word you have heard at home, am I right? Your fathers and perhaps your brothers descend into the body of the earth to find those streaks of ore. If you think about it, copper is the blood of Butte."

As I said so, a part of my mind filled with visions of what lay ahead of these youngsters in this veined city. By all odds, at least one among the fresh-faced boys who would follow the family path into the mines would die underground in that relentless toll of a death a week. A greater number of their classmates in pigtails and curls, women-to-be, would experience perilous childbirth and the innumerable ills of the Hill. Yet others sitting here today would go on uneventfully to what passed for average life in Butte. Those flashes of precognition were hypnotic; I could see as if it were written in me the circlings of fate which would single these young lives out, as always happens in the human story, within the rushing bloodstream of time.

"Mr. Morgan?" Rab prompted me out of my trance. "You were saying . . . ?"

"Ah." I scrambled for new ground. "Blood provides life to our language, too, doesn't it. Shakespeare could scarcely write a page without bloodshed ahead or behind. Poets would have nothing to rhyme perfectly with *flood*. Who can tell me some everyday ways we use this essential word?"

"Bloody murder!" blurted a freckled scamp who seemed to relish the thought.

"Red-blooded," a bossy girl overrode that, impatient at not having been first.

"The blood of our Lord," said a cauliflower-ear tough who nonetheless must have been an altar boy.

"Bloodshot eyes!" rang out from one end of the increasingly enthusiastic audience, and from the other, "Blood poisoning!"

Amid the hubbub came a muted utterance from the back row. Everyone looked around. I encouraged: "A little louder, please?"

Russian Famine wriggled in his seat, scratched behind his ear, gazed over our heads as though that would make us go away, and finally muttered:

"No getting blood out of a turnip."

"A well-known saying, thank you very much," I honored that. Before I could get another word out, a hand was up and waving strenuously. Its owner was the impish enthusiast for bloody murder. "I perceive you have a question."

"Sure do. Back there a ways when you had us taking our pulse, how come we couldn't do it on our veins just as good as on those archeries?"

"Clean out your ears, dummy," the girl next to him jumped on that. "It's not *arch*eries. That's bows and arrows. It's *arth*ries, like *arthritis*. Isn't that right, Mr. Teacher?"

"You are both nearly correct." But not near enough. While explaining that the returning blood in veins was too dispersed to register a pulse, I despaired of ever making my words stick in minds as flighty as these. Then an idea hatched.

"Miss Rellis?" Rabrab was startled to hear me call her that for the first time since she was the age of these students. "Do your young scholars ever sing?"

"They most certainly do. Why?"

"Can they sing this one?" I whistled a snatch of it.

Confidently, Rab swept to the front to lead the command performance. "Class, serenade Mr. Morgan such as he has never heard."

Whether it was the song's mischievous endorsement of betting

on bobtail nags or the familiar sassy tune or simply the chance to
bawl at the top of their adolescent voices, the sixth-graders attacked
the old favorite with gusto, making the auditorium ring with the
final galloping chorus:

> Camptown ladies sing this song, doo dah, doo dah!
> Camptown racetrack's five miles long, oh the doo dah day!

"Unforgettable," I said with a congratulatory bow to the class
when the last high-pitched note had pierced the rafters. "And would
you believe, the exact things we have been talking about go nicely
with that same tune. Hum it for me and I'll show you." With the
room practically vibrating to Stephen Foster's jingle-jangle rhythm
that practically anything can be fitted to, I improvised:

> Arteries and veins and pulse, heartbeat, heartbeat!
> They all deliver life to us, that's the job of blood!

"Ready to try it?" I challenged. They couldn't be held back. Rab
looked radiant as the young voices romped through my version a number of times.

"One last thing." I rolled my sleeves down at the conclusion of the
songfest. "At next week's story hour, I am sure Miss Runyon will be
happy to show you the knack of the tourniquet."

"I HOPE YOU DIDN'T do too much damage to the minds of the
youngsters."

Sandison was back to prowling the mezzanine when I came
upstairs. "Just imagine"—he swept a hand over the scene of the

miners tucked in every conceivable sitting place in the Reading Room below—"if we had this kind of patronage on a usual day. The trustees would think we're geniuses." He looked resentfully at the Roman-numeraled clock high on the wall. "And at one minute past noon, ninety out of a hundred of our involuntary scholars will hightail it out of here to the nearest speakeasy. The poor fools."

"That's an altogether gloomy view of humanity, isn't it, Sandy?" I protested. "Surely a good many of the men apply their minds while they're in here like this."

"Hah." He rested his bulk against one of the grand bookcases, the gilt-edged works of George Eliot over one shoulder and Ralph Waldo Emerson over the other. "Let me tell you a story, Morgan." A distant look came into those iceberg-blue eyes. "It was back when I was just starting out in the cattle business, before I could get things built up into the Triple S. I was wintering in by myself—Dora and I hadn't been to a preacher yet. It was a bad winter, down around zero a lot of mornings when I'd have to pitch hay to the cows. Other than the feeding, I had all the time in the world on my hands, and the winter wasn't half over before I'd memorized every damn word of all the reading material in the house." He turned his hands up empty, still in the distance of remembering. "There wasn't a library or bookstore in fifty miles in those days. The only neighbor was an old prospector, up a gulch a couple of miles away. I'd seen a beat-up copy of *Robinson Crusoe* in his cabin." Sandison fixed his disturbing gaze on me. "You're a bookworm, maybe you savvy: I had to have that book or go crazy. I saddled up to go get it. Snow was starting to come down heavy, but I didn't give a damn, I wanted something to read. When I got there the old coot drove a hard bargain—I had to promise him a veal calf in the spring. Anyhow, he finally handed over the book and I wrapped it good in a piece of oilcloth and stuck it under my coat. Rode all the way home in a blizzard, and both ears were frostbitten, but I still thought it was worth it." One more time he scowled down at the mineworkers, some of whom were starting to watch the clock. "See there? Do you think any of these would have gone through that for the sake of a book? Look at them, they'd rather educate their tonsils than their brains."

Maybe I thought he was scanting the capacities of the Quins and the Jareds and others from the Hill whose minds were as lively as could be asked for. Maybe I was still sailing on air after my session with Rab's young minds. In any case, I indignantly invoked the bard of us all, presiding open-eyed as an owl above the entrance to the jam-packed Reading Room. "You leave me no choice but to bring down Shakespeare on you, Sandy. 'The music of men's lives' is not so easy to call the tune of, we must remember."

At that, the expression under Sandison's beard was unreadable, but the rest was plain enough. Shaking his head conclusively, he moved off toward his office, leaving these words over his shoulder: "You're an optimist, Morgan. That's always dangerous."

"You have a caller."

Along with Grace's knock on my door came the distinct note of curiosity in her tone. I was as inquisitive as she was. With my head still full from that day in the library, I could think of hardly anyone in the entire city who would be paying me a call here, with two shadowy exceptions. But Grace, of all people, would know an Anaconda goon when she saw one. Wouldn't she? To be on the safe side, I made sure the brass knuckles were in my pockets before I went downstairs.

The parlor was empty, as was the dining room; no caller, no Grace, anywhere.

Just as panic was setting in on me, she called from the kitchen: "In here, Morrie. Your visitor is making me tired just looking at him."

At the first glimpse of my guest, I relaxed the grip on my weaponry. Dealing with a twelve-year-old may take a lot of one's resources, but usually not brass knuckles.

Skinny as the sticks of kindling in the woodbox behind him, in dusty patched pants and a hand-me-down shirt, Russian Famine was only barely occupying a chair, one leg jittering and then the other, ready to bolt. Grace, as usual in crisp apron and a dress so clean it practically squeaked, was looking at him as if one or the other of them was at the wrong costume party. So as not to confound her even further, I retrieved the boy's given name with a smile: "Wladislaw, we meet again. What brings you?"

Even his words were thin and fidgety. "Miss Rellis needs to see you. At that Poority place."

"It's another long story," I fended off Grace's quizzical look. Gesturing toward our surprise caller, I made a supping motion. "Perhaps . . . ?"

"Good heavens, yes." She cut a thick slice of bread, put it on a plate, and set it in front of the famished-looking youngster. Pouring from the syrup can, she said, "Say when."

"I like it sogged."

The syrup pooled on the plate before the boy nodded. As he tucked in to the food, Grace wordlessly cut another slab of bread for him. I excused myself to fetch my hat from upstairs. When I came back down, Grace's guest reluctantly licked his fork and edged out of the chair to go with me. "I may be a while," I told her. "Skip me at supper."

"The larder can stand a chance to recover," she bade us off, still looking mystified.

Another side of Butte showed itself in the route I was now led on. With a nonchalance you might not expect in a sixth-grader, my guide took an immediate shortcut through Venus Alley. Overhead in one of the red-curtained windows, the sash was flung up and a woman in a kimono leaned out. "Hey, kid! How about running over to Betty the bootlegger's and getting us a bottle of her best?"

"I'm busy, can't you see?" the boy called back importantly.

"Then how about you, Mustachio? Come on up and we'll cure what ails you."

"I'm busy keeping up with him," I tipped my hat, "thank you very much anyway."

Block after block, we wound our way past buildings that put all their respectability out front, their back ends grimy with the detritus of coal chutes and the leavings of garbage. Around every other corner a view of the Hill was framed between brick walls, the tower over a mineshaft like a spiked ornament on the roof of the city. I could hear the throb of ore lifts and other machinery, so pronounced after the silence left behind when the morning shift walked off; Jared and his tactic of work actions was turning the Hill off and on like a master switch. If, that is, the Anaconda Company didn't find a way to break his hold on the matter. Or already had. I wondered again why Rab was summoning me.

Suddenly my hotfooted escort was talkative. "How come you work at the library 'stead of the schoolhouse? I was just telling Miss Rellis she's the best teacher in the whole world and she said not as long as you're on two legs."

That touched me deeply. Yet it also mandated an answer. "Life likes to surprise us, Wladislaw, and so—"

"I hate getting called that," he muttered, squirming as if to dodge the name. "It sounds too much like *coleslaw*."

"Russian Famine, then—"

"Don't like that no better. I ain't any kind of a Russian. My unk says if we're anything, it's Glishians." I tried to remember if Galicia was central to what the Europeans from time immemorial called the Polish Problem, and whether that part of Poland was another jigsaw piece on the table in front of Wilson and Clemenceau and Lloyd George as they sought to remake the world with the peace treaty. In any case, the Old Country was forever off the map of a peddler whose only ware was the sharpening of knives, and a skin-and-bones street tough nephew, wasn't it. The thought clutched at me: the fostering places that we are exiled from, in the irreversible twists of life.

Back to the question at hand, though. "Young citizen of the world, we are running out of possibilities—what would you like to be called?"

He thought for the next some steps, slowing his pace to mine. "Famine ain't too bad. It'd be one of those nicked names, huh?"

Gravely I took off my hat and in due ceremony tapped him on a narrow shoulder with it. "By whatever authority is vested in me, I dub thee Famine." He bounced a little higher his next couple of steps. "Now, then, Famine, as I was saying. Sometimes a person finds himself doing the unexpected. And so you give each job everything you have, but stay on your toes for what comes next. Isn't it that way with you at school?"

A shrug. "I guess. Miss Rellis's flame says it's the same in the army—now you're peeling spuds and next thing you're shooting back at somebody."

"Jared is at the Purity with her?"

"Uh-huh." The boy flopped his hair out of his eyes and looked around at me hopefully. "That sure was good about blood. Are you gonna do story hour some more?"

"We'll see," I said, smiling. "That's up to the man who runs the library."

"With all the whiskers? The one they call the Earl of Hell?"

That stopped me in my tracks.

"Where did you hear that?"

Famine slowed himself to wait for me by walking backwards. "Down around the stockyards. Those cowboys riding the fence are always yakking about something."

I felt relieved. I could easily believe Samuel Sandison had been high-handed in his ranch days and gained that name in the Triple S bunkhouse. That had me thinking about the doggedness of reputation, fair or not, when Famine, curiosity on as much of his face as there was, wanted to know:

"What's a earl?"

"Someone who owns everything but a good name, usually. That other word, I'd advise you not to use around Miss Rellis."

"Uh-huh, she's death on cussing." Restless as a hummingbird, Famine now was talking to the top of my head. I had frowned him off clambering on fire escapes along our backstreet route, but he couldn't resist hopping up onto the loading docks at rear entries to stores. He teetered along the planked edge of this latest one, his sense of balance making a mockery of gravity. I watched with the envy of those of us who have outgrown the blind bravery of a twelve-year-old. Perhaps it was the pale sharp cheeks or the flatly factual eyes beneath the toss of uncombed yellow hair, but he looked oddly pristine up there, more like a trainee in an acrobats' academy than a schoolboy. I thought back to the blood enthusiasts among his classmates, and to the black eyes, bent noses, scabs, and bruises that my Marias Coulee pupils accumulated in the average mayhem of the schoolyard. Skinny and milk-skinned as he was, my young friend seemingly would be a bullies' delight, yet there was not a mark on him. "Famine, I'm not trying to be nosy, but the bigger boys don't give you trouble?"

"Would if they could catch me."

"You're quite the runner, then. Don't they ever catch you?"

"Huh-uh." He continued along the outmost inch of the loading platform with the aplomb of a tightrope walker. "I run until they drop."

AFTER DEPOSITING ME at the entrance to the Purity Cafeteria, Famine vanished at a high lope. The owner, a scarlet bow tie blazing under his set of chins, met me with a glad cry. "I knew you'd be back," the gust of welcome nearly parted my hair. "Your appetite wouldn't let you stay away! Help yourself, this is the spot to fill that hollow leg!" I slipped in line behind a broad-beamed couple who obviously had partaken of the menu many times before. First things first, as ever; I peeked from behind the glassware breakfront to make sure the Typhoon goon was not on the premises, then gathered a meal for myself and joined Rab and Jared at their corner table.

Fatigue showed on Jared, but so did something like the sheen of a winning streak; Rab's pride in him stuck out all over her. He had not backed down after the dynamiting of the Flying Dutchman pay office, simply skipped aside from any blame with the kind of remark Butte loved—even the *Daily Post* could not resist quoting him—to the effect that anybody who worked for Anaconda maybe should have his head examined, but no miner was dumb enough to blow up the place his wages came from. In boxing parlance, I knew, he and the union were winning the early rounds on points, with the shift stoppages he was invoking about some faulty working condition or another in the mineshafts; the danger was whether the company would be provoked into unloading a haymaker, such as a lockout or a show of force, brutal and bloody, by its goons. Well, he was the tactician and I wasn't. I simply remarked, "On behalf of the library, I should thank you for our unprecedented number of users, lately."

"Always glad to encourage the cause of learning," Jared responded, wearing that droll expression somewhere between pious and piratical. "I hear you're quite the expert on blood." He eyed me as if curious to find any evidence to back that up.

"In a pedagogical sense," I said, between bites of my food. "All in all, though, that is likely the wisest approach to the substance. For instance, Shakespeare invoked the word some seven hundred times in his works, but there is no evidence he ever actually experienced the shedding of blood. Christopher Marlowe, now, sadly did undergo—"

"My pupils want you back next week to talk about skulls and skeletons," Rab sought to pin me down.

"While you're handing out favors," Jared was quick on the heels of that, "I could use one, too. Rab tells me you're a whiz with figures."

With a modest gesture I admitted to something of the sort.

"Good. Anaconda has us bamboozled on the production figures." As if scouting a battlefield, he scanned the entirety of the restaurant to make sure we were not being observed. "Show him, Rab."

Covertly she cracked open her sizable purse to give me a peek at a vivid sheaf of papers. "Those are the pink sheets the mine managers hand in at the end of each week," Jared went on in a low voice.

"The janitor at the Hennessy Building is supposed to burn them, but he has a nephew working in the Neversweat shafts, so he slips the batch to us." Rapidly he explained that the famously fought-over wage was tied to the Hill's production total and subsequent price of copper, but the union was suspicious of the company's numbers in the negotiations. "They're playing it cute on us, we're pretty sure. It seems like the bulk tons that come out of the mine"—he indicated Rab's trove of pink sheets—"ought to add up to more processed tons at the smelter than the company tells us. But the differential is the problem. No two mines assay out at the same percent of copper in the ore, and there are three dozen Anaconda mines on the Hill." Jared tugged ruefully at his lopped ear. "It's driving us batty trying to come up with a complete figure to argue against theirs."

"I told you Mr. Morgan would have a solution," Rab snuggled nearer him with the scheming expression I remembered so well, "just wait and see."

With the situation delineated to their satisfaction, the two of them, ravens of collusion, waited me out.

This, I realized with a churning in my stomach that caused me to lose interest in my meal, was another of those moments when choice was forced upon me. What was being asked of me was exactly what Sandison inveighed against, taking sides in the dogfight, as he not inaccurately characterized the Butte feud of labor and capital. Here was where a headful of learning was a burden. Intuition, instinct, some mental gremlin, whispered to me that the library's extensive mineralogy section, complete with the annual mining reports of the state industrial board, with a bit of calculation might yield the set of ore differentials the union needed. But why should it be up to me to coax out that magic arithmetic? Unfortunately the answer kept coming back: *Who else?* Resist it as I tried, a certain line of reasoning insisted that the Anaconda Company had an army of bookkeepers on its side and the union deserved at least one.

Besides, around Jared Evans you felt you were made of stronger stuff than you previously imagined, and Rab's guile was as infectious as ever.

"All right," I sighed as she glowed in triumph, "let me see what I can do." Jared watched keenly as she slipped me the pink sheets and I tucked them well out of sight inside my vest. "I may live to regret this, but I'll help out in the name of the holy cause of the lost dollar."

"Oh, we have the wage back up to where it was," he answered matter-of-factly. "Now we need to fight to hang on to it."

"You have the— Since when?"

"Since some Anaconda bigwig with a lick of sense looked at a calendar and realized Miners Day is almost here." He grinned fully for the first time. "Just after the next payday."

"It's Butte's biggest doings of the year," Rab leapt in on that. "The whole town turns out for Miners Day. You'll have to, too, Mr. Morgan."

My brain felt weak. "Are you telling me the Anaconda Company gave in about the dollar because a holiday is coming?"

"Look at it from their side," Jared instructed. "Every miner in Butte will be perfectly legally parading through town that day. If you were up there on the top floor of the Hennessy Building, would you rather have them happy or ready to tear things up?"

"Then this is a kind of truce," I wanted to make sure of what I was hearing, "of the moment?"

"That's not a bad way of putting it," he commended in his best sergeant manner. "The one thing sure about dealing with Anaconda is that the war is never over."

WHATEVER LUNAR POWER Miners Day possessed that the year's other three hundred and sixty-four did not, things settled down ahead of it. Work actions ceased and the Hill pulsed day and night with the excavation of rich copper ore. The coveted dollar a day, as Jared had said, was added back in to the wages of ten thousand temporarily soothed union men. Without the morning tide of miners, library life quieted to its usual seashell tone of whispers. Miraculously, I nearly caught up with the chores Sandison pushed my way. He himself, of course, constituted a sizable task as often as not.

This day I came back into the office after some errand to find him pacing from his desk to the window and back, his bootsteps sharp as a march beat. Barely acknowledging me with a glance, he delivered: "That robber Gardiner in New York I deal with has a fine copy of *The Bride of Lammermoor.* What do you think?"

Quick as a fingersnap, I calculated what a transaction of that sort would do to the delicate balance I had achieved in the library's ledger. "Sir Walter Scott himself regarded that as one of his lesser works," I responded breezily. "Rather like *Ivanhoe*, but done with a trowel."

He grunted. "All right, I'll think it over." The boots retraced their route as if following dance steps imprinted on the floor. I grew uneasy as he prowled the room, more often than not a signal that something was on his mind. I could only hope no one had blabbed to him that I was staying late after the Jabberwockians and other evening groups packed up and went home, and immersing myself suspiciously deep in the mineralogy section.

Just then Miss Mitchell from the cataloguing section, young and rather pretty and somewhat of a flirt, came in with a question. I dealt with it in no time and she pranced out.

Sandison watched the back of her until she shimmied out of sight, then turned to me with a frown. "Morgan, I don't see you making eyes at young things like that even when they're asking for it. What are you, some kind of buck nun?"

This turn of topic took me off guard. Good grief, did my social situation look that dusty to someone whose own idea of mating in life was the grandee and grandora sort? Trying not to show how much that smarted, I stiffly assured my white-bearded interrogator: "I enjoy female companionship when it presents itself, never fear."

"THIS DAY GOT AWAY FROM ME." Grace guiltily bustled past me, trying to tie her apron and control her braid at the same time, when I came in at the end of my own hectic day. "How do you feel about cold turkey for supper?"

"Rather tepid. Let me see what can be done." Following her to the kitchen, I scrounged the cupboard, coming up with cheese that was mostly rind, some shelled walnuts, and macaroni. Yielding the culinary arena gracefully, so to speak, Grace stood aside while I whacked chunks of the turkey into smaller pieces and set those to simmering in cream and flour in a baking pan.

"Such talent." She watched with folded arms as I did my imitation of Escoffier. "If all else fails, you can get on as a cook at the Purity," she ventured.

Up until then, I had not offered any explanation of Rab mysteriously summoning me to the cafeteria, nor, for that matter, of Rab herself. "Yes, well, Miss Rellis you heard mentioned by our fleet young friend the other day," I fussed with the meal makings some more while coming up with a judicious version of the past, "and to make a long story short," by which time a pot of water was boiling merrily and

I dumped in the macaroni for what was going to approximate turkey tetrazzini, "someone I knew when she was just a girl ends up as the fiancée of none other than Jared Evans. Isn't it surprising how things turn out?"

Grace's expression had gradually changed from puzzlement to a ghost of a smile. "You lead an interesting life, Morrie."

As I combined the macaroni and turkey and added the walnuts, I took the opportunity to bring up the question that was in my mind and doubtless Hoop's and Griff's these past many suppers. "Now you tell me something—why is a holiday bird like this such a perpetual bargain at this time of year?"

Razor-sharp shopper that she was, Grace looked at me as if I did not understand basic commerce. "Don't you know? The homesteaders' crops dried up, so they tried raising turkeys. The whole dryland country is gobblers these days, and what that does to the price, you see, is—"

"I can guess, thank you." I tried not to show it, but the news of hard times in the other Montana, the prairie part of the state where agriculture drank dust if rain did not come, hit into me all the way to the hilt. My hands took over to grate the cheese atop the other ingredients while the remembering part of myself was transported to Marias Coulee and the parting of the ways there, Rose's and mine. So deep in thought was I that I barely heard Grace's expression of relief as the turkey dish went into the oven looking fit for a feast. "You've turned the trick again, how do you do it?" She patted my shoulder as she passed. "I'll call you and the Gold Dust Twins to the table when it's done."

My mood refused to lift during supper; the boardinghouse blues are not easily shaken once they get hold of you. The same exact faces that had seemed so companionable three times a day now surrounded me like random passengers in a dining car, right, left, and center. The four of us were at that table because nowhere in our solitary lives was there a setting for just two. I knew Hooper was a widower, and no one had ever been willing to put up with Griffith as a matrimonial mate. Grace still was beholden to her knightly Arthur, touchy as she was about any appearance of being "taken up with" by an unworthy successor. And I, I had to be classified as something like an obligatory bachelor, always mindful that for a woman to be married to me would be like strapping her to a lightning rod. A quartet of solitudes, sharing only a tasty meal.

Tired from brooding—tired *of* brooding—I excused myself from small talk after eating and went up to my room to lose myself in a book. The one I had brought home was a lovely blue-and-gold volume of letters titled *Let Me Count the Ways.* The illustrious surname incised twice on the cover caused me a rueful moment; Casper used to tease me whenever he caught sight of my Browning collection, asking if I was reading up on how to get a suntan.

I tucked into a pillow and the coverlet, hoping to be transported, and was. In the marriage of poets, I found from the very first page, each wrote with the point of a diamond. Dazzled and dazzling, Robert Browning was a suitor beyond any that Elizabeth of Wimpole Street could have dreamt of:

> *I love your verses with all my heart, dear Miss Barrett . . . the fresh strange music, the affluent language, the exquisite pathos and true new brave thought; but in this addressing myself to you—your own self, and for the first time, my feeling rises altogether.*
>
> *I do, as I say, love these books with all my heart—and I love you too.*

The quality in that. The pages fell still in my hands as I thought of such a matching of souls. The ceiling became a fresco of Marias Coulee as I sank back on the pillow and imagined my version.

"Morrie! You're back! Even though you promised not to be."

"Rose, run away with me."

"Oh, I can't."

"You did before."

"I did, didn't I. But that was to save our skins, remember?"

"You might be surprised how little the situation has changed."

"Tsk, don't spoof like that. I know you. That tongue of yours calls whatever tune it wants to."

"If you won't listen to reason, my dear, let me try passion. We have ten lost years to make up."

"Where's the clock that can do that?"

Rose always did know how to stump a good argument.

Wincing, I put away reverie and sat up. My mind took a resolute new posture as well. You don't need to be an Ecclesiastes devotee to realize there is a time to equivocate and a time to do something.

Still in my slippers, I trotted down the stairs. In the living room, Grace whirled from the sideboard where she was putting away her mending, looking flustered at my hurried arrival. I halted at the foot of the stairs, she braced at her end of the room. Practically in chorus, we blurted:

"I was wondering if you might want to—"

"If you don't have anything better to do—"

Both of us stumbled to a pause. She caught her breath and expelled it in saying, "You first."

"I'd be impolite."

"Morrie, out with it, whatever it is—we can't beat around the bush all night."

"I suppose not. I, ah, I wondered if you might like to go to Miners Day. With me, that is."

Grace covered her mouth against a wild laugh. I felt ridiculous and, calling myself every kind of a fool, was ready to slink back upstairs when she put out a hand to stop me. "Great minds run in similar tracks. I was about to knock on your door and ask you."

8

N ever seen you quite so dolled up, Morrie. Mrs. Faraday will have to go some to keep up with you."

I smoothed the fabric of my new checked vest and adjusted the silk necktie bought to match it. "Everyone tells me Miners Day is a holiday like no other. You are quite the fashion plate yourself, Griff."

"Better be, on account of the parade. We've marched in every one of them, haven't we, Hoop."

"Since parades was invented."

The brand-new work overalls on both of them looked stiff enough to creak, and underneath were the churchgoing white shirts and ties. Their headgear, though, was the distinctive part. Each wore a dingy dented helmet that must have seen hard duty in the mineshafts.

"Are you expecting a hailstorm?" I asked with a straight face.

Hoop proudly tapped his headpiece. "The Hill tried to knock my brains out any number of times, but nothing ever got past this lid. Anymore we only wear it the one day a year, don't we, Griff."

Telling me they had to form up early with the other marchers or spend the entire parade looking at hundreds of behinds, the pair hustled out while I waited for Grace to come down from her room. With the Hill not operating due to the holiday, a stillness had settled over the city, and the boardinghouse was in rare quiet. A silent room that is not your own tends to breed long thoughts. Around me now, the boardinghouse's furnishings seemed to sit in arrested attitude, as if arranged in a villa in Pompeii. The mood of timeless delibera- tion drew me in and I became more aware than ever of the wedding photograph on the sideboard, where Arthur Faraday stared levelly at me. Something in that everlasting straight gaze reminded me of Casper, likewise gone too early from life and a bride who idolized him. Introspection is a rude visitor. An unsparing look into myself went to the heart, in more ways than one. I know myself fairly well: I am solo by nature. Incurably so, on the evidence thus far. But what a hard-eyed trick of fate—perhaps reflected in Arthur's stare?—if I was destined, around women, always to be a stand-in for better men.

"Sorry to keep you waiting," I heard Grace behind me, her foot- steps quick on the stairs. "I had about forgotten how to dress up."

I turned to look at her, and looked again. She had gone some, in Griff's phrase for it. Her hair was done up in a crown braid, and atop that sat a broad-brimmed summer hat with a nice little swoop to it and a sprig of red ribbon. Her dress, attractively tailored to her com- pact form, was of a sea green with a shimmer to it. Even her complex- ion had a new glow, assisted by just enough rouge to give her cheeks a hint of blush.

"Very nice," I fumbled out.

"You, too," she managed.

With Arthur in the room, we stood there, shying away from fur- ther compliments, until she remembered to check the clock. "We should get a move on," landlady back in her voice, "everyone turns out for the parade. I hope we can still find a place to see."

"Spare yourself that worry," I rallied. "I know just the spot."

MAN, WOMAN, AND CHILD, the populace of Butte lined the downtown streets a dozen thick. I shouldered a way for us, Grace with a grip on the tail of my coat, to the block by the library. She looked dubious as I led her past people picnicking on the steps to the big arched doorway. "Isn't the library closed for today?"

"Except to the privileged." I displayed the key.

We slipped in, the ornate front door sweeping closed behind us. Inside the thick walls, the din of the outside world was shut out. The foyer, its Tuscan paneling and dark timbered beams as royal as ever, stood staidly empty. I glanced up to see whether Shakespeare winked at us as we passed through the Reading Room doorway, and he may have. Grace gazed around the elegant quiescent chamber with a trace of awe, and then at me. "Sam Sandison must trust you."

"Mmm, I suspect he simply doesn't want me to have any excuse day or night for not being in here doing all the things he piles on me to do."

As we passed through the Reading Room, I could not help but stop for a minute and run my eyes over the mezzanine's ranks of books, silent but eloquent. I was smitten every time by the finest collection west of Chicago, and to have its literary riches almost to myself this way seemed like a scene in a dream. Housed in their volumes, the souls of writers waited in this great room to come out into the light of day. I would not have been surprised right then if Joseph Conrad materialized at the railing like a stalwart first mate on the deck watch, or Emily Dickinson came tiptoeing out of the shelves to peer down to the unattainable life below.

"My. It's so different in here without anyone around, isn't it."

"Grace, you needn't whisper."

"Oh, right." She trilled a laugh in relief. "If you promise not to shush me."

A last lingering moment, I gazed at the varicolored bindings as a person would cast a final glance at the jeweled colors of a cathedral window. Then I motioned Grace to the stairway, but she stayed as she was, studying me. "This is the love of your life, isn't it. What's in these books."

"I suppose it is," I conceded. "As the phrase goes, for better and for worse."

OFF THE CORRIDOR to Sandison's office was a small balcony, like a flex in the stonework over the main entrance's keystone arch, and the parade coming down Broadway would pass practically beneath us. Grace went straight to the balustrade and took a full look around, adjusting the swoop of her hat to keep the sun out of her eyes. Smiling her best, she plucked at the cuff of my suitcoat. "This is such a treat, you devil."

The rising roar from the street announced that things were under way. The copper capital of the known world knew how to stage a spectacle. Everything in shoes walked in the parade. The lodges— Masons, Elks, Templars, Odd Fellows, you name it—all of them sashed, some plumed. The firemen, prideful of their new hook-and-ladder Ford. The suffragists, resolute with their signs championing the correction to the Constitution that would give women the vote. The trade unions, and in Butte that was every trade; bakers,

tailors, cooks, carpenters, even blacksmiths went by with their banners in the breeze. Most groups were led by a drum, the boom of
march step resounding off the buildings. Then behind those marchers came the big horses, the brass of their harnesses gleaming, pulling delivery vans of every sort, and other horse-drawn conveyances
polished up for the occasion. A traveling carnival, calliope and all,
rolled past in gold-spoked wagons; a stiltwalker ambulated by nearly
at eye level with us. The next group on wheels were putt-putting
automobiles with dignitaries trying to maintain dignity in the herky-
jerky progress.

Eventually, more pedestrianly, came contingents of schoolchildren. Rab, gaily dressed, went by in charge of a flock of beribboned
girls representing her school. She spotted me, waved, and blew me a
kiss. Grace looked at me with a slightly raised eyebrow. "She must
have been quite something as a girl."

By now the Miners Day processional had gone on for a considerable time, and I leaned out to see how much more there could possibly
be. "Good heavens!" was all I could say.

Bearing down on us was what looked like an army of toy sol-
diers magnified to heroic size. Each marching man wore a uniform
of emerald green with gold-thread embossing across the chest and
down the sleeves, and their cap visors were set identically low to their
brows. The mix of gaudy uniforms and shiny musical instruments
suggested an orchestra conscripted onto the stage of an operetta. As
the marching mass neared the library, its leader spun in his tracks
and, walking backward, lifted his arms. Instantly instruments sprang
to lips, and at his signal, a Sousa march roared to life. Sun glinted
off a tuba, the extensions of trombones, the squadron of cornets. The
bass drums produced a beat that could be felt on the body.

"The Miners' Band," Grace managed to make herself heard into my ear. "They're nationally known. Not for lullabies, as you might guess."

And in the wake of the powerful music, here came the miners in their hundreds and hundreds, beneath a forest of banners with the union council proudly at the front. Leading them with his level stride was Jared Evans, in suit and tie and a snappy hat that might as well have been a crown. With his triumph in the wage battle, he was the hero of the day; Caesar coming home to Rome after victory could have received no greater tribute from the crowd. Grace and I added our cheers. The banners dipped and rose and swirled in back of Jared and the other council members, where the ranks of men who worked in the mineshafts stretched for blocks, each national group distinct to itself as I had seen them that first day on the Hill, but now scrubbed and tidied and in their best clothing. We strained to see, and tucked in between the Finns and the Serbs were the retired miners, with Griffith and Hooper and dozens of stooped replicas all in their vintage helmets.

By now the band had wheeled about and strutted back, facing the mineworkers. The resplendent bandleader lifted his arms and everything halted. He bowed from the waist toward the council, and a great cheer went up for the union and the restored wage. The other council members pushed Jared, grinning and not objecting too much, out for recognition by himself. The bandleader spun, up went the arms, and in tribute the band thundered into the mighty Welsh anthem "Men of Harlech."

> Men of Harlech, march to glory!
> Victory is hov'ring o'er ye!
> Bright-eyed freedom stands before ye—
> Hear ye not her call?

"I've never been within five thousand miles, of Wales," Grace was sniffling when it was over, "and that old thing always makes me want to bawl."

I was somewhat misty myself. "A very wise man once said mankind's two great magics are words and music."

Meanwhile Jared had doffed his hat to the band and the crowd, and the marchers were starting to shuffle into motion again.

Then it happened.

From somewhere, perhaps an alley or a rooftop, came a lone singing voice, just short of a yodel but with a devilish lilt to it. The refrain sliced through the parade mood:

> Wear the copper collar,
> Swallow dirt for your dollar.
> You'll get pie in the sky
> When you die.

Jared looked up as if the mocking ditty had hit him like an arrow. A squad of policemen at the intersection, whom I had assumed were on hand to hold back the crowd, jumped into action toward where the derisive singing seemed to come from. Before they made much headway, the invisible songster was at it again.

> Work and pray,
> Live on hay.
> You'll get pie in the sky
> When you die.

Now a couple of the council members shouted to the bandleader, a march tune was struck up, and the parade slowly snaked into motion once again. Looking back from now, what strikes me in the whole episode was that although I had never heard the pie-in-the-sky stanza before, I knew its origin almost from the first few insidiously catchy notes. So did Jared, according to his reaction. That kind of serenade rose straight from the Little Red Songbook.

"That's Butte for you." Grace had been waiting as patiently as she could for me to return to myself. "The top of the world one minute, the glory hole the next."

Now IT WAS her turn to surprise. With the parade over, I assumed we would follow the crowd to the next attraction, down at the depot. Butte was a regular stop for political speakers traveling through, in that ritual of a suspender-bursting oration from the rear platform of a train. Today's portable statesman was the imported variety, Eamon de Valera, a leader in Ireland's struggle against British rule, and judging by the sprigs of green in lapels and bonnets of everyone rushing by us, Dublin Gulch was avalanching off the Hill to hear him. Grace, though, firmly headed us the other direction. She would not tell me our destination—"You know what curiosity did to the cat, don't you?"—as we bundled onto a trolley. All I saw ahead as the trolley tracks continued past the outskirts of the city were mine dumps and the wall of mountains that topped out at the Continental Divide. Yet Grace and the other holiday-goers packed in with us were as merry as if we were bound for paradise.

The last stop on the line, in the tuck of a valley at the foot of the mountains, may not have been my notion of paradise, but it was somebody's idea of a fantasy land. We stepped off into an enormous amusement park, with COLUMBIA GARDENS spelled out in floral design against an entire hillside. Everything but the flowers seemed to be in excited motion. As I tried to take it all in, a roller coaster galloped through the treetops, and beyond, a Ferris wheel spun against the sky. Across acres and acres of the only green grass I had seen since coming to Butte, there were picnic groves; a playground featuring a brilliantly striped maypole and high-flying swings and a labyrinth of monkey bars; a merry-go-round; a zoo; a baseball diamond; a boxing ring; a trout pond; flower gardens; on and on. And the populace of the city had arrived in force to absorb the pleasures, it looked like. There is an unforgettable painting by Bruegel of swarms of children, serious about their fun, each bunch engaged in a different game and oblivious to the larger world. This panorama was like that.

Directly ahead from where Grace and I stood was a huge central pavilion, vaguely Italianate, surrounded by a soda parlor and other refreshment stands. "Pinch me," I told her, "I seem to have been whisked off to Coney Island. Who runs this?" She only gave me a certain kind of look.

"Don't tell me," I groaned. "The Anaconda Company."

"You're getting better at the facts of life," she awarded me.

The extravaganza surrounding us, then, was the other side of the copper coin, at least for this one day. Shaking my head at the turnabout of Anaconda's conduct, I asked Grace what she would like to do first. "Stroll the gardens," she chose without hesitation. "I haven't had an outing like this since—it's been a few years."

For as long as there are men and women, some things in life will best be done arm in arm, and strolling a flower garden is one. We exclaimed together at a hillside burst of blooms planted in the design of a giant lyre, as if a Gulliver had temporarily laid aside his music-making. Grace's grip on my arm was an exclamation in itself as we happily competed in naming off blossoms while we walked. Under the spell of the aromatic surroundings, we soon were sharing more than just the pleasure of the day. Grace's story was entirely rooted in Butte, I learned. "The mapmakers don't get rich on some of us, Morrie." To help support the family she had been a bucket girl, selling sandwich lunches from a pail as the men trooped to the mines on the Hill. There she caught the eye of a young miner on the same shift with her father; Arthur Faraday, as patient as he was gallant, had his reward when she reached marriageable age. The toils of Butte took her parents before their time—heart and lungs worked to death—leaving the young couple the gift of property. I listened raptly, the makings of a life always casting a spell on me. "We thought we had it made, Arthur and I, with the house in our name and his job in the Speculator." Instead, the fire, the worst in American mining history, widowed her overnight. There had been no children. "Nature did not provide." Left on her own, Grace used what resource she had—the house—and boarders such as present company were the result. "You and the matched pair are good about the rent," she patted my arm, "but it's still a hard go. The taxes and the upkeep and all. I get by, though. No sense in waiting for my ship to come in when there's none in sight, I've decided." She tilted her head in my direction, putting the question lightly enough. "What about yours, is the library it? You seem at home there." I cocked the same kind of look to her. "Do I? I don't always have the Butte Public Library all to myself, understand."

We laughed, duly self-conscious about the day's unexpected glimpses into each other. So much private time on the most public day of the year surely was too good to last. "Aren't Hoop and Griff joining us?" I checked. "It's not like them to miss this kind of spree."

"They're off to their own pursuits, they told me," Grace reported in that tone of fond exasperation the pair customarily produced in her. All at once she clutched my arm hard enough to leave a mark. "Look, dear!"

Companionable as our promenade was, I was surprised silly by the sudden endearment. I had to wonder if I was keeping up with developments. Was this a forward side of Grace Faraday, hitherto hidden in the house rules of landlady and boarder? Then, thoroughly abashed, I saw the deer she meant, several does and fawns flitting through a stand of blue spruce in the near distance.

"Cutlets on the hoof," I jested feebly and drew a swat on the arm, but also Grace's teasing smile.

Something surprising seemed to be the constant at Columbia Gardens. Fresh riots of flora in exuberant designs kept showing up as we strolled. Around any curve of the path, we were apt to be met with flower-holding ceramic gnomes of the European sort. And down at a pond off to our side, evincing great interest in the ducks, was Typhoon Tolliver.

There in broad daylight, the awful sensation of being stalked by shadows came over me. Luckily, Grace was distracted by the next riot of flowers. Taking a neck-stretching look around as if I could not get enough of admiring the grounds, I caught sight of Eel Eyes behind us, lurking around a corner of the soda fountain.

Apprehension rose in me like the mercury in a thermometer with a match under it. There is no law that goons have to take holidays like the rest of us, but why was this pair of dunces on my tail at all? The miners and the Anaconda Company were at peace, at least temporarily. Were Typhoon and his sidekick simply in the habit of following my every move? Whatever the notion in their thick heads, I didn't like it.

I scanned around some more. Back toward the pavilion and its huddle of refreshment stands, a photographer with his hood and flash powder was busily taking pictures of posing couples. "Let's," I said, pointing. "What's a day like this without a keepsake? My treat."

Grace hesitated, no doubt hearing from the spirit of Arthur. Verve won out. She primped her extensive hat and provided me a practice smile. "I suppose we shouldn't let all this gussying up go to waste."

The waiting line to be photographed was considerable, as I was counting on. "You hold our place," was my next proposal. "How about a root beer fizz?"

"Morrie, are you made of money all of a sudden?"

"I hope you're not turning down a root beer fizz."

"Of course not."

Off I strode, nonchalantly enough, to the soda parlor and its line of customers. The instant the angle of the building concealed me from Eel Eyes, I darted around to the back.

I crept along until I could sneak a look around the far corner. Eel Eyes, his back to me, was slouched against the building, dully watching for me to return to the photography line. I was scared to do what I was about to do, but more scared not to. The one advantage I had was musical; the Miners' Band had arrived somewhere on the park premises, and the triumphal march from *Aïda* was blaring loudly enough to drown any sound I could possibly make. Whatever Nile god is in charge of brass knuckles I said a quick prayer to, and fitted the metal onto my fists. Coming up unheard behind the bored goon, I clipped him hard on the crazy bone of his left elbow.

He yelped like a coyote and flopped around clutching the elbow, his business hand unable to reach for the blackjack or gun or whatever he carried in his coat. Grabbing hold of his shirtfront, I backed him against the rear of the soda parlor. While he was still squirming in pain, I rested a fist on the point of his chin, where at any sharp move the brass knuckles could knock out his front teeth.

"Typhoon isn't close enough to be any help to you," I uttered with so much bravado I hardly recognized my voice, "so you're going to have to tell me a thing or two. Why do the pair of you keep following me around like collie dogs?"

"Coincidence," he said sullenly, looking down his nose at the brass knobs threatening his teeth.

"Come now, Roland. Before one of us gets hurt"—I tapped his chin hard enough to make him wince—"you need to rid yourself of this ridiculous notion that I'm worth tagging after. Where does it come from, anyway?"

"How am I supposed to talk with those things half in my mouth?"

"Try."

He drew his lips over his teeth and munched out the words. "Let's square with each other, Morgan, or whoever you are. You're up to something, but Ty and me are on to you—so what do you say we cut a deal?"

"I am not 'up' to anything, you idiot, and whatever the pair of you think you're 'on to' is a figment of your overcooked imaginations."

"Oh yeah? Try this for size," he mustered hardily for a person in his situation. "Butte ain't been quite the same since you showed up. You got off that train and funny stuff started happening. Wildcat strikes. That old mug who runs the library wakes up and throws his weight around. And today you're up there on that balcony like a royal highness and at just the right time some Wobbly belts out a song and throws the whole parade bunch into a fit. Don't that add up to something in anybody's book?"

"That is all coinci—" I caught myself from using his exculpatory word. "I swear to you, man to man, I did not come to Butte to stir up trouble. What more can I do to convince you?"

"Leave town. Vamoose."

I hated to admit it, considering the source, but there was a lot of sense in that. Something else outweighed it, though. Maybe this was a wrong reading of the human condition, but it seemed to me there ought to be a limit to the number of times in life a person was obligated to vamoose.

Eel Eyes took my brief silence to mean I was thinking it over. "Ty and me will put you on a train tomorrow, how about?" he blurted. "We won't lift a hand to you except to wave good riddance, I promise. Him and me can find better things to do with ourselves than trailing you around."

"Then go find those, starting about now. But I'm not leaving. Butte is too interesting at the moment." His left hand was creeping toward the inside of his coat, so I rapped his knuckles with my brass ones. "Ow!" He sucked his lips over his teeth again. "And one more thing while we're at this," I leaned in on him instructively. "In case you're told to deliver any messages about a glory hole to a certain boardinghouse, save yourself the trouble on that, too. Now go collect your fellow idiot and"—I have to admit, I took nasty pleasure in the word—"vamoose."

I gave him room, and he backed around away from me. At a safe distance, he spat out: "Okay, we're done following you since you're on to it, but that ain't the only way to nail you. We'll get the goods on you yet."

"Tsk, Roland. You really ought to take up some other line of work."

He looked at me with sneering pity. "There's goods to be got on anybody, sucker."

"DID YOU HAVE to brew the root beer for those?" Grace inquired when I came back. We sipped our fizzes while the last few couples ahead of us in line were posed to wait for the click of the shutter, then it was our turn.

If memory serves me right, it was Balzac who believed that the human body has layers of self, and each time we are photographed one of those ghostly images is peeled off us irreparably onto the photographic print. In our case, Grace posed cautiously beneath the shelter of her hat, and I'm sure I looked as though I had too many things on my mind, which I did.

"Perfect!" cried the photographer as the flash powder went off with a *poof.*

He emerged from under his black cloth to hand me a numbered receipt. "Here you go, you can pick up your picture at the gate when you leave."

Grace startled me by taking my arm again. "Now I have a surprise for you."

Surprises come in two sizes, good and bad. Hers remained indeterminate while she steered me through the holiday throng toward the grandstand by the playing fields. The area was buzzing with activity as sporting events took shape; I could not help but notice two boxers going at it in the ring at a corner of the grassy expanse. After Eel Eyes, a boxing match appealed to me as restful. But Grace did not guide me up into the stands to spectate the various contests as I expected. With a flourish, she led me to the lip of the grass where the surprise came into sight.

I laughed helplessly. "Why didn't I think of this?"

"You must be slipping," she teased.

"I'll try to make up for it. Wait here, I'll be right back."

She frowned. "Has anyone ever told you, Morrie, you are restless company?"

Off I went in search of a gnome that moved, and found him circulating in the vicinity of the men's lavatory, as expected.

"What's up, buddy?" the halfpint messenger, in Sunday suit and bow tie for the day, called out when he spotted me. "Hey, how about those White Sox? They're burning up the league."

I sighed. Chicago follows a person like a botanical name. "The Comiskey Cheap Sox," I scoffed as I came up to him. "They'll unravel."

"You Cubs guys don't know real baseball when you see it."

"I shall keep looking." I left it at that and got down to business. "Skinner, I believe you might know how a man could place a bet."

"Think so?" He scanned the grounds. Satisfied that no strolling policeman was going to intrude on his working territory, he whipped out a much-used notebook. "What's your pleasure? The boxing matches? The mucking contest?"

"The boys' hundred-yard dash."

Indignantly Skinner pushed away the money I held out to him. "You kidding me? Use your noggin, buddy. Not till I look this over. How do I know you're not running some junior-size Jim Thorpe in on me."

RUSSIAN FAMINE was shambling back and forth at the edge of the field of contestants like a stray keeping his distance from the herd. All the boys in the race wore jerseys cut down; the stenciled FARADAY BOARDING HOUSE practically wrapped around him.

I went over to lend encouragement. I needed some myself after a closer look at our entrant. His gangly arms and legs were as pale as if the bones beneath were reflecting through, the strawy hair had not been combed in days, and for lack of a handkerchief in his racing outfit he was busily wiping his nose with the tail of the jersey. I had to hope the rest of him was as runny as his nose. Bending down to him, I urged in a low voice: "When you're in the race, Famine, just imagine the other boys are trying to catch you and beat you up."

"Doesn't take much imagination," he said stoically.

"To the victor belongs the spoils, remember."

"Huh?"

"Just run like the wind." I patted him on a barely existent shoulder, then joined Grace on the sidelines. She looked worriedly at the bigger boys in the race. "You're the one who told me he's lightning on two legs. He'll need to be." She inclined her head indicatively at a lanky redheaded lad, Irish as Saint Paddy, wearing a jersey with PETERSON'S MODERN MORTUARY across his chest, and on the back: AND FUNERAL HOME. "Look at that one, he makes two of poor Famine. This had better be worth the five dollars," she muttered, meaning the sponsoring fee.

"At the very least, it will distinguish the boardinghouse." I did not need to say with precision that it would distinguish it from the different sort of houses a block or so away in Venus Alley.

Catching Skinner's eye, I stepped over to place my bet. Observing this wagering side of me, Grace bit her lip but said nothing. Skinner wasn't happy to see me either. He shook his head, squinting skeptically at the assortment of boys, and Famine in particular. "Huh-uh, I don't bet blind. How do I know this kid of yours isn't some kind of freak of nature?"

The gambling spirit took another leap in me. "Then let's try this. I'll bet he wins by at least ten yards."

"Ten out of a hundred?" Skinner exclaimed. "A racehorse couldn't do that. You're on, let's see the color of your money."

He bolted for the far end of the track to gauge the finish, and I swept Grace along, despite a little protesting squeal. Meanwhile at the starting line, eleven of the dozen boys took determined stances while the Faraday Boarding House entrant stood there, fidgeting from one scuffed foot to the other. Somewhere the band played "When You and I Were Young." The starter's pistol fired. And Russian Famine was in full flight while the others were getting their speed up. He ran as if the devils of the steppes were pursuing him with red-hot pitchforks. He ran however fast it is a boy can run. Down the track he came, flying toward us, leaving the puffing pack of other runners in his dust, if there had been any. He crossed the finish line so far ahead of the others that Skinner simply turned away.

While Grace hurried over to congratulate her winner, I stepped aside to settle up with Skinner. Disgusted, he ponied up my bet. "Hardly fair. That skin-and-bones kid is like a streak."

"Exactly." I made a show of taking out my wallet and plucking the money from his bookmaker hands. "Don't you think he would make a messenger, if the right someone were to put in a word for him?" Skinner was giving the money hovering over my wallet a sad farewell gaze. "Who knows, I might forgive the bet if that were to happen."

Skinner perked up. "I guess I could see about it."

"At," I emphasized with a riffle of the money, "the Hennessy Building."

"At the Hen? Whoo, that's tough." He scratched his head as if digging out a thought. "They do hire an office kid for the summer. Usually it's some bigwig's fat nephew."

"Put it to them that in the relay of their messages, they have a choice between a flatfooted chair-warmer and winged Mercury."

"I'll skip that lingo, but those top-floor guys are always on fire to get their messages delivered fast." He watched in dismay as I tucked the wagered sum into my wallet. "Hey, when do I get my bet back?"

"At the time my friend Wladislaw becomes a messenger you-know-where."

WHILE I WAS AT THAT, Grace had flagged down a vendor and provided our victor with a feast of salami and cheese. Famine was devouring the victuals as if living up to his name when I joined them. I ruffled his hair, telling him that's where the laurel wreath should reside for a race so splendidly run and won, and in professional interest asked what he was going to do with his winnings.

He burped. "Eat some ice cream. Then go on the rolly coaster."

Grace and I watched him bound away. By then our own next diversion was hammering at us, literally. At the end of the field was what seemed to be a carnival of clang and clamor—even in its entertainment, Butte flexed its muscles—where contests of mining skills were being held. Arm in arm without thinking about it, we strolled over to spectate as the Miners' Band set the mood with "The Anvil Chorus." I saw Grace turn somber amid the displays of strenuous skills that had been her husband's working life. The mucking contest was almost too fatiguing to watch, as men competed to see who could shovel a ton of ore into an ore car the fastest. Moving on, we came to a series of drilling contests, divided, I was interested to note, into weight classes like those of prizefighting—lightweight, middleweight, heavyweight—and competitors stripped to the waist readying for the match. Fit, muscular, confident of their skill, plainly these were the pick of the Hill, which meant of all the copper miners on earth.

Which is why I thought I was seeing wrong—Grace's reaction was even more pronounced than mine—when just ahead of us, swinging a sledgehammer and hoisting a drilling bar to loosen up, were Griffith and Hooper, shirts off, in their overalls and long underwear.

The weight of years defined this competition, as the placard bluntly announced: OLDTIMERS DRILLING CONTEST.

"No wonder they were so full of themselves this morning," Grace burst out. "I hope they don't fall over dead, the old fools."

Across on the other side, there seemed to be no similar trepidation around their competitors, a pair of Finns who had lost no huskiness to age. Their supporters were whooping and clapping and singing in Finnish as if the contest already was won.

Wordlessly I assessed the matchup, although it didn't take much study. I reminded myself that the gambling spirit should be harkened to only when the gamble carries a discernible chance of reward. I protectively patted the winnings Russian Famine had supplied to my wallet. In short, I took myself through the whole breviary of common sense, then told Grace I would be right back and went in search of Skinner again. She bit her lip even harder this time.

THE RIVAL TEAMS were poised to start by the time I rejoined Grace, each pair of men at a block of bluish granite the size of a packing crate. These drilling matches were of the old classic type, before compressors and air hoses replaced muscle and diligence at the rockface; in other words, by hand. Two sets of hands, and two steel tools. The holder knelt with a five-foot drill of tempered metal, like a slim crowbar, gingerly in his grasp. The hammerman, swinging a sledge, would strike the end of it, and as he drew back for the next stroke, the holder twirled the steel a quarter-turn for the drill head to make another flaking cut. In the early rise of Butte to mining eminence, I gathered, this blow-by-blow assault on rock—offhandedly called "breaking ground"—was an essential skill; the hole drilled in this laborious but effective way would be tamped with dynamite and the resulting blast would bring down the wall of rock for the ore to be separated out. Life tells tales as strange as those we can make up: the copper that wired the world for electricity was set loose, like fresh water from a struck stone in a fable, by those pairs of hands and driven steel in the chinks of the Hill.

Fortunately, dynamite was not involved in this match, which was to be a race to see which team could drive the deeper hole in a given time. Grace and I, already tense, watched intently as the judge fondled his stopwatch and instructed the two teams to get ready. Hoop, the hammerman, spat in his hands; Griff, the drill holder, flexed his fingers. The hardy Finns at the other block of rock did the same.

"Ready," the judge chanted, "set . . . DRILL!"

The ear-ringing sound of steel hitting steel echoed off the hill where flowers spelled out COLUMBIA GARDENS, on up into the mountains beyond, and in not many seconds resounded again. The strokes of the sledgehammers set up a clanging rhythm best described as Hell's bells. Yet the process was strangely hypnotic and suspenseful to watch; the hammerman had to hit, each and every time, a target no bigger than a nickel, while the holder had to absorb the sting of the blow and make his fingers turn the drill the correct fraction. It was inherently dangerous, the eight-pound head of the sledgehammer arcing at the holder if the hammerman missed, the shaft of steel thrusting spearlike toward the man with the hammer if the holder mishandled it. I watched in fascination as Hoop, scrawny as he was, swung his sledge in a pace steady as a pendulum, and Griff, equally meager, knelt fearlessly over the drill as if his life depended on its next turn. Their opponents meanwhile seemed built for the job. One of them gravely white-haired, the other with a mustache that would have been white except for tobacco stains, both Finnlanders looked as sturdy as the granite.

As the clamor of the hammers went on and the drills chewed into the rock particle by particle, Grace nudged me hard enough to make me grunt. "Tell me, you," she fanned herself with her hat as though the exertion of the competitors was getting to her, "which team did you bet on?"

"I'm surprised at you, Grace. How could I not be loyal to the boardinghouse?" She was not the only skeptic. Skinner had chortled as he took the money I put on Hooper and Griffith. "Don't know how to quit while you're ahead, huh? Those old gimps have seen their day. You better stick to footraces and baseball, pal."

"Loyalty is one thing, using your head is another," Grace now added to that, fretfully watching the spectacle of old men attacking hard rock.

"Never fear, I still have enough to pay my rent."

"I wasn't worried about that." She fanned herself more rapidly, giving me a sidelong look. "Well, maybe a little."

It was no doubt true that in a world where chance operated as surely as gravity, I would have bet on the Finns. And perhaps regretted it, for Hoop was matching the mustached Finn blow for blow, their sledgehammers chorusing together. I was no stranger to contests, and this one could not have been closer, one team ahead by a fraction of an inch, then the other.

"Switch!" cried the judge at the five-minute mark, and,

fantastically, the men of both teams changed jobs without missing a stroke. That fast, Hoop was on his knees minding the drill, Griff was banging away with the sledgehammer, and the race into the rock thundered on.

Grace sat on the edge of her seat, urging Griff on and muttering aside to me about the bawling-out he and Hoop were going to get from her at home. Griff's long underwear darkened with sweat across the shoulders as his turn at hammering went on. It was incredible to think of, the human muscle that had gone into the extraction of ore before machinery came to the mines, and Griff and Hoop and their opponents were part of it then as they were now.

"Switch!" cried the judge again, and like the flash team Hoop had told me they were, he and Griff switched jobs for the last stint of the quarter-hour contest.

"If only they don't kill themselves," Grace breathed. My concern, too, with money thrown in. As the contest drew down, Hoop was red with effort. I ached in some of my parts just from watching his exertion. Yet the beat of his hammer stayed steady. By the time the judge shouted that they were coming to the final minute, I could see no measurable difference in the extent of the drills into the blocks of stone.

Then, like a broken note between the rhythm of the hammers, came an anguished cry from Griff. His hand had cramped, freezing onto the drill and pulling him, bent by the pain, toward the path of the sledgehammer. Grace gasped and started to her feet and I vaulted toward the scene along with several other men. Hoop with miraculous presence of mind buckled his back leg at the last second, driving the hammer head into the dirt instead of Griff. The two of them stayed hunched that way, gulping for air, to the sounds of the Finnish team driving its drill the last inch to victory.

———

IN THE AFTERMATH, Grace and I consoled Hoop. Griff was avoiding everyone, staring at the hand that had betrayed him. I saw him wipe his eyes with his shirttail. "We'll see you at breakfast," Hoop told us wearily as we watched Griff disappear, shoulders bowed, into the holidaying crowd. "He's gonna need some liquid refreshment to get over this. Me, too."

"I'M SPENT," Grace sighed, sounding already wistful when we ended our stay after a silent last tour of the gardens.

"Wait, we have to see how we're immortalized." I plucked the photographer's result out of the envelope I'd picked up at the amusement park exit and she pressed close to me. At the sight, we both burst out laughing and teasing. She claimed I looked like a scared preacher, and I expressed amazement that Queen Marie of Romania had got into the picture with me.

"Such a day, Morrie," Grace wound down as the trolley back to town toddled along the tracks to us. Her violet eyes sought mine. "I feel as if I've been on that roller coaster with our star runner."

With a pensive smile to match hers, I provided my arm to help her up the step as the trolley rattled to a halt. "I know the feeling."

9

"Now we can get back to business," Sandison met me with as the staff reluctantly queued up on the library steps to be let in, the morning after. "I never have understood the meaning of holiday. Didn't have time for loafing of that sort on the ranch. Cows never took time off from eating."

"The nomenclature, Sandy, I think you'll find goes back to Middle English—the term recognizably became 'holy day,' and subsequent centuries of quickening pronunciation have given us—"

"Damn it, Morgan, did I ask for the history of the universe? Didn't think so." His shaggy gray eyebrows knitted, he contemplated me in either amazement or extreme irritation, it was always hard to tell which. "You have the damnedest brainbox ever created, I swear. Anyhow, get yourself caught up on the usual chores"—a near impossibility the way he kept adding to them—"the next couple of days. I have something I want you to do. Tell you when the time comes."

GRACE HAD BEEN QUIET as a mouse at breakfast, as had I, out of respect for the kingsize hangovers Hoop and Griff brought to the table. I was unprepared, then, when I came home from the library and heard the urgent stage-whisper from the kitchen: "*Hsst*. In here, Morrie."

Expecting to perform an act of rescue on whatever was cooking for supper, I stepped in and found Grace miserably seated at the kitchen table, her face a smeared mask of white. A bottle of calamine lotion was standing ready for more application. Wrapped around her forehead was a rag soaked, according to its eye-stinging odor, in vinegar. Not that I needed any further evidence, but the red welts on any inch of her skin not yet daubed with calamine told me I was seeing a prime case of hives.

"What on earth—?" I sat down quickly and reached over to hold her hand, trying madly to think what to do beyond that. If the goons had shown up here on a glory hole mission despite my warning, I was going to have to find some way to make them regret it; I did not look forward to that. She continued to gaze at me with a forlorn expression, her eyes smarting from the acrid vinegar cloth, which, truth to tell, did not seem to be cooling her troubled brow appreciably. "Grace, you have to put it into words. What's the matter?"

"You are."

This was worse than if she had said, "The goons were here, breathing fire." My hand withdrew. Apprehensively, I asked, "How so?"

"By being you, whoever, whatever—" She started to scratch her arms, thought better of it, and instead dug her elbows into the table and leaned practically flat across to confront me. "I tossed and turned all night trying to figure out who am I with when I'm with you. Take yesterday. One minute I'm on the arm of someone I enjoy thoroughly"—her reddened eyes blinked more rapidly at that emotion—"and the next, you're gambling away money like you're feeding the chickens."

"Russian Famine won by at least eleven yards," I pointed out.

"All right, then," she said, no less miserable, "half the time when you're busy getting rid of any wrinkled money, the wind blows a little back."

Still trying to catch up, I asked hoarsely: "What brought this on? Just a few bets I happened to place when the opportunity seemed ripe?"

Wordlessly she gazed past me, through the kitchen doorway, to the wedding portrait on the sideboard, and my heart sank. The ghost of Arthur hovered in from the next room, and how could I ever compete with such a paragon of domestic virtue? Her whitened, rag-wrapped countenance as tragic as a mummy's, Grace leaned farther toward me as if to deliver that verdict more fiercely. But what came out was practically a whisper.

"Arthur was a betting man."

Silence followed this shocking news. Grace sat back as if exhausted, scratched under an arm, and with an angry swipe slathered on more calamine. I still was trying to imagine which competitions of skill so manly a miner would be enticed to wager on. "Boxing matches? Drilling contests?"

"Dogs."

My jaw dropped. "Believe me, I never have and never shall put money on the velocity of a canine."

"Arthur was hopeless about it," she half-whispered again, her voice carrying the strain of the memory. "He would be perfectly fine for a while, bringing his wages home, sweet as anything. Then would come a payday when he didn't show up for supper and I knew he'd gone to the dogs again. The races, that is." She folded her arms, wincing as she did so. "And there you were yesterday, one minute as perfect a companion as a woman could ask for, and the next, behaving as if you were trying to break the bank at Monte Carlo. Which one is the real you? I can't tell from one moment to the next whether you're the best creature that ever wore pants, or, or—I don't know what." Her tirade ran down. "How can a person ever hope to get a straight line on you, Morrie?"

I nervously smoothed my mustache, dreading where this was leading. It had to be faced, it always does.

"Grace"—I used her name as if patting it before putting it away for good—"I don't know any cure for being myself. The lotion for that hasn't been concocted yet." The next had to be said past the lump in my throat. "Do you want me to pack my satchel and go?"

No man is a hero to his butler, it is said; nor is any boarder a model of perfection to his landlady. Grace Faraday straightened up and scrutinized me, blinking harder. "If I had a lick of sense, I should push you out the door right now, shouldn't I." As I watched, her dubious self struggled with the proprietorial side of her. "But when you're not a pile of trouble, you're no trouble. You're on time with the rent every week, although heaven knows how. You aren't a steaming drunk, at least since you gave up wakes. You don't throw a fit when dynamite goes off under the place. And Griff and Hoop don't seem to drive you crazy. That counts."

Had she been ticking these off on her fingers, she now was out of fingers. Looking as doubtful as she sounded, she concluded:

"For now, you may as well stay. One more thing, though. We need to be as clear as we can about each other. Yesterday was too, um, too forward of me, Morrie, and it wasn't really fair to you." Something more than an itch was making her chalky face twitch. "You shouldn't get the wrong idea and feel . . ." There she faltered.

"Taken up with," I finished for her, and I was surprised at how sad it sounded.

THIS WAS ONE of the nights of the week when I had to go back to the library and lock up after the evening groups, and I trudged off to do it with the old weight of disappointment on me.

First Rose, now Grace. Rejection as soon as someone personable and pretty took a good look into me, whatever it was they thought they saw.

Women were the fairer sex? What was fair about their finger-snap judgments of me? Even Sandison, grumpy and flatfooted around women, had found someone to put up with him, the redoubtable Dora. While my best efforts caused them to dust their hands of me or break out in hives.

I felt lonely as a castaway, and, what was worse, from present indications I had better get used to it.

My acidic mood was at odds with the gentle summer dusk, spreading down from the Hill over the brick canyons of the city, casting the streets into picturesque shadow. That sank through to me, and a couple of times I whipped into a doorway and looked back. There was no sign of goons, at least. Brass knuckles seemed to get the job done, although I couldn't see how to apply that to courtship.

In the library basement when I arrived, the Ladies' and Gentlemen's Literary and Social Circle was still going strong. A balding young man with the look of a bank clerk was onstage, reciting in round tones: ". . . *now when heaven holds starry night in its keep / and on moonlit Olympus, the Muses gently sleep.*" Ordinarily I am all in favor of the Muses, but tonight I shooed the literature lovers mercilessly, and they filed out of the auditorium in shy pairings. The big room echoing with emptiness now, I was stacking away the chairs when I heard a single set of footsteps rapid on the stairs. The goons always traveled as a pair. Or did they? Just in case, I hefted a chair, ready to hurl.

"What the devil," Jared stopped short as he came through the doorway and saw me with the chair in my hands, "are you cutting the janitor out of his job?"

"It's his lodge night, so he's excused early," I said crossly. "My employer has a habit of bending the rules for this, that, and the other, except where I'm concerned."

"You need a union," he joked, or not, lending a hand with the stray chairs. He looked at me curiously. "That poor thing who's your landlady told me you've about taken up residence in the library."

"It's a long story."

"I imagine. Anyway, I'm glad I could track you down." He glanced around to every corner of the auditorium even though we were alone. "Any luck with you know what?"

"Luck is the residue of endeavor, in some situations," I responded, still not in my best mood. "Come on up to the office."

Our footsteps were magnified in the empty darkened building as we went upstairs, and I sensed Jared was jumpy in the unfamiliar surroundings. But if situations were reversed, I would not be particularly at ease in a mineshaft, would I. When I switched on a light in the office, he stayed by the door and took everything in. "So this is the lion's den." His gaze came to rest on me, with that flavoring of curiosity again. "I have to hand it to you, you've got guts, holed up in here with him all day long. I've heard about old Triple S since I was a kid."

"He hasn't taken my head off my shoulders, so far," I muttered, my attention on the contents of the hiding spot in the cabinet where the ledgers were kept, the one place I was sure Sandison would not go near now that he had shed the bookkeeping to me. I brought out the pink sheets and my pages of calculations of each mine's differential between raw tons of ore and tally of processed copper. "Is this what you had in mind?"

Not wasting a moment, Jared laid out my pages on the nearest desk—Sandison's—and ran his finger down the figures. When he reached my totals, he pulled a slip of paper from his shirt pocket and compared. His whoop startled me, and probably the pigeons on the library roof. "You've nailed it! Anaconda's been feeding us low numbers on the finished copper. We'll give them holy hell in the negotiations now and they won't even know how we figured it out." Exuberantly he batted my shoulder. "Rab thinks you're the greatest thing going. I'm starting to see why, Professor, if I can call you that."

"I'm flattered, I suppose."

As the two of us headed downstairs, I could make out just enough of Jared in the library's moonlit atmosphere to know he could hardly wait to turn the tables on Anaconda. Now I was curious. "You have the lost dollar back. What are you still negotiating about so urgently?"

"You name it. Working conditions. Hiring and firing. Safety." His voice turned hollow. "On first shift, just this morning, one of our men in the Muckaroo was killed when a tunnel roof fell in on him. Left a wife and six kids." I recalled his delivering the union tribute—cash and consolation—to the widow at my first wake as a cryer; again and again, from the sound of it, he faced that duty.

Mustering himself now, Jared went on with what he had been saying. "All of it causes bad feelings in the union. There are those who say getting the wage back is what counted, let's don't beat our heads against the shed on these other matters until we get some pay-days behind us. And then there's plenty who are ready to shut down the Hill again like that"—he snapped his fingers—"if the company doesn't give us every last thing we want."

He glanced sideways at me. "Professor?" In the splendid acoustics—we were in the foyer by now—he sounded like a messenger of fate in a Greek drama as he laid matters out. "I wouldn't guess you're a military man at heart, but you maybe know what an accelerated march is. It covers ground a lot faster than parade cadence, but it's not a run that makes your tongue hang out. That's about what I'm trying for. We can't let up much on Anaconda or things slip back. But we're never going to turn copper mining into a picnic, no matter what we try. Either way, as I see it, those of us on the council have to keep things moving, just fast enough." The next came out as if he were thinking to himself. "Particularly now."

When I halted short of the front door and gave him a questioning look, Jared hesitated. "All right," he granted, "Rab will probably blab this to you if I don't. Anaconda isn't our only problem—we're scrambling to stay ahead of the Wobblies. The word is, they're going to make a big push to take away our members." He tilted his head to one side as if trying to see the situation from a fresh angle. "Who knows, if things had been different, maybe I'd be on their side. But I was born a union man. The union stuck up for the workingman on the Butte Hill all those years, every day of my father's life when he went down into the mine. The Wobs always say they would, too, and take over the mines and everything else besides." He shook his head. "I don't trust that, Professor. It would go to hell in no time, I think. Look at Russia. The Bolshies did away with the Czar, and now they're knocking off anybody they don't like the looks of."

I just listened, Jared needing to get the weight of fate off his chest;

he had earned the right in the trenches that were the maw of the Great War.

"I have to hand it to the IWW," he was saying ruefully, "they're a persistent damn bunch. The last time they sent a bigtime organizer in here, the goons hung him from the railroad trestle. Lynched him. The old remedy, the Montana necktie." With a laugh that had no humor in it, he gazed around at the grandeur of the library as though wondering how it and a lynching site a dozen blocks away could exist in the same realm of time. "Maybe I have Wobs on the brain," he mused. "That one at the parade yesterday, singing that damn thing?" Jared Evans startled me again by mimicking, quite presentably, the phantom voice that had mocked the parading miners' union with *pie in the sky, when you die*. He banged his head with the heel of his hand. "It gets in there and I can't get it out."

"It's called a mnemonic effect," I informed him. "Something that prompts remembering, usually voluntary but not necessarily. A musical phrase is particularly suited. For instance, 'Camptown—'"

At the library door now, Jared put up his hands to hold off my discourse.

"I appreciate the definition. But I'll just call it trouble. Good night, Professor."

I WAS WARY in every direction I could think of, those next few days. But there was no sign of lurking goons, and on the home front, Grace—still a picture of misery, under the ghostly layer of lotion— did not come up with any further charges against my personality. She and I were painfully polite with one another, to the point where Hoop and Griff grew nervous around us. They talked a blue streak at mealtimes to cover our silences, and while I learned a lot about assorted topics of interest to retired Welsh miners, it was a relief each morning to go off to work at the library.

Until, that is, the pertinent day when Sandison spun around in his chair as soon as I stepped into the office and announced, "Morgan, it's time we get some ammunition to use on the trustees."

I knew "we" meant me, so I simply cocked my head to listen.

"You've done a good enough job of balancing the ledger, the board can't find anything to kick about in there," he went on. "Now they're fretting about where the money is going to come from for new carpets, all the wear and tear we've had in here lately. I keep telling them any board of trustees worth its name would just pony it up, but they want to steal it out of the book budget, the damn thieves."

He hunched forward as if about to rake in a poker pot. "That's where you come in. I want to remind that pack of meddling fools which side their bread is buttered on." He looked at me craftily. "I've never signed my book collection over to the library," there was a sly note in his voice I had not detected before, "it's here on loan, like museums have with paintings of people with their clothes off." That explained much: for Butte to house the finest collection west of Chicago, the obsessive keeper of the books came along with it.

"Told you there's something I have for you to do," he was saying, as though I were looking for a way to fill my time. "Draw up an inventory of what's mine out there on the shelves," he waved in the direction of the prized books on the mezzanine. "That'll bring the trustees to their senses," the grandee of the library finished, sitting back and cracking his knuckles in satisfaction.

"I shall need a helper."

That caught him by surprise, and before he could cloud up enough to tell me I was out of my mind, I said, "Fortunately, Sandy, the staffing has been a little light for some time, hasn't it." I flipped to

the ledger page that listed library positions and wages, his piggybank
for those *Miscellaneous* expenditures when irresistible books showed
up in dealers' catalogues. He eyed me as my finger singled out positions budgeted for but chronically unfilled. "Very wise of you," I
drove the point home with a final finger tap, "to leave leeway for an
occasion just such as this."

Sandison coughed. "Let's be reasonable about this. We can't be
cluttering up the place with some moron we don't absolutely need,
just because—"

"No, no," I headed off that objection, "summer help will do. A
teacher, perhaps, with free time now that school is out. In fact, I think
I know of one."

"Don't waste time talking about it, then." He heaved himself
around in his seat as if compelling business awaited on his desk.
"Hire this summer wonder you have your eye on, and get going on
the inventory. You have to make decisions in this life, Morgan."

"THIS IS EXCITING, working for Sam Sandison. It's like being on a
pirate ship."

"Rab, contain your imagination. This is a library."

"You know what I mean," she whispered back secretively, there on
the mezzanine. "Everyone in Butte has an opinion about him. What's
yours, Mr. Morgan?"

"It's too deep to go into. Pull down *Pride and Prejudice* and see if
it has the bookplate."

She took a peek inside the tanned leather cover and giggled. "It
does. Just like on a heifer." Volume by volume, our library lord's collection bore the bookplate lettered in bold SSS, with the smaller,
uncompromising line below, *Property of Samuel S. Sandison.* I hadn't

put this together until Rab's remark, but now my first conversation with the man came back to mind, when he berated me for not knowing that the most famous cattle herd in Montana history had borne the Triple S brand. Leave it to him to put a brandabetical stamp on the world's literature.

Rabrab—or Miss Rellis, as I had to make myself call her in front of other staff members—was a diligent worker, as we were both going to need to be. Already we each had a heaping armful of exquisite books, and this was only Adams, Arnold, and Austen. As we tottered off to the sorting room, where Sandison had let us set up shop for the inventorying, she marveled: "Say what they will about him, he really does have a soft spot for books, doesn't he."

And Ivan the Terrible perhaps loved his staghounds. My private opinion of Sandison, inconstant in the best of times, varied almost hourly during those first busy weeks of summer. He was as demanding as ever in the office chores he foisted onto me, the Earl of Hell with a list in his head, and between those I would dash back to the sorting room to work with Rab on the inventory. Sometimes we would look up and see the snowy beard and cowlick pass by as he came stalking out of his office to stand there on the mezzanine and contemplate the ranks of books on the shelves. When he loomed there in one of these trances, white as a sacred elephant, Rab and I simply detoured around him in our task. I was certain as anything that *bibliomania* did not mean a maniac loose in a library, but there were times Sandison made me wonder whether the definition needed adjusting. Yet, fume at him and his high-handed ways as I so often did, there were the immortal books, which would not have graced the Constantinople of the Rockies but for him. In life's list of complications, this one seemed to carry an acceptable price.

Volume by plated volume, Rab and I kept compiling and adding up the Sandison library-within-the-library. If the edition in hand matched a listing in a rare books catalogue, it was no problem to assign a value. Any we could find no listing for, one or the other of us would take, several at a time, for appraisal by old Adamson, the coldblooded antiquarian book dealer across town. As you might guess, there is a secret satisfaction in going through the streets with your arms around the Artful Dodger and Natty Bumppo and Emma Bovary, no one knowing you are hugging a monetary fortune as well as a literary one.

So, its hectic moments aside, the inventorying was the most pleasant kind of work, engaging the mind, and no unduly heavy lifting involved. Rab was sparkling company, as I had counted on. She showed up each morning bright-eyed for whatever the day might bring, and in plucking the SSS books from the shelves, she whisked in and out of the mezzanine stacks as if on jeweled skates. From the number of upturned male heads among the Reading Room patrons as she winged past overhead, I was not the only one appreciative of her presence.

I suppose I should not have been surprised when Sandison called me in to his office, and there, like one of the frowning Easter Island stone heads, was Miss Runyon.

"It seems there is a distraction in our otherwise flawless service to the reading public," Sandison addressed me pontifically from behind his desk. "State your case, Miss Runyon."

She drew herself up as if to huff and puff and blow me away. "It's that helper of yours. She wears those little dresses, you can see everything she has."

"You can? I mean, I had not noticed."

"Then you are the only man breathing who hasn't," she declared.

I looked from her to Sandison and back again, both of them

dressed twenty years behind the times. "Perhaps it is natural that the younger people take a different view of wardrobe than, ah, we do."

Rousing himself, Sandison abandoned his chair and clomped out from behind the desk. "Your concern for propriety is notable, Miss Runyon," he said soothingly as he escorted her to the door, "and I'm sure Morgan can deal with the issue."

When she was gone, he rounded on me. "The next couple of days, you be the one to prance out there on the mezzanine and fetch the books," he directed, "just on the chance that people may not be quite as interested in seeing everything you have." His frosty eyebrows were hoisted high as he studied me. "You're a sharper operator than I thought, Morgan." He laughed bawdily. "Make the most of your time with Miss Rellis."

I LOOK BACK on that midsummer stretch of weeks as a season of life that went up and down with the regularity of a carousel. Each day divided itself according to the female company of the time. At the boardinghouse, Grace and I stayed as self-consciously civil as schoolchildren who had been told to mind their manners or else; her hives had gone away, but her allergy to being taken up with me had not. Then I would go off to the library and the short-hemmed zephyr that was Rabrab Rellis.

With her keenness for being in on things, Rab was as intrigued with the inventory books as I was, both of us beaming like babies at the chance to handle lovely volumes that even the most omnivorous reader would miss out on in a lifetime. On nice days we carried the mood outside, joking to one another, and ate lunch on the library steps. Butte sunned itself those noon hours, as if storing up for rougher weather ahead. Gangs of boys swarmed down from the

Hill neighborhoods, heading for the swampy attractions along Silver Bow Creek. On the next street, the *Post* building had put up a
baseball scoreboard on its front, and the amplified voice of the sports
telegraphist relaying diamond drama as it took place in Cincinnati
and Washington and other major-league outposts carried to us like
opera arias: *"Flash! It's a home run! The Redlegs lead one to nothing!"*
Sometimes Russian Famine, scrubbed and neatened, would stop by
on his errands as a Hennessy Building runner, and one of us would
share a sandwich with him before he sprang to his duty again.

"Mr. Morgan, there's something I've been puzzling about," Rab
broached during one of those pleasant noontimes when we were
alone. "I noticed it all the way back at Henry Adams and his *Education*. That was published only last year." She had her old look of a
schoolgirl circling what might be a trick question. "Aren't the Sandison books supposed to be what he collected when he was on the ranch,
ages ago?"

That had tickled my interest, too. By now we were at Kafka, Keats,
and Kipling. The romantic poet was sadly gone, but the other two
were up and writing and I had just catalogued recent contributions to
literature by both that also carried the SSS bookplate.

So as not to heat up Rab's instinct for intrigue, which never needed
encouragement, I shrugged past the matter of newly minted books
among the old: "An occasional stray may have wandered into his literary herd, large as it is. Isn't there a ranching word for that?"

"Maverick, you mean? An unbranded cow that someone slaps
their own brand on?" Rab wrinkled her nose as if sniffing something
spicy. "Oh, that's so funny."

It was more so than she knew. Possibly Sandison, from long habit,
was simply buying valuable books out of his own pocket and folding
them into his collection, as he had every right to do. But the more

tantalizing possibility, I sensed, was that those *Miscellaneous* purchases drawn from the library's payroll budget were being cunningly mingled into his earlier holdings. If I knew anything about Samuel S. Sandison by now, it was that he never saw a thing of worth that didn't look better to him with SSS on it.

Brushing away lunch crumbs as though that took care of the topic, I told Rab, "We had better get back at it, there's a shelf of Longfellow ahead."

"How's THAT INVENTORY COMING?" Sandison rumbled when I passed by the office that afternoon.

"Sandy, you are to be commended for your buying eye," I stuck to what I could honestly say. "The books you have gathered amount to a financial fortune as well as a literary one."

"They damn well ought to," he said as he hunched over an antiquarian catalogue and some notations to himself which, I was quite sure, added up to more books for the Sandison collection.

"Oh, by the way," the issue of expenditure reminded me, "a cyclopedia salesman this morning left us a sample of his newest." I stepped to my desk for the brochure as Sandison groaned at the distraction. "Here you go, the sales pitch for *Prominent Figures of Montana, Past and Present*. He assured me no self-respecting library should be without such a volume. As an added inducement, he told me you will find yourself prominently in it, Sandy." I passed the brochure to him for inspection.

He took one look, informed me it was nothing more than the usual attempt by some robber to steal names and sell them back to flattered fools, and tossed it aside. "Bury it in Section 37," I thought I heard him mutter as he turned back to what he had been doing.

"Excuse me, please"—by then I thought I knew every corner of the library—"but you'll have to tell me where that section is."

"Eh?" His head jerked up and around as if I had been eavesdropping. Catching up with himself, he waved me off the subject. "Never mind. Get back to the inventory and making eyes at Miss Rellis, why don't you."

NOT LONG AFTER, I was met at the breakfast table by two long faces. Griff asked mournfully, "You heard what they're doing to us now?"

"I am barely out of bed, Griff, how could I?"

"They're cracking down," said Hoop, equally doleful.

I waited, but both informants were too overcome to provide anything more. Mystified, I had to look to Grace for an explanation.

"The police have heard from a higher power," she said with a frown. From the look on her, I translated that to mean the top floor of the Hennessy Building, home of the copper collar. "They're arresting characters who hang out downtown without any business for being there." For a change, she spoke to me in the old dulcet way, I supposed to make two sets of deaf ears perk up and listen in. "A couple of those come to mind at this table, don't they."

"Spitting on the sidewalk, the cops call it," Hoop said with disgust.

"Vagrancy is another way of putting it," Grace provided for my benefit.

Griff burst out, "It's that 'unlawful assembly' crap"—Grace did not rebuke him—"whatever name the buzzards put on it."

Still behind, I asked around the table: "What put the authorities on this rampage?"

"The Wobblies," Hoop and Griff answered together, while Grace's expression said she had heard all this too many times, and she went off to the kitchen. The IWW wanted to cut in and take the lead in the miners' struggle with Anaconda—it just wasn't right, my tablemates stated. From what they heard, the specter of operatives filtering into town to mold discontented workers of the Hill into a radical legion had thrown Butte's powers that be into a tizzy. Hence, jail awaited anyone deemed a "vagrant."

When the law is bent that way, a detour around it is sometimes needed. That morning I went to the library by the back-alley route shown me by Russian Famine, just to be on the safe side.

To MY SURPRISE, that lunchtime, Rab was mum about this newest tussle over who would contol the Hill. I don't know what I expected to be in sight when we settled at the top of the library steps as usual—the Hennessy Building being stormed like the Bastille by maddened Wobblies, perhaps—but the streets were placid, only punctuated here and there by strolling policemen who looked vaguely embarrassed. Rab was chattering on about Melville and whether anyone who wasn't vitally interested in blubber actually ever read every page of *Moby-Dick*, but there was something bubbling under that which should have alerted me. Nonetheless, I was caught by surprise when a lean figure, brisk and businesslike in a somber suit but with his hat pulled low, peeled away from the concourse of patrons in and out of the library and dropped onto the steps beside us. "See what I mean about the Wobs spelling trouble, Professor?"

"I suppose I do, Jared," I answered him as equably as I could.

"There seem to be a lot of ways to spell that in Butte." I watched with envy as he nestled in next to Rab and was rewarded with a kiss and a sandwich. Curious as to why he was dressed up, I asked: "What's the occasion?"

"None in particular," Jared provided between bites. "I just don't want to look like somebody who might spit on the sidewalk." A policeman went by on leadfooted patrol, giving us hardly a glance. "You can almost feel sorry for the dumb cops," he mused. "Almost."

The police on puppet strings were not the only ones entitled to sympathy in the situation, I could tell; the crackdown plainly hindered the activities of the miners' union, and I charitably said something of the sort to Jared.

"An opportunity for a strategic withdrawal, we called it in the army," came the dry response.

"Extra syllables aside, I believe that means 'retreat'?" I made sure.

"You might say that," he granted. "But going a different direction, even backwards," he munched on the matter along with his sandwich, "gives a chance to gain some ground somewhere else, doesn't it?"

Rab, eyes alight, had been flicking glances back and forth between us. "You'd better ask him, love," she prompted. "Mr. Morgan and I have to get back to whaling all too soon."

The ancients who invented storytelling knew to the instant when drama must put on a human mask. The soaring ambition of Icarus to consort with the sun, before the first feather melted from his wings and wafted down and down to the waiting Aegean Sea. The echo of the knight's heartbeat within his armor before he slays the dragon. Some such flutter in the curtain of fate, now that I look back on everything that was about to happen, came with Jared Evans that noontime.

"You brought this on yourself, Professor," he said as though I didn't know any better. His dark eyes held a glimmer as he went on: "Remember when you were telling me why 'pie in the sky' gets in a person's head and won't leave? The 'nimo gizmo' side of things, you called it?"

"The mnemonic aspect," I was glad to clarify. "It derives from Mnemosyne, the Greek goddess of memory, and—"

"That's what I'm saying, the union needs that kind of brain food." Past the brim of his hat I could see Rab glistening with interest. Jared scanned around as if scouting enemy terrain and lowered his voice. "I got to thinking about what you'd said and it hit me—why shouldn't the union have a song like that?" He made a fist. "Something that shows our spirit. There on Miners Day, when the band played 'Men of Harlech,' I damn near bawled and I wasn't the only one. That kind of thing. I mean, hell, up against Anaconda, we're in a fight just as much as any army." I practically had to shield my eyes in the face of his fiery determination. It took only one look at Jared to know he was purposeful as a harpoon, and another at Rab to remind me that the whiff of anything venturesome was catnip to her. I had to admit, the two of them were made for Butte.

"Professor?" He spoke now as if taking me deep into his confidence. "You see where I'm going with this?"

"Vaguely. You have in mind musical phraseology that will rally—"

He didn't wait for me to finish. "A song of our own that will make the Wobblies sound like sick cats. And that's where you come in."

Well, who would not want to be the author of "La Marseillaise" or "Marching Through Georgia" or even "Yankee Doodle"? However, sometimes I know my limits. "Jared, that's generous of you, but songwriting is actually not among my talents."

"Doesn't matter," he sped right over that. "All I want you to do

is to make the case to a few people for a hell of a good song for
the Hill. Miners can be contrary. We have more factions than a
henhouse." He gazed up at the dark strutworks over the mineshafts
and the spill of neighborhoods between. "The Finns would join up
with the Wobblies lickety-split if the union gives them any least
excuse. The Italians think the union is getting too radical. The Irish
are itching to run things themselves, and the Cornish think they
could do a better job than the Irish or any of the rest of us. So on
down the line." Abruptly he batted my shoulder, which was going
to develop a callus if this kept on. "You're just the right one to set
the bunch of them thinking about a song that will pull everybody
together instead of their own grumbles. Rab swears you're a wonder
when you get going." Her smile ratified that.

"Ah." Flattery is a quick worker. "I suppose I could lend whatever
modicum of musical knowledge I have. If you'd like, the next time
you hold a meeting, I could come by the union hall and—"

"That's the rub," Jared said quickly. "The bunch we want won't
come near the union hall, the way everyone is being watched like sin
these days."

The rogue had already calculated the next, I later realized, but he
offered it as if the notion just then strolled up to him.

"Come to think of it, though, there's one place in all of Butte
where the cops and goons know better than to go. Down the shaft."

No three words in the language could have been more unwelcome
to me. I am not subterranean by nature. Quite the opposite; I tend to
look up, not down, in life. The sky has held fascination for me since I
was a boy sneaking out to the Lake Michigan shore on clearest nights,
tracing out the constellations shimmering over the water. Above me
in the hypnotic dark, Sagittarius the archer bent his everlasting bow
while Pegasus flew on wings of light; those and all the other patterns

etched in star-silver define heaven to me. I know of no mine pit in the sky. Now I was being asked to reverse my basic inclination and point myself into the blind paths under the ground. Down where a glory hole led to.

"Must we?"

Jared brushed aside my quavery question. "It's our only shot at getting the right people in one place at the same time." Rabrab watched him with adoration as he tackled tactics. "How are you at being somebody else?" he asked me and didn't wait for an answer. "Your pals Griff and Hoop never took themselves off the extra gang list, it makes them feel like they're still miners. We can sneak you onto the night shift on one of their work tickets." He wrinkled his brow. "First we have to get you past that pair of apes at the gate."

I groaned. "Big and bigger? One of them with eyes that belong on a sea creature?"

Jared showed surprise. "How'd you know? The company stuck them there to watch for Wobs."

"It's too long a story to go into." I felt a guilty kind of relief as I explained that Eel Eyes and Typhoon Tolliver would know me on sight; with them on lookout at the gate, it was impossible for me to enter the mine.

During this, Rabrab had been studying me.

"Your mustache, Mr. Morgan. If that were to come off, you'd look like a different you."

My upper lip smarting, I trudged up the Hill in the company of Griff the next night. I felt undressed without the mustache, although I was in the same regalia as the hundreds of other miners around us: substantial trousers, a workman's jumper, and an old hat.

Griff was practically hopping with anticipation. "You're in luck," he had me know as we trooped along. "The Muckaroo is as nice a digging as there is on the Hill."

"Is it," I responded without enthusiasm; doubtless there was a similarly prime spot in the salt mines of Siberia, too. To try to bolster myself for this, after the library closed I had gone down on my knees and examined the mine model in the glass case long and hard, but right now that seemed like no preparation whatsoever for the real thing. The screeching of pulleys and the throb of machinery sounded louder than in the daytime. Ahead of us, lit harshly, the headframe of the Muckaroo mineshaft towered into the darkness. The graveyard shift—how I wished it wasn't called that—converged at the pinch of the mine gate and then spread out as men filed off to their eight hours of labor beneath the surface of the earth. Jared was a steady but discreet number of strides behind us, which was somewhat reassuring, but Griff hustling along next to me, madly eager to redeem himself after the Miners Day drilling contest, was not. I kept hearing Grace's strained words when my conscience made me draw her aside after supper and confess what we were up to: "Think twice about this, Morrie, please? The Hill is the most dangerous place on earth, even for those who know what they're doing."

By now I'd had those second thoughts and many more, with no result but Griff to show for it. Allegiance to a cause is a prickly thing. Put your hand to it just right, and there is the matchless feeling of being part of something greater than yourself. Grab on to it the wrong way, though, and it draws blood. Back and forth this scheme of Jared's wavered in me as our rough-dressed procession tromped out of the dark to the mine entrance.

The enemy was at the gate, the oversize pair of them scrutinizing every passing face, Eel Eyes with that sideways stare, Typhoon with

192 · IVAN DOIG

doggish concentration. Griff braced up beside me as we neared that inspection. "Here we go, Mor—Hoop, that is." He sneaked a look toward the weedy shadows along the high fence, muttering: "If that kid's gonna do it, he better be doing it."

"He will," I said with more confidence than I felt.

Just then a rock clanged off the tin siding of the gatehouse behind the goons. "Scabs!" came the taunt. "Anaconda stinks and so do you!"

As hoped, Tolliver reflexively bolted off after the stone thrower, although he had no chance in the world of catching up with Russian Famine. Eel Eyes angrily stayed sentry, but his gaze kept dodging toward the darkness or in search of the jeering laughs from the rank of passing miners, while Griff and I, prim as monks, flashed our work tickets and slouched past him.

Jared caught up to us in the mine yard.

"Nice work. When we get in the lamp room, stay at the back"—he was addressing me—"and keep your head down. Griff, you know what to do."

The lamp room, jam-packed with men and equipment, was where we were to outfit ourselves with helmets with a small headlamp atop like a bright Cyclops eye. Finding one that more or less fit, I plopped it on, hoping it would help to hide me. No sooner was it down around my brow than the night supervisor stepped into the room, a list of names in his hand.

"Hooper and Griffith on the extra gang," he sang out. "Oldtimers' night, is this?"

"Don't fret yourself, Delaney," Griff bridled. "We can still turn out the work."

"We'll see about that." The mine overseer peered to the right and left of Griffith. "Where's Hoop?"

"Taking a leak against the office."

"He would be." Comparing the rest of the names on his list to the crowded roomful of faces, now the supervisor craned to see to the back, where I was keeping my head down. "Who else we got here, anybody I don't know?"

Jared broke in on that. "Just so you have it in mind, Delaney—we voted not to go on the twenty-hundred level until more shoring gets put in."

"Nobody's asked you to yet," the mine boss said sourly. "Don't push it, Evans."

"You call that pushing, when it's our necks at risk?" Jared harped on the matter to create a distraction. "I'm just saying, that shoring better go in before any of us set foot onto that level or—" During this, Griff and I slipped out.

The open air of the mine yard chilled me. With the helmet weighing on me, I felt even more like a blockhead for agreeing to this scheme. Happy as if he had good sense, Griff gimped along ahead of me, carrying on about the old days on the Hill and this rare chance to have a look at the workings of the Muckaroo. "So, all we need to do," he chatted over his shoulder as if we were out for a stroll, "is get ourselves down to the thirty-hundred level."

That snatch of enthusiasm sounded reassuring. Wait, though; multiply those offhand numbers and the result is—

"Three thousand feet?" I jammed to a halt as if an abyss of that depth had cracked open beneath the toes of my shoes. "I just can't. You'll have to tell Jared."

Without saying a word, Griff circled back and clamped a sinewy old hand on my shoulder, steering me toward the mineshaft.

The Muckaroo's headframe stood over us, black metal casting blacker shadows in the glare of the night lights, as we approached.

Griff headed us straight in under the girders toward a narrow plate-metal box hung from a steel cable. "Here we go, Morrie, I mean Hoop. Hop in the cage."

Rust-spotted and dented, the thing looked like some torture chamber left over from the Spanish Inquisition. Rationally I knew it was simply an elevator, a way to travel to work the same way an accountant in a celluloid collar would step into wood-paneled circumstances downtown and pleasantly tell the operator, "Fourth floor, please." Except that this express traveled more than half a mile between stops, straight down. With Griff's firm aid I edged in and stood rigid against the back plating, as far away from the flimsy accordion gate across the doorway as possible. He shouldered in next to me as other miners packed in with us.

The hoistman peeked in, counting heads, then snicked the gate closed. He called out, "Everybody ready for China?"

"Let 'er drop," the miner nearest the front called back.

No sooner were the words out than the cage plunged like a shot, for about a dozen feet. Then stopped with the kind of yank that comes at the end of a scaffold rope.

Everything dangled there, shuddering wildly; I include myself in that. The walls of the mineshaft had closed in around us and overhead there was a terrific clatter and continuing commotion. I believe I would have whimpered if the power of voice hadn't been scared out of me.

"It's okey-doke," Griff tried to soothe me with a whisper. "They're loading a couple more cages over us, is all."

Oh, was that all. Merely piling people on top of our heads, to make sure of calamity if anything went wrong in the descent. Hearing Griff's rushed words or perhaps my breathing, the other passengers glanced over their shoulders curiously at us.

"My partner here is a greenhorn, I'm breaking him in," Griff confided to them. "He's got a little case of heebie-jeebies." That brought knowing laughs and a round of wisecracks about how lucky I'd be if I didn't get anything worse than that from digging copper.

In a minute came another sickening jolt downward and one more shuddering wait. Then *swish*! The next thing I knew, the cage was dropping at top speed, so fast that I feared we had been cut loose and were free-falling to our doom. I shut my eyes, not wanting to see death coming. Then, though, I heard the steady whine of the cable, and I cautiously peeped past the darkened outline of Griff and the others. Down and down and down, the shaft walls flew past in a terrifying black blur. My ears popped. I was trying to work my jaw when everything stopped with a hard bounce. The cage yo-yoed for long seconds as the springiness of three thousand feet of cable settled down.

Someone outside flung open the cage gate and I was blinking into a harshly lighted concrete chamber. Hot air rushed into the elevator shaft as the other men clambered out ahead of Griff and myself. A staccato chorus, like invisible riveters, emanated from various tunnels where compressed-air drills were noisily cutting into walls of ore. "Here we are," Griff announced as if it were a tourist destination, "as deep as it goes in the Muckaroo."

As I gawked around, the next cage settled to a stop and Jared climbed out. Giving us a thumbs-up, he disappeared off into a timbered tunnel across the way. By now the underground traffic was thick, files of miners passing us by, their talk trailing away as they vanished into various tunnel portals. Griff had been orienting himself. "C'mon, we want to scoot off over here."

He had picked out what looked to me like an abandoned tunnel, except that steel rails were aligned in the center of it. Our headlamps cast bobbing beams as we hiked deeper into the darkness. Every so often, the light caught a gleam where water dripped down a rock wall. The stammer of drilling followed us at first, gradually dropping to a distant murmur that was simply in the air, like the metallic smell that smarted in my nose. I kept waiting for where this burrow led to, some larger cavern, timbered and more secure, where actual mining was done. Then something occurred to me, from my session of studying the mine model in the library.

"Griff?" I sounded like I was in the bottom of a well. "I believe this is what is called a drift tunnel—"

"Righto. You know more about this than a person might think."

"—and if I am not mistaken, the only purpose of a drift tunnel is the excavation of ore. It isn't a passageway to any of the rest of the mine."

"Right again. You are a whiz."

"Then where's the crew that's supposed to be in here doing that digging? I don't see or hear anyone."

"That's because we're it."

I stopped almost in mid-step.

Griff plowed along for a few more paces before noticing I was missing. Turning around, he examined me critically. "I don't want to worry you, Morrie, but you look kind of milky."

"Where did this notion come from that you and I are going to dig copper in this crypt?" I burst out. "My understanding was, I came down here to meet with the men from the other mines."

"Well, yeah, sure," Griff said, patience and reason combined. "When meal break rolls around, Jared is gonna see to that. I bet he's got it worked out slick, don't worry. But we need to make some kind of showing until then. We get caught loafing around"—the beam of his helmet lamp shined past me as if in search of assailants following us through the tunnel—"and Anaconda will make it rough for us. I don't know how you feel about it, but getting turned over to their goons doesn't appeal to me."

"Lead on," I said with resignation.

Like tramps on a railroad track, we trudged along the narrow set of rails deeper and deeper into the reaches of the mine. It was hellishly hot; I would not have been surprised to see lava oozing out at us. Every so often, small rocks dribbled down disconcertingly beside us. At last a covey of ore cars, squarish troughs on wheels, showed up in our lamp beams. Here we were, Griff declared with a flourish, at the ledge of ore. Above us the tunnel wall opened into an arched excavation, and he skimmed up the ladder to it, with me gulping and following.

What awaited at the top was a large cave; blasting had hollowed out the far wall of the ledge and left a litter of ore. I clambered in behind Griff, barking my shin in the dark as I did so. "Whoopsie-daisy," he advised absently, "watch your footing." As I stepped over to a rock where I could sit and rub the sore spot, he cautioned: "Let's just sort of hang back and look things over before—"

At that instant I felt a familiar tremble. Not my own, but the kind of glory-hole tremor that shook the boardinghouse every so often; somewhere in the catacombs of copper, dynamite had been routinely set off. I had just started to say to Griff, more than a little nervously, that I supposed I'd better get used to that down here, when half the cavern ceiling caved in, with an avalanche roar and a blinding boil of dust.

Choking on dust and my ears ringing, I staggered a few steps this way and that in the murky cavern. My headlamp barely penetrated the filth, thick as smoke. Desperately I tried to fan away the cloud and find Griff, or what was left of him.

In the gloom, something darker yet appeared, also disturbing the dust. It stopped and I stopped. Through a swirl of murk, Griff and I became visible to each other by the whites of our eyes.

Wiping off a mask of dirt, he said, "That's why it's not a good idea to rush into this kind of place." He squinted around as the dust settled. "Lucky thing is, it was the ceiling toward the back that came down." Turning to say something more to me, he stopped, and very slowly raised a pointing finger. "Morrie," he said quietly, "don't be passing the time of day under a Creeping Pete like that." I looked up, to where he was indicating. Overhanging me was a wicked-looking slab of rock, which, if it dropped on a person, definitely would necessitate the services of the undertaker.

Hurriedly I backed away from beneath it as Griff explained that blasting throughout the mine loosened overhead rock in unpredictable places. Studying this cracked mass, he concluded: "Nasty. We're gonna have to bar it down."

He went over to the tool stash in the corner and fished out what looked like a very long, skinny crowbar. Armed with that, he began to pry at the slab. After many thrusts and grunts, he succeeded in breaking it loose. When it hit the floor of the mine with a deafening crash, he grinned at me. "There's one that won't come down on our heads."

Griff moved on to the next overhang, eyes peeled to find the right crack to insert his bar. I stood back as far as I could, spitting out dust, and watched him jab away at the rock until I noticed he was favoring a hand. Remembering the cramp that had done him in during the drilling contest, I took a deep breath and shuffled over to relieve him of the rod. "Here, let me give it a try."

Poking and prodding as if I were using a lance to find chinks in
a dragon's hide, eventually I was rewarded with the fall of a chunk
about the size of a gravestone. "See there, we'll make a miner out of
you yet," Griff commended from the far corner where he was sitting
in apparent contentment.

"Not if I can help it." I fanned away more dust and scanned
the ominously uneven surface overhead. Trading back and forth,
we pried more chunks down until Griff at last called a halt. "Let's
have a listen." He took the bar from me and struck the rock ceiling
with it. The timbre was surprisingly musical, a high lingering note
that resounded rather sweetly. "There, hear that nice clean sound?
It ought to be safe now." He tossed the bar aside with satisfaction.
"Now we better get to work."

"Digging, you mean?"

"Nope. Mucking."

I waited, but that seemed to be the entire explanation.

"Griff, really, not only aren't we anywhere in the same pew on
any of this, we're not even in the same church. The best thing I can
see for us to do is to go back and get on that elevator and—"

"Don't worry none, you'll get the hang of mucking in no time."

That turned out to be true if a person had brains enough to operate a shovel. The loose ore strewn on the floor of the ledge had to
be scooped—"mucked out," in Griff's terminology—into those ore
cars waiting in the tunnel.

"We might as well get at it. The sooner done, the sooner finished,"
he philosophized unarguably.

We commenced shoveling. Copper ore proved to be the peacock of rocks, mottled blue and green showing off the mineral
wealth within. I was up to my shoetops in the wealth of the Richest Hill on the planet, but in raw lump form. As the task heated

up, with Griff tossing two shovelfuls to my every one, he remarked sympathetically:

"It's kind of tough on the muscles at first. Some people can't stay with it."

"I can sweat with the best of them."

"Sweating isn't necessarily the same as hard work, in my experience."

That pricked my pride. "I'll have you know, I am not a total stranger to manual labor."

He eyed me. "Lately?"

There he had a point. As time wore on, I wore down. I thought our amount of copper-bearing rock flung into the ore cars was heroic, but Griff was not inspired by it. He shook his head reminiscently. "Hoop and me could fill an ore car while other guys was standing there thinking about it."

"I'm not the second coming of Hoop," I panted.

Just then a baby-faced flunky stuck his head above the edge of the ledge. "Jared says to tell you," he piped in a high voice, "the shifter is coming through."

The youngster vanished while that was still sinking in on me. "Quick!" Griff rubbed dust on my face, even though I already felt grimy as a coal stoker. "Keep those lily hands of yours out of sight."

We heard the crunch of heavy footsteps, and then the shift fore-man came climbing the ladder to us. Our helmet lights dimly lit the chamber as he stepped in. Long-faced and gray-mustached, he had the same miner's stoop as Griffith; they leaned toward each other like apostrophes. "Griff, you old poot. I heard you were on the extra gang—can't stay away, eh?"

"You know how it is, Smitty. It gets in your blood."

I was standing back as far as I could in the shadows. It didn't help. The shift boss cocked an unblinking look in my direction. "Who's this?"

"Hoop's kid," Griff said blandly. "He's trying his hand as a fill-in. Been down on his luck, haven't you, Junior." He confided as if I weren't there: "A little too much of the booze."

The shift boss shook his head. "The company let us know it doesn't want stew bums down here anymore. These aren't the old days, Griff."

Trying to backtrack from his mistake, Griff scuffed at the mine floor. "Aw, Smitty. What am I gonna tell Hoop, that our old buddy from when we was all working in the Neversweat tied a can to his kid? Hardly seems fair, after Hoop told me: 'Make sure to get Junior in at the thirty-hundred level, I don't want him on anybody's shift but Smitty's. Smitty'll understand, he's had a few under his belt himself, like the time you and me and him were celebrating payday in the Bucket of Blood and—'"

"Don't pour it on," the shift boss managed to stem the tide. He sucked at his mustache as if straining the dubious impression of me through it. "So, Junior, how do you like mining so far?"

"It's a sobering experience."

He grunted, still studying me skeptically. Walking over to the brink of the ledge, he peered down at our loaded ore cars. I held my breath and could see Griff doing the same. With a last doubtful look at us, the shift chief backed around and started descending the ladder. "Keep the rock flying, you two."

We more or less did, although even Griff eased off somewhat now that we had survived inspection. Still, I was sweating so much I felt like a sponge, and every muscle on me was protesting. I was nearly done in by the time a bell signaled somewhere in the distant tunnels.

"Chow time! Here we go." Griff bounded down the ladder and scuttled off, and I followed as best I could.

The route he led me on was as twisty and unpredictable as the wildest of the streets of Butte somewhere over us. Here, however, the thoroughfares were a mere few yards wide, and all the way there was the encroaching roof of solid rock or splintery timbering barely overhead. People speak of the ends of the earth, places beyond all normal geography: the South Pole, the Amazon, the Sahara. The deep mine was that extreme to me; even though I knew the Hill was as pierced as the catacombs of Rome, the unending tunnels we were trekking through made me feel trapped in a maze. That feeling redoubled when we came to a place where borehole pathways diverged left and right and Griff abruptly halted. "Let me just kind of sort this out a little."

I waited, twitching, while he studied the two choices, fidgeting considerably himself. At last he swayed into motion in one direction, declaring, "The left one's the right one." Was I imagining, or did I hear him mutter to himself, "I think"?

This passage showed no signs of recent mining; the dead air of abandonment was unpleasant to breathe. Except when our boots met rocks on the uneven footing, the silence was absolute. And the going became increasingly narrow; I did not have to put out either arm very far to touch a side of the tunnel. This was what the circle of Hell for claustrophobics must be like. Long minutes passed, and as far as I could tell, we were not getting anywhere except deeper into a labyrinth.

"Griff, are you sure this is the way?"

"Pretty sure. Watch your head on that overhang."

You wonder sometimes where your common sense disappeared to, just when you most needed it. Over and over I asked myself that as I followed Griff toward nowhere. I could not stop remembering the Miners Day drilling contest when his hand had so miserably failed him. My only hope was that the part of his brain which held the instinct of a badger wasn't similarly cramping up.

The tunnel, though, seemed to have no end, and I was frantically wondering whether we had left the Hill behind and were doomed to roam some crevice of the earth where no other human existed. Finally I could contain my doubts no longer.

"I really and truly think we ought to turn back and—"

"Shh. Don't talk so much, Morrie. Let's just have a listen."

We did. Water dripped somewhere. Our own breathing was loud. But faintly, some immeasurable distance ahead, there were voices.

In the beam of my helmet lamp, my guide gave me a silent frog-mouth grin. For the life of me, I couldn't tell whether he was as relieved as I was or just being the essential Griff.

WE EMERGED into a musty chamber which had been mucked out and abandoned. A few glowing helmet lamps hanging from spikes driven into the rock walls illuminated this cavern, showing a scene of open lunch buckets and grimy faces as darkened as my own, as though the bunch of us were in vaudeville. Naturally Griff seemed acquainted with everyone in sight. There were a dozen or so of these miners of various persuasions and nationalities, Jared in their middle. The only other one I recognized was Quinlan, who grinned a wolfish welcome. I couldn't care about manners, I was famished. Collapsing onto a convenient rock, I grappled open my lunch bucket and tore into a turkey sandwich Grace had fixed. Jared cleared his throat and announced: "Here's the gent I was telling you about."

After a silence broken only by my munching, someone in the jury-like assembly posed the question prevailing in them all: "He's the brains?"

Quinlan chortled. "They're running out his ears. He has to stick corks in at bedtime, don't you, Morgan."

Swallowing a major bite of sandwich, I managed to respond: "Mental miracles are in short supply with me at the moment. Music lore, I perhaps can provide as Jared has requested."

A man built like a small haystack stirred from where he was squatting against the inmost side of the cavern. "Why should we fiddle around with music," he demanded of Jared in the declarative accent of Cornwall, "when there's every kind of thing to fight Anaconda about?"

"Tell it to the Wobblies, Jack. I can't get to sleep at night without hearing about pie in the sky. Can you?"

"Thee be right, it's somewhat like a bug in the ear," the Cornishman acknowledged, "but a ditty is just a ditty."

"Ah, but it is much more than that," I was roused in defense of melody and lyric. "A song says something to us that we can't hear in any other way. There is a kind of magic to it. Music does not simply soothe the savage breast, it reaches to our better nature, wouldn't we all agree?"

Not a word nor nod from this uncooperative audience.

"A tune keeps us company," I refined that, "when we need a bit of cheer. We don't whistle just to let air out of ourselves, do we?"

Whistlers in their spare time or not, the entire bunch sat there with lips firmly clamped.

"Or," I tried a different tack, "sing in the church choir merely to show off the starch in our shirts?"

Even Griff was looking stony now, in the frieze of unmoved faces.

Frustration giving way to desperation, I burst out: "How else was the Erie Canal dug but to the chant of workmen who had come from the world over *'to see what they could see / on the Ee-rye-ee'*? Nor would railroads such as the Union Pacific have conquered the continent without the chorus of Irish tracklayers"—a hopeful glance toward Quinlan here—"swinging their sledgehammers to the rhythm of *'No leshure in your day, / no sugar in your tay, / working for the U Pay Railway.'*" By then I was onto my feet. "And I would bet any amount some of you lately marched in the service of your country to the memorable strains of *'You might forget the gas and shell, parlee voo! / You might forget the gas and shell, / but you'll never forget the Mademoiselle, / hinky dinky parlee voo!'*" Head up, chest out, I tramped in place to make the point. Jared's expression said he remembered that anthem of soldiery all too well.

In the dim and shadowed light, expression among my other listeners was mostly limited to brows and eyeballs, and I could see some widened gazes by the time I registered a final ringing *parlee voo*!

After that died away, one of the most grizzled miners spoke up. "All them songs you been reaming our ears out with are for bunchwork, while we're scattered just a few at a time in every mine on the Hill. So what kind of thing are you talking about that would ever fit us?"

"Mmm." Inspiration is hard to produce on demand. "A work song does have to fit the job and its circumstances, you could not be more right," I stalled. "In our instance here, now don't hold me to this as a finished product, but perhaps something along the lines of—" Insidious as ever, the catchy rhythm of "Camptown Races" crept to mind, and in what I like to think of as a passable tenor voice, I improvised:

> I'm a miner through and through; you too, you too!
> We dig all day and nighttime too, in the Muckaroo!

Utter stillness met the finish of my performance. Eyebrows came down like dropping curtains, and I saw a wince on Griff. "That was merely one of many possible examples," I offered up feebly. Shaking their heads, the miners began gathering themselves, lunchboxes were snapping shut—Jared looked as defeated as I felt. Any hope for a song for the union cause was walking out with these men.

"Wait!" The requisite bar for breaking treacherous slabs loose lay in a corner. Grabbing it up, I stepped front and center in the cavern and struck the ceiling as hard as I could.

The same high sweet tone that Griff had produced in our workspot filled the cavern. Its clarion call halted everyone in mid-motion.

"There, hear that?" I hurried to capitalize on the frozen moment: "That sound—let us call it a musical note, because it has such a ring—is one you would know anywhere, any time of day or night, am I correct?" I noticed both Quinlan and the Cornishman now looking sharply interested, and other faces attentive as well. "The point is, the right kind of song stays in the mind that same way. It's a melodic message that never wears out, in there. And that's what I was endeavoring to tell you about the magic of a work song."

"A work song for us against Anaconda," Quinlan said slowly, the rest of the miners letting him speak for them. "I like that." Off to one side, Griff rocked on his heels as if he knew all along it would come out this way.

Jared jumped in. "We've got Morgan here for brains, we've got over ten thousand voices on this Hill if we just had the right song for them. It's worth a shot, everybody agree?" One by one around the disparate circle of men, heads nodded and *yes*, *yup*, and *aye* were heard.

"With one understanding," I made sure to have this generally known. "Your response to my first little ditty was indicative. The work song will have to come from you and the men themselves."

"How's that supposed to happen?" a bearded miner demanded. "If any big bunch of us try to get together for it, the cops will be right on us for unlawful assembly."

Jared's gaze of appeal was more than I could turn down. I said: "Leave that to me."

10

You meet yourself in the mirror one morning and wonder if you know the revealed face in the glass. My reflection, after the night spent three thousand feet beneath the surface of the earth, seemed to mockingly remind me that the head on my shoulders is mostly bone, not brain. What had dropped away from me, due to Jared's tricky scheme hatched down there in the Muckaroo, was the visage of self-confidence, the appearance of a sure-thinking person that had carried me largely unscathed through the world. Now as I blinked dumbly at myself in the light of day, I seemed to be missing the countenance I had always counted on. Although perhaps it was only the absence of my mustache.

By the time I pulled myself together sufficiently, I was late to breakfast. Griffith and Hooper were done with theirs, but lingered at the table to greet me. Hoop hopped up from his chair and shook my hand as if operating a pump handle. "So you're pitching in with the union, Griff says. We knew you came to Butte for some good reason."

"That remains to be seen," I said woodenly.

"Don't worry," said Griff, he and Hoop grinning their ears off. "We'll help out on the work song business. You just tell us when and where."

Off they went to their day's puttering, and Grace emerged from the kitchen with my warmed-over breakfast. Her arched eyebrows expressed all that was needed.

"I know, I know," I responded to what had not been said. "You told me the Hill is a dangerous place."

Shaking her head, she slipped into a chair and passed me the jam for my cold toast. "What an honor for the Faraday Boarding House to have the singing master for the union on the premises," she said apprehensively.

"I am not the—" I gave up and poked at my plate. "Butte has a way of making a person line up on one side or the other, you may have noticed."

"You like to place a bet now and then," she observed, as though I might not have noticed this about myself. "You've just placed a big one."

"It is only a bit of music," I tried to convince us both. "Who is going to be overly bothered by that?"

"Other than the police, the Anaconda goons, and the Wobblies, do you mean?" She crimped a worried frown at me, scratching under an arm. I hoped she was not going to have to reach for the calamine. No, the affliction of the moment was entirely mine, her attitude made clear. "You really have taken on trouble, Morrie, with this. Just where do you think you're going to hold these sing-alongs and no one will notice?"

"Somewhere near the surface of the earth, definitely." I stroked my upper lip nervously. My eyes met hers. That violet gaze cast its spell on me even when she was being severe. "Your honest opinion, please. Should I grow the mustache back or not?"

Grace being Grace, she provided a deeper reckoning than I had asked for. She smiled the old bright way, or at least close to it. "Try life without it, why don't you. Men are lucky, you can change your face overnight. That's not bad for a start."

HERS WAS A MORE LENIENT view of me than Sandison's opinion, which was that I looked like a skinned rabbit.

With that, he dismissed my presence in the office and went back to opening the small bundle on his desk that had come in the day's mail. With practiced flicks of his jackknife, probably learned from skinning cows, he slit open the brown paper. There the treasure lay, the latest from a rare book dealer, swaddled in cotton wrap. Sandison lifted it out tenderly. I could see it was an exquisitely tanned edition of *David Copperfield*. "This does it!" Sandison congratulated himself. "The complete Dickens in leather and gold." Deftly he opened the novel to the sumptuous first page. "'*Whether I shall turn out to be the hero of my own life, or whether that station will be held by anybody else, these pages must show.*' Heh heh. The old scribbler knew his business, wouldn't you say, Morgan?"

He always was in his best mood at such moments, so this was my chance. Hovering at the bulwark of his back, I spoke with forced casualness. "Just so you are apprised, Sandy, there's a new group that will be meeting in the basement."

"What is it now," he drawled without turning around, "some weak-kneed bunch that wants to hold seances?"

212 · IVAN DOIG

"These are not spiritualists, although now that you mention it, spirit is of interest to them."

"Don't let me die of suspense—what's the name of this pack?"

"I believe it is the, um, Lyre Club."

"Liars?" His shoulders shook as he laughed long and loud. "You slay me, Morgan. The majority of Butte is already a liars' club."

"No, no, you misconstrue. The meaning in this instance is the stringed instrument that accompanied the words of bards. When Homer smote his lyre, he heard men sing by land and sea, remember?" I drew a breath. "To launch this group, I have been asked to be the guest speaker for a series of sessions."

"You're the main attraction? They must be hard up. What are you going to yatter to them about?"

"Versification," I said, honest enough as far as it went.

"Aren't there enough bad poets in the world already?"

"You never know where the next bard will derive from, Sandy."

"If you want to spend your nights making up nursery rhymes, I guess I can't bring you to your senses." He looked around at me as though I had lately lost more than my mustache. "If you ask me, you're going about things all wrong. Why don't you spend your nights sparking Miss Rellis like a red-blooded human being, instead of preaching verse to some bunch of sissies?"

"Actually, she will be on hand at these meetings."

"Oho. Maybe there's hope for you yet, Morgan. Make the most of your Homeric opportunity." Chortling into his beard, he turned back to fondling his latest bound-and-engraved prize.

Rab was lingering near the office doorway when I came out. "Is he going to let you?"

"We have his blessing," I said moodily.

"I knew you'd make things click. Jared will get word to the others and we're in business, presto!"

"I can hardly wait," I said, my mood not at all improved.

"AHA! THERE YOU ARE."

Dora Sandison made it sound as if I had been hiding from her, when in point of fact she was the one lurking like a lioness at a watering hole as I emerged from the lavatory later that morning.

"Everyone is somewhere, nature's way of housekeeping," I responded, skipping back a bit from her overpowering height. "I expect you're in search of your husband, and I believe I just saw him disappear into the mezzanine stacks. May I escort you to—"

"Not at all," she crushed that with a smile. "My evening group has a wee problem that is beneath Sandy's notice."

"I see. How wee would that be, Mrs. Sandison?"

"Simply a book we are in desperate need of," she said airily. Her enunciation of the title lacked only a drum roll: *The Gilbert and Sullivan Musical Treasury, Complete and Illustrated.*

"You're in luck!" I exulted, really meaning that I was. "If I am not mistaken, such a volume already exists at the reference desk."

"That is precisely the point," she said, that sly note coming into her voice. "The book can't leave the Reading Room. But our meetings are held not there but in the auditorium." She fixed me with the look I had come to dread. "A downstairs copy of our own is absolutely essential when major questions arise, such as what costumes the three little girls from school wore in the original Shaftesbury production of *The Mikado.*" Confident that even I could see the justice of that argument, she added, generously: "Storing it would be no problem whatsoever for you. It could fit with the music stands, could it not?"

My mind was whirring with the cost of a fat reference book of that sort, the kind of duplicate expenditure that would send Sandison through the roof. Fortunately, though, there were a lot of Gilberts in the world, and if I slipped merely the author's last name and a reference like *costumery in foreign lands* into the general book budget, chances were our mutual bugaboo wouldn't pay any attention to it.

"Mrs. Sandison, I think I can accommodate you."

"Good. You haven't disappointed me yet." She pursed the smile of one weaned on a pickle, and turned to go.

"Now I have a favor to ask of you," I halted her.

A pause. "And what would that be?"

"A dual favor, actually. I need to squeeze a new group into the meetings calendar. So, I would like your group to change its meeting night for the next several weeks, and to amalgamate with another group during that period."

Dora Sandison looked at me as if I had lost my mind.

"Preposterous," she snorted when she had regained enough breath for it. "We could not possibly—"

"The other group," I sped on, "is the Ladies' and Gentlemen's Literary and Social Circle. Your husband rather scoffs at them as junior aesthetes, but just between us, Mrs. Sandison, they would make ideal new adherents to Gilbert and Sullivan. Think of it: maidens and swains, already listening hard for the music that makes a heart go pit-a-pat. You'd be doing them a favor, really."

The sniff of conspiracy had its effect on her. I swear, her nostrils widened a tiny bit with anticipation as she eyed me. "This might work to everyone's benefit, am I to understand? Yours included?"

"Your understanding is pitch-perfect."

She gave me the queen of smiles, as lofty as it was crafty. "You still have not disappointed me." With that, she swept out of the library.

When I got back to the inventorying, Rabrab looked at me curiously and asked where I had been.

"Reinventing the calendar," I said, mopping my brow.

"GOOD EVENING, FELLOW LYRISTS."

Among the upturned faces as I took center stage in the auditorium only a faithful few showed any appreciation of my greeting. Rab sent back a warm conniving smile, and Jared grinned gamely. In the front row Hoop and Griff looked eager for whatever mischief the night might bring; Quinlan's expression was similarly keen, but with a sardonic edge. Most of the others, union stalwarts coaxed by Jared and his council to represent their neighborhoods, showed curiosity at best, and at worst a variety of misgivings. These hardened miners had sifted into the library basement one by one or in pairs; several had brought their wives, weathered women in dark-dyed dresses usually worn to weddings, wakes, and funerals. Life on the Hill was written in the creased faces staring up at me in my blue serge, and I needed to tap into whatever inspiration I could find, without delay.

"Why the lyre, you may be wondering, as a fitting symbol for our musical quest?" I whirled to the blackboard I had rigged up on Miss Runyon's story-hour tripod and sketched the flowing curves of the instrument, then chalked in the strings. "Poets and singers of ancient Greece took up the lyre to accompany their recitations, wisely enough. It is a civilized instrument that honors a song's words without drowning the intonations out."

"You draw a pretty picture," Quinlan called out, "but come right down to it, Morgan my man, the thing is only a midget harp. How's that going to compete with anything in the Little Red Songbook"—in back of him Jared pained up at those words—"where all you have to do is oil your tonsils a little and bawl out the verse?"

"Just the question I was hoping for, Quin. What the lyre gives us is the word we must strive toward."

There was a waiting silence, which I could tell would not last beyond one more fidget from the audience.

"Lyrical," I pronounced, and drove the matter home. "The lyrics of the work song for the union cause must sing to the heart as well as the mind."

A miner with a bristling mustache objected. "What'd be wrong with a song that just out and out gives Anaconda hell?"

"I believe that already exists." I warbled the first few lines of "The Old Copper Collar" in illustration. "As apt as that may be, it seems to have had no measurable effect on the top floor of the Hennessy Building, do we agree?" Griff looked hurt.

The audience absorbed my performance uncertainly until the Cornish miner from the Muckaroo called out. "Thee speak a good spoke. But what's the first bite of the bun to get this done?"

"Aha! You have just put your tongue to it." I spun to the blackboard and wrote *bun* and *done*. "Rhyme is the mother of song."

THAT WAS THE OVERTURE, musically speaking, in the quest for a battle hymn for the miners of the Hill.

With the union contingent now regularly showing up, a martial set to their jaws and unpredictable stirrings in their throats, I had to enlist Hoop and Griff to direct traffic in and out of the library; it would not do for top-hatted downtowners to come face-to-face with restive Dublin Gulch and Finntown, for example. (I could just imagine Quinlan at close quarters with a library trustee.) No, at all costs I needed to keep the so-called Lyre Club from being brought to Sandison's attention by any complainers. Only too well I remembered how he fumed against "taking sides" when the idled miners sought shelter in the library during the work actions. If he ever divined that the crowd of us in the basement were, shall we say, less than legally assembled to generate a rallying song for the union, all he had to do to be rid of us was to summon the authorities. What other choice would he have?

Jail was only one worry. Authoritative in their own way and answering to their own shadowy purposes, there were always the goons.

BUT WHERE WERE THEY?

Jared reported that the pair of them had vanished from the mine gate, replaced by uniformed guards not so apt to be taunted as scabs and bombarded with rocks in the night. Accordingly, I watched the shadows more sharply on my way home from the library in the dark, but the inky shapes at alley mouths and lightless doorways never once materialized into Eel Eyes and Typhoon Tolliver. Which did not put to rest my sense of apprehension. In broad daylight, I was carrying a beautiful matched set of Shakespeare plays to the antiquarian shop for appraisal when I rounded a corner and nearly bumped into a hulking figure with an upraised club. I jumped back, shielding myself and the works of the Bard against a blow from Typhoon, but it was merely a hod carrier transporting bricks into the building. So, maybe the goons were nowhere to be seen, but to my mind that didn't mean they were not, as the one called Roland had said of me, up to something.

My imagination kept asking: Up to what?

———

"Do me a favor, please, Rab," I felt compelled to ask, when I was sure we would not be overheard in the book stacks as we tackled Tennyson, Thoreau, and Tolstoy. "Just as a hypothetical exercise, mind you, find out from Jared how much granite it takes to withstand dynamite."

"Mr. Morgan, since when are you such a scaredy-cat?" she scolded. She clucked as if I were one of her more dismaying schoolboys. "Besides, I already checked. The walls of the basement auditorium are three feet thick."

"Rhythm." I turned to the next session of miners and wives sitting immobile as birds on a wire while I paced the stage. "The ebb and rise of sounds, the heartbeat that gives life to the alphabet."

I paused, which never hurts in building up drama.

"In other words, the vital pattern within each line of a verse. Art imitates nature in this, for we live amid natural rhythms, don't we? For instance, the *pit-pat, pit-pat* of rain," I clapped gently in time with that.

Climatology evidently did not stir this audience. Not even Hoop and Griff in the front row responded with more than stifled yawns.

"Or," I resorted to, "let us take the example of oceanic sound, the anticipatory *swish* of the tide coming in"—I illustrated with my elbows out and my hands sweeping grandly to my chest—"and the conclusive *hiss* of it going out," my arms spreading wide to imaginary watery horizons.

High tide did not seem to register in Butte. Clearing my throat as though the problem of communication might be there in the wind-pipe, I tried once more:

"In strictly musical terms, a song can attain a distinctive rhythm with repetition of certain syllables or sets of sounds. An example, please, anyone?"

I had not encountered that many mute faces since trying to explain the Pythagorean theorem in the Marias Coulee schoolroom.

Walking a circle on the stage as if surrounding the problem, I thought out loud for the benefit of the passive gathering:

"I assume many of you have children at home? A show of hands, please."

A good proportion of the audience admitted to parenthood.

"And all of us here are former children, am I correct?"

An unsettled chuckle went around the room.

"Therefore, let us approach this matter from that younger time. We are fortunate to have with us someone who, I happen to know, excelled in schoolyard serenade. Miss Rellis? Would you come up, please, and demonstrate?"

Rab colored prettily. Beside her, Jared tried to look as though he was not present during this. "You're too kind, Mr. Morgan," she made a show of demurring, "I'm badly out of practice."

"One never forgets one's specialty. Recess was never complete without it, I have reason to believe."

"Ooh, that. Do you really want me to?"

"Desperately."

"You asked for it, then."

Rab sprang from her seat and paraded up onto the stage. As I had counted on, she showed the admirable zeal of a schoolgirl, but of more interest to this mostly male audience, also the chest and legs

of a Ziegfeld chorine. She proceeded to deliver the playground song
in a voice as pretty as she was, her hands instinctively hoisting the
hem of her dress a trifle at just the right words:

> Two little lovebirds sitting in a tree,
> K-I-S-S-I-N-G!
> First comes love!
> Then comes marriage!
> Then comes a baby in a baby carriage!
> That's not all! That's not it!
> Now there's another before they quit!
> That's not it! That's not all!
> Now comes twins, Peter and Paul!

I had no more trouble explaining the vital nature of rhythm.

HECTIC NIGHTS OR NOT, the library went about its daytime business
at its own whirligig pace. Rab and I were kept hopping to finish the
inventory before she went back to teaching in a few weeks, and on
top of that was my never-ending round of chores devised by Sandison. Reaching the end of a typically crammed week, I was somewhat
behind in tabulating the most popular books of the past seven days
and typing up the list for the *Daily Post*, and still was slaving away at
the checkout slips when I heard footsteps approaching the office at a
near trot. Why, just once in his life, couldn't the courier be less than
prompt? Glancing up to say something of the sort, I discovered the
speed demon coming in the door was not Skinner, but an even skin-
nier messenger.

"He's busy running bets on some fight," Russian Famine explained nonchalantly. "Said it don't take any brains to do this kind of thing."

"Nice to see you, Famine. Make yourself comfortable," I pointed him to a chair, "I'll be a little while yet at this."

Making himself comfortable was the opposite of sitting still, as I should have known. After a bit of trying to put up with his fidgets, I suggested he work off that energy on the back staircase and I'd meet him there. Bouncing up to go, he spun into the doorway and collided with Sandison's belly. The boy gawked up the slope of body, gasped out a strangled "'Scuse me," and darted into the hallway.

Sandison stared after him. "What the hell now, do you have us taking in orphans?"

"You have just met our current messenger to the *Daily Post*, Sandy. Butte's version of winged Mercury."

"If he was any scrawnier, he'd be transparent. Where's he off to?"

"Oh, just out among the books. Fam—Wladislaw is interested in higher learning."

Only barely assuaged, Sandison steamed on into the room, took charge of his chair, and wheeled it around to face me. Lately he seemed even more testy than usual. "Something's not quite right around here, and for once I don't just mean the library. You've got ears like a donkey when it comes to what's going on in this town. Catch me up."

I hesitated. Saying anything about the rising resolve of the miners' union might brush too close to the fact of the sessions in the basement. I chose to concentrate on the Wobblies and recited the gossip about the arrival of phantom operatives to poach membership from the miners' union.

"Outsiders," Sandison pronounced flatly. "They're always trouble." With that, he heaved himself out of the chair and marched over to the

stained-glass window to broodily peer out as if watching for trouble
to come.

RUSSIAN FAMINE WAS FLYING UP the top steps when I went to the
back staircase with the book list for him to deliver to the newspaper
office. For a minute I stood watching, not daring to interrupt the dizzying ballet on the stairs. As before, the scissor-thin legs flashed up
the steps three and almost four at a time, then straddled the banister
and rode gravity *zip-zip-zip* to the bottom. Reluctantly I called to
him after one of these precipitous rides, and, shaking his thatch of
hair as if coming awake, he trotted over to me.

"Has anyone ever told you, my young friend, you give new meaning to the word *restless*?"

"Huh-uh. You're the only one who talks that way."

I thought it best to walk him out of the building, lest he run into
Sandison again. While we made our way through the standing ranks
of books Rab and I had tallied, the turn of season was on my mind,
with her impending departure back to the classroom, and, as adults
always foolishly do, I asked Famine if he was ready for school to
start.

The boy put on a long face. "Flunked is what I shoulda done.
Hung on in Miss Rellis's class. Now I'll get some old biddy for a
teacher." He sent me a sideward look, his eyes as quick as the rest
of him. "I maybe won't be going to school too much longer anyway.
Skinner says I'm in luck, the Hennessy bunch has its eye on me when
they do any more hiring."

That knifed through me. So much for my bright idea of having
posted him to the almighty top floor, just for the summer, to watch

for any message of a certain sort dispatched by the goons; true to its nature, Anaconda was ready to swallow him up.

"What does your uncle think?" I asked, afraid I knew the answer.

"He says it's up to me." Famine scuffed along, head down. "I don't much want to, but a kid has got to eat."

So, things flew at me like that during those days; and the hours after work the fledgling lyricists of the Lyre Club were steadily ready to consume. "You're quite a night owl again," Grace waylaid me as I was about to hustle back to the library one of these times.

My spirits instantly shot upward. How good to have her popping out of the kitchen to trade small talk as she used to. "These evenings, though," I responded in relief, "everyone involved is healthy enough not to require a casket."

"That's not bad—"

"—for a start, yes, yes, you needn't remind me." That drew nothing more from Grace; she just hovered in the hallway. The recent distance between us had shrunk to within reach. I chanced hopefully: "If you're feeling daring, would you like to come with me tonight?"

She shook her head, but still made no move to let me by.

"Hoop and Griff, bless their incurably Welsh souls, have taken practically a proprietary interest in the song sessions," I gabbed to break the silence.

Grace pinched her lip, restricting her response to a careful "Mm-hmm." I waited, willing her to find whatever words she needed to put us back on the good terms of Miners Day.

Finally she wound her hands in her apron and said:

"Rent day was three days ago, Morrie."

Deflated, I paid up and exited into the night.

AT MY SECOND HOME, the library, once more the miners and wives and Rab and Jared and Hoop and Griff and I filed into the basement without the whole passel of us being hauled off for unlawful assembly. It was a critical night: by dint of my tugging and hauling, we had reached melody, in the steps of song construction. However, I was making scant progress by standing on the stage and humming famous melodies as illustration, and in frustration I bemoaned the auditorium's lack of any means of musical accompaniment.

To my surprise, that put life in my audience. For once, there was unanimity in the knowing grins of everyone but me, even Jared and Rab.

It was left to the Cornishman to ask:

"Has thee not heard of the Butte Stradivarius?"

"I confess I have not."

"Thee shall have that remedied."

THE CONCERTINA, rapidly fetched and in Cornish hands, could produce any melody I could think of, and plenty more. The wheezebox, as I came to think of it, made my point that a good tune was essential to a good song.

"That completes the three parts of musical invention," I announced exultantly as the last wheezy strains of "Camptown Races" wafted away into the plaster foliage atop the auditorium walls.

"Rhyme, rhythm," I smacked my fist into my hand with each word, "and melody. Keep those in mind and the Hill and its union

shall sing a work song to rival that of the angels in their airy labors."
(Or, in my mind and Jared's, to challenge that infernally mocking
ballad of pie in the sky.)

This was a proud moment, and the craggy miners who had man-
fully sat through nights of musical instruction now slapped their
knees and batted their neighbors on the shoulders and shouted out,
"Good job, Professor!"

I took a modest bow. "I have done my utmost, and now it is
up to you. Appropriately enough, creating the right song will take
work, don't think it won't," I exhorted further. "Inspiration most
often follows perspiration. Now, then," I advanced to the lip of the
stage and made a beckoning gesture to the group, "what ideas do I
hear for that song?"

Discord ensued.

The Finns wanted something grand and sonorous, in the manner
of a saga.

The Cornish wanted something brisk.

The Irish wanted something rollicking that would tear the hide
off Anaconda.

The Welsh, who legitimately had music in their blood, were outnumbered and outshouted by the others, as usual in history.

The Serbs wanted something that dripped blood.

What the Italians wanted was not clear, but it was nowhere close
to what the other nationalities had in mind.

Standing up there trying to referee the musical wrangle, I wondered
what it took to get committed to a mental institution in Montana.

At last Jared dutifully climbed onto the stage beside me and in his
best top-sergeant manner managed to institute some order.

"This is a start," he took command of the chaos in an unarguable
style Napoleon might have admired. "There are a few differences of

opinion, but talk those over with each other, with your shift partners and anybody who can carry a tune, all right? We'll sort out what's promising and what isn't, next time. After that, we'll get the union delegates from each shift at every mine together, and settle on the best song." Without breaking his cadence of being in charge he asked over his shoulder: "How many people does this place hold, Professor?"

"Hmm? Perhaps two hundred. But you can't—"

"It'll be the damnedest thing they ever heard on the top floor of the Hennessy Building," Jared vowed with a fist, "our song when we get it. Folks will sing it in this town as long as there's a chunk of copper left in the Hill." He clapped his hands, once, sharply. "Now let's go home and get to working on the work song, everybody."

As the group dispersed, I stood by numbly, still jolted by Jared's fervent promise to assemble two hundred miners here in a library space where they were not supposed to assemble at all. Knowing perfectly well that if I asked him, "How?" the reply was going to be, "Professor, I leave that to you."

Quinlan passed by me with a troublesome grin, humming to himself. That tune at least was unmistakable. *Same song, second verse. / Could get better, but it's gonna get worse.*

WHEN I CLOSED UP THE LIBRARY, Rab and Jared were waiting for me down on the steps. "Come with us to the Purity for pie," he invited, direct even when he was being pleasant. "I'll even buy."

I joined them, and the sound of our footsteps was our only company on the lamplit streets. Of course Rab had a dozen enthusiasms about what the sought-after song should be like, and Jared winnowed those in his wry fashion. I contributed what I could, although my head was a swirl. A crowd of a couple hundred, to get past the police, the goons, and, perhaps most consequential, Samuel Sandison, without attracting attention? My mind went back and forth over this, which simply dug the problem in deeper. My mood was not helped when we passed the *Daily Post* building and I saw that even the so-called autumn classic, the World Series, was jinxed this wayward year; the scoreboard being set up for the forthcoming games announced the Chicago White Sox—Skinner would crow to me unmercifully—versus the Cincinnati Red Stockings, as purists knew the team that sports pages habitually shrunk to the Redlegs or Reds. The Anklet Series, I thought of it with disgust. Where were the teams with good sound contentious names, Cubs, Tigers, Pirates? When even baseball starts to go downhill, I grieved, there's no telling what will follow.

My brooding spell was broken by Jared as we neared the cafeteria. He tugged at his short ear as he did when thinking hard, and Rab attentively shut up. Looking around to make sure we couldn't be overheard, he said in a voice low but firm:

"Just so you know, Professor. The Hill might have to go on strike, maybe pretty damn quick."

I hoped his wording was a slip of the tongue. "Another work action, you mean."

"That's the farthest thing from what he means, Mr. Morgan," said Rab.

"She's right as usual," Jared acknowledged, giving her a wink. He was all seriousness as he turned to me again. "We've negotiated until we're blue in the face, and Anaconda still won't meet us halfway on anything that counts. Worse than that, those of us on the council have a hunch the company is getting ready to cut the dollar off the wage again. If that happens," his tone became even more resolved, "we won't have any choice. The union will either have to curl up and die or call a strike." In the streetlight there outside the cafeteria, I saw Jared square his shoulders as he looked up at the lights of the Hill and listened for a moment to the drivewheel sound of the mines at work. In another battle, of another sort, he must have sized up Dead Man's Hill similarly before the attack up the slope. Now he shifted his gaze to the slumbering city around us. "It's always tough on the town, to shut everything down," he said solemnly. "But Butte has been through strikes before. They're part of life here. Everybody understands it's our only way to fight back against Anaconda."

"Jared, I must know," another apprehension creeping up on me, "how quick is pretty damn quick?"

"After the next payday, more than likely. Doesn't leave you any too much time, does it."

I blanched. That soon? To come up with the union song necessary to rally his forces? From an aggregate of miners who didn't agree on anything musically except the sublime charm of the concertina?

Jared nodded as if reading my mind. "I know it'll take some doing. But we'll need all the ammunition we can get when the strike comes." He touched my shoulder. "The song counts for a lot, Professor. I want it in the head of every miner on the Hill, to hold us together."

"Inspiration follows perspiration, you did say, Mr. Morgan," Rab contributed all too helpfully.

At least one thing stayed the same in the Butte night: the owner of the Purity with a glad cry ushered us in to serve ourselves.

THUS, there was everything but library business on my mind during business hours at the library the following day. Which may explain the next thing to happen. My thoughts elsewhere, I was on my way between one chore and another in a rear hallway when a shadow not my own loomed on the wall beside me. In a fit of panic, I whirled and put my back against the wall, digging with both hands for my brass defenders.

"Famine!" I exhaled with relief. "You surprised me a little."

"Didn't mean to spook you." He handed me an envelope. "Told me you wanted to see anything with Shycago on it."

I glanced at the Chicago postmark and the kind of chill that supposedly occurs when some creature of the night treads across one's gravesite came over me.

"Have yourself some ice cream," I rewarded my trustworthy messenger with enough money for a vat of it, "and then come back." He vanished in leaps and bounds, and I trotted downstairs to the auditorium. The Theosophists' electric tea kettle steamed the envelope open quite nicely.

Two pieces of paper shook out, dire as loaded dice.

"There's goods to be got on anybody, sucker." Eel Eyes' parting shot resounded in me like a cannonade as I examined the sheets one by one. You should never underestimate even the most thickheaded adversary. The goons had been a lot more determined to get something on me than I imagined. Who knew how many underworlds they'd had to try, but they hit pay dirt in a certain den of high rollers beside Lake Michigan. What I was holding was a print of the photograph from Miners Day, Grace and myself frozen-faced as missionaries with the splendor of Columbia Gardens around us. My head was circled in red crayon like a target.

The letter that came with was even worse.

"Photo you sent is positive identification: real name Morgan Llewellyn. Capture him and deliver him to us. We have an old score to settle."

There was more, but that told the story. The Chicago gambling mob did not forgive; it never even forgot. Like hounds stirred from sleep by an old hunting scent, the betting sharpies were roused all over again about Casper's last fight and our winnings, and I had to act fast.

Reflex and logic agreed on the same piece of advice: take the next train out of town. Put all possible distance between the contents of the envelope and myself. But that left Grace, literally in the picture next to me, and in for nasty interrogation by Eel Eyes and Typhoon if I wasn't available. Besides, if I fled now I would be leaving other loose ends flapping in this Butte chapter of life, and that would bother me for the rest of my days.

With the troublesome pieces of paper tucked inside my suitcoat, I made my way upstairs to the mezzanine, thinking as hard as it is possible to think. Rab had gone out with an armload of books for appraisal by the antiquarian dealer; that helped. And further luck: Sandison was down there in the Reading Room, trying to deal with Miss Runyon, highly indignant over something, and would have his hands full for a while. My path was clear, and indicatively it led through an aisle of fiction. Passing through the ranks of Twain and Defoe and the others as I slipped into the office, I was in the company of those who best knew that a greater truth can sometimes be told by making things up. And those wise old heads did not even have my magic kit to work with, the typewriter and fountain pen.

I had two envelopes waiting for Famine to deliver when he scampered back. In the one from Chicago, the goons now were informed in nice fresh typing with a copied signature that, alas, this was a case of mistaken identity, no one back there had ever laid eyes on the nobodies in the photo. In the one to go into the mail to Chicago, the gambling mob was notified that, regrettably, its message had arrived too late, the miscreant Morgan Llewellyn had vanished from Butte.

"You look sunny this morning," Grace observed.

As I sat down to breakfast that next day, it was all I could do not to reach over and pat her on the dimpled cheek in celebration of our mutual survival. "A sound night's sleep does wonders," I restricted myself to. She herself looked refreshed by something, taking time off from the kitchen to sit and sip coffee until Hoop and Griff appeared. I still was only a boarder and she still was the landlady, but when Grace wasn't having to doctor herself against her own nerves, she also was a very attractive companion at the table. Right now, with her freshly braided hair a coil of gold, she resembled the sunshiny maiden on the lid of tinned shortbread. The sovereign maiden in charge of all such tinned goods, that is. While I was in the midst of such thoughts, she gave me, in the words of the poet, a brightening glance, and I smiled gamely back. Maybe this was only a mild degree of thaw between us, but it improved the climate. She watched me expectantly as I settled into eating. "Well, have you noticed?"

Whatever it was, it hadn't caught my attention yet; certainly the cold toast was the same as ever.

"The house, Morrie," she prompted, "the house!"

"Ah." I scanned around. "New curtains?"

"All right, you," she said in mock exasperation—at least I hoped it was mock. "There hasn't been any dynamiting for days and days, has there?" She knocked on wood, but her smile was triumphant. "I was curious," she continued in a confiding tone, "so I had Arthur's old partner in the mines look into it for me. And guess what? The shaft under here is played out and Anaconda has had to seal it off. You can quit worrying about sleeping in a glory hole," she teased.

Little did she know that the Chicago watery version had just passed me by. "Grace, that's nice news," I could say unreservedly. "Butte would not be the same without the Faraday Boarding House."

Bouncing up when she heard Hoop and Griff on the stairs, she went off to fry their breakfast.

The two of them came in grinning, grinned at each other, then grinned at me some more as they sat at the table.

"We been thinking," said Hoop as if it was something new.

"You've got yourself a lulu of a problem, slipping a couple hundred people into the library the night the song gets voted on," Griff said as if that fact might have escaped me.

"Wouldn't be the first time the cops broke up a meeting and arrested everybody in sight," Hoop went on, tucking in his napkin.

"Righto," Griff confirmed, spooning sugar into his coffee. "So we figure what you need, Morrie, is an *eisteddfod*."

I did not want to say that something pronounced *eye-steth-vod* stumped me as much as if he had been speaking mumbo-jumbo. But it did.

"Perhaps you could elaborate on that just a bit, Griff."

"Glad to. Like everybody knows, an *eisteddfod* is when the finest singers and the greatest bards in Wales gather from the hills and the valleys and every mine pit from Caernarvon to Caerphilly"—he swept a knobby hand around like an impresario—"and try to outdo one another."

"Kind of a jollification," Hoop put in. "Like Miners Day that just don't stop."

With that, my tablemates sat back and slurped coffee, magnanimously ready for all due praise.

"I see," I coughed out. "Actually, I don't. The Welsh miners are the only ones who would have any idea what an *eye—eisteddfod* is,

and they're just a handful among the song bunch. Everyone else—?"
I spread my hands.

Griff squinted at me. "You're a little slow on the uptake today,
Morrie. Everyone else *outside* of the song bunch, after we clue those in."

"Nobody is gonna go near the thing," Hoop expanded on that,
"who don't know the lingo."

Thinking back to the Welsh minister and the tongue-tying eternity of *tragwyddoldeb*, I couldn't argue with that.

Somewhat against my better judgment, I tested the matter out
loud.

"Such as the public at large and the police, you mean." Both
wrinkled heads bobbed at my response, gratified that I was catching
up. My tablemates now took turns expanding on why an indecipher-
able event that would unobtrusively slip a couple of hundred people
into the basement of the Butte Public Library was such a surefire
idea.

Grace came from the kitchen with a plate in each hand, stopping
short at Griff's grand culmination:

"Hoop and me can handle the whole proceedings for you, don't
worry none."

I had not really started to, until he said that.

It WAS LIKE TRYING to rein in runaway horses, but I managed to make
the pair promise to contain their eisteddfod enthusiasm until I could
test the notion on Jared. Meanwhile, I was late and had to bolt for the
library. People were out and about in unusual numbers, I couldn't help
but notice, all heading down toward the railroad tracks where a sizable crowd had already gathered. I presumed another political figure
was arriving to make a speech off the back of a train; but President

Wilson himself would not be a shield against Sandison's displeasure if I weren't in the head count of staff before he opened the library.

Too late. When I got there, everyone had gone in but Rab, who was practically dancing with impatience as I hastened up the steps.

"Mr. Morgan, you came from that direction," she spoke so fast it was nearly all one word, "did you see it?"

This was not my day, linguistically. "Do you suppose, Rab, you could take a deep breath and define *it* for me?"

She was as disappointed in me as Hooper and Griffith had been. "Oh, here." Whisking over to a stack of newly delivered *Daily Post*s beside the doorway, she handed me one with fresh ink practically oozing from the EXTRA! atop the front page.

Beneath that, the even larger headline:

OUTSIDE AGITATORS WARNED

And below that, a jolting photograph of the railroad overpass where the IWW organizer had been lynched a few years before. From the middle of the trestle girders dangled a hangman's noose. Attached to the rope was a sign readable even in the grainy newsprint reproduction:

THE MONTANA NECKTIE

YOU ONLY WEAR IT ONCE

WOBS AND OTHER TROUBLEMAKERS—

LEAVE TOWN BEFORE THIS FITS YOU

Digesting this, I had mixed reactions. Plainly the goons, stymied about me after Chicago was no help, had broadened their approach to include any other strangers in the vicinity of the Hill; when you are a target, I have to say, you do appreciate having that kind of attention shared around. On the other hand, a noose just down the street from where you lay your head at night is still too close for comfort.

"Jared says the police are taking their sweet time about removing it," Rab confided over my shoulder, again as fast as words could follow one another, "so Anaconda gets to scare everybody."

"We have to let Jared handle that," I stated, "while we have to get inside and handle books or face the wrath of our employer."

Her mischievous laugh surprised me. "We wouldn't want that, heaven knows."

DISPATCHING RAB TO TAKE OUT her ardor on the book collection, I had to tend to a few office matters before joining her. If I was in luck, Sandison would be out on one of his prowls of the building. But, no. There he sat, stormy as thunder. Before I could utter any excuse for being late, he flapped the *Post*'s front page at me. "Did you see this damn thing?"

"By this hour of the day, I believe everyone in the city has seen either the newspaper or the actual piece of rope, Sandy."

"This town," he said in a tone that it hurt to hear. "It just can't resist having dirty laundry out in the open. Hell, anyone knows outsiders are asking for it, that's where rope law comes from." Saying that, he took another furious look at the front page photograph, his gaze so hot I thought the paper might singe.

"The 'Montana necktie,'" he ground out the words, "what's the sense of dragging that up?" He started to say something more, but instead crushed the newspaper in the vise of his hands and thrust it into the wastebasket.

I stood there, gaping at the outburst, until his glare shifted to me. "Don't you have anything to do but stand there with your face hanging out?"

I left in a hurry. The calm ranks of the books on the mezzanine were particularly welcome after that. Was there any way in this world to predict the actions of their combustible collector?

Hearing me come, Rab spun from the shelf where she had been flicking open covers to look for the SSS bookplates. "This is the day, you know."

From my experience, that could be said about every twenty-four hours in Butte. But I did know what she meant.

"The sixth grade is about to meet its match," I said with a smile. Tomorrow was the start of school and the teaching year of Miss Rellis, as she had to turn into. I was going to miss Rab's company and the noble ranks of the inventory. Reaching to the shelf nearest her, I asked: "Ready?" She nodded. Into her waiting arms I stacked the plump volumes of *Thérèse Raquin, Nana, Germinal,* and on top the slim, elegant masterpiece *J'accuse*; Zola, the end of the inventory alphabet.

"The ones we've been looking for," she joked a little sadly as we went to the sorting room to tally these treasures in with the rest.

"Maybe the full inventory will improve Sandison's disposition," I thought out loud. "The commotion about the noose seems to offend his civic sensibilities."

The mischievous laugh again. "Quit being funny, Mr. Morgan."

"Rab, really, you are not being fair to our employer." For whatever reason, I felt tender toward Sandison in his upset mood. "I grant you he has a bit of a temper, but we shouldn't judge him entirely on that.

It is a truth as old as humankind that the presence of a shortcoming in a person does not preclude the existence of other worthier attributes in that same— Why are you looking at me like that?"

Rab had the magpie gleam of possessing the hidden morsel. "Don't you know who Sam Sandison is? He's the Strangler."

11

Rabrab's words went directly to my windpipe.

When I recovered enough air to speak, it was little more than a squeak. "Rab, you might have said so before now. Are you telling me the man I share an office with goes around throttling people?"

"Not that he was ever caught at it himself," she said, as if explaining etiquette to a child. "He had mugs who worked for him do the dirty work. 'Necktie makers,' they were called. Vigilantes." She looked at me closely. "You know: types who hang first and ask questions later."

"I grasp the terminology," I fumbled out. "What I am uninformed about is who my employer has had strangled, and why?"

"Cattle rustlers," she answered both of those. "Or anybody who looked like one, to those cowboys of his." Rabrab calculated with the aplomb of a hanging judge herself. "Plenty of them had it coming, probably. But some might have been small operators whose herds some Triple S cows and calves just got mixed in with. You know the saying about a rope"—she looked at me as if I likely did not—"one size fits all."

"But—" Still stunned, I tried to reconcile the two Samuel Sandi-sons, the one who petted rare books as if they were living things and the other who used lethal means without thinking twice. "How can a, a vigilante be permitted to run a public institution such as this?"

"Oh, I suppose people think those old hangings were a long time ago," Rab reasoned. "After all, Butte is where a lot of people get over their past. Mr. Morgan, are you feeling all right?"

"The start of a headache," I replied, truthfully enough. It was scarcely twenty-four hours since I had wriggled free from the grasp of the goons and the Chicago betting mob, and now I found out my library refuge was in the grip of a hangman. Whose method of tap-ping the library payroll budget to accumulate literary treasures in his own name was known only to me. This was an unhealthy turn of events, to say the least.

"MORGAN!"

I nearly jumped out of my hide, but managed to face around to the white-maned figure looming at the end of the aisle of bookshelves. Sandison looked as if he had grown even more enormous since I saw him minutes before.

"Drag your carcass to the office," he bawled out, turning away, "I want to talk to you."

Rab bade me off by wrinkling her nose prettily. "He really is something, isn't he."

I WENT IN, determined not to tremble. I suppose the blindfolded man facing a firing squad tries that, too. At the other end of the office, Sandison's black suit was the darkest kind of outline against the stained-glass window jeweled with colors. He swung around to face me, saying nothing, sizing me up. Between us, on his desk, lay the smoothed-out newspaper with the emphatic photograph of the noose.

"Sandy?" I gambled, not for the first time, by taking the initiative. "I believe you wanted to see me about some minor matter?"

He grunted and advanced toward me as if he needed a closer look. The gleam in his eye seemed diamond-sharp. "You're an odd duck, Morgan," he declared, halting an uncomfortably short distance from me, "but you're cultured, I have to hand you that. You damn well mean it when you jabber about the music of men's lives, don't you."

A weird hope sprang up in me. Maybe he had discovered I was flouting his orders against "taking sides" by letting the miners congregate in the basement in search of a song and was merely going to fire me. I would take that instead of a death sentence any day.

"Anyhow," he immediately brushed aside that hope, "we can talk about that tomorrow. You're coming with me in the morning."

"Where to?" I asked over the thump of my heart.

The white whiskers aimed at me. "A place you ought to see. Section 37."

WAS THAT A JOKE from Samuel Sandison? If so, it was his first. I cleared my throat, to try to speak without a quaver.

"Perhaps, Sandy, you could elaborate a bit on that destina—"

Somewhere within the whisker cloud he snorted. "What's the matter, sissy, coming down with a case of *Hic sunt dracones*?"

I had to bridle at that. A measure of caution about traveling in the company of someone nicknamed the Strangler did not equate me with skittish mariners of old who feared sailing off the edge of the map into the abyss that carried the warning *Here be dragons*.

"That's hardly fair, I am only naturally curious as to—"

Sandison didn't pause over my hurt feelings. "Never mind." He briefly stared at me again with that strange gleam. "Don't tell anyone we're going, eh? Tongues are already too busy in this town." Turning back impatiently to the newspaper spread on his desk, he told me to meet him at the depot, good and sharp, for the six a.m. westbound train.

THERE WAS A MIDNIGHT TRAIN. Eastbound.

Why not be on it? the ceiling posed the question, a certain seam in the plaster straight as a railtrack as I lay fully clothed on my bed. I was as alone as ever in this latest dilemma. At supper, Hoop and Griff had been as animated as carnival pitchmen, while Grace put actual cutlets on the table in evident celebration of the boarding-house's new lease on life. No one seemed to pay particular attention to my unmoored state of mind; when that happens, it makes you wonder about your normal mien.

The bed was crowded with debate. Sandison was a latent noose-wielding unpredictable madman. Or not. He'd had the perfectly sound sense to hire me, I tried telling myself. Just to be on the safe side, though, pack the satchel for the train; saying a permanent goodbye to Butte would be only a strategic withdrawal, after all. But so was Napoleon's retreat from Moscow.

My head now really did ache from going back and forth. I checked my pocket watch again. Midnight was not far off. Abruptly my mind made itself up, almost as if I had not participated. I scrambled off the bed.

Quietly as I could, I opened the door of my room and tiptoed into the hall. Snores emanated from Griff's room, and Hoop's next to his; at the end of the hall, Grace's bedroom kept a silence. Feeling like a burglar in the darkened house, I slipped past one door. Then another. And stealthily turned the doorknob of the end one.

I crept to the sleeping form and, hesitating just a bit, shook the bare shoulder where the nightdress had slipped down.

"Grace, I hate to interrupt your slumber. But I must talk to you."

My whisper penetrated as if I had jabbed her. Bolting upright in the bed, she clutched the coverlet around her, huskily reciting: "In the name of decency, Morrie, we really ought not—"

"This is imperative or"—I looked at the ivory slope of shoulder still showing—"I would not come uninvited. Please just listen, Grace."

Vigilantly, she did so while I told her she had to be my witness, to attest that I was alive and in one piece before boarding the train early in the morning with Samuel Sandison. "Just in case worse should come to worst."

"Worse coming to worst, is it." There was just enough light in the room that I could see she had let down her flaxen hair when she went to bed, and now she ran a hand through the long tresses. "Morrie, you are the most complicated boarder there ever was."

"I wish I could dispute that."

"Why do I have the honor of this, why not Griff and Hoop?"

"They've been at a union meeting, and you know the condition they come home in after that."

Grace gave an extended sigh. "All right, you want a sober witness. But why go with Sandison at all?"

"He's the kind who will not let loose of an idea—the man is a bulldog. If I don't humor him on this, he'll do away with my job at the library. Then I won't have charge of the auditorium. Then the eisteddfod can't be held in the— It's, well, complicated."

All that was wordlessly weighed on the landlady scale of things.

244 · IVAN DOIG

Then she reached to the bedside table, opened the drawer, and took something out. "Here."

In the dimness of the bedroom, I peered down stupidly at the cold metallic item, with some dull opalescence to it, that she put in the palm of my hand. If I was not mistaken, it was the type of small pearl-handled pistol called a Lady's Special.

"You're—you're armed," I stammered.

"I'm a widow, sleeping alone," she said quietly. "And Butte is a rough and tough place, as you may have noticed." Again she passed a hand through her hair, looking at me as if memorizing me. "That little thing is called an equalizer for a reason, don't forget, Morrie."

I hesitated, then pocketed the gun. "I'm sure I am in better health than when I came in here, thanks to you."

An expectant silence. She patted my hand there in the dark, in a feathery way that was either shy or sly. "I would only be telling the truth if I said you had life in you the last I saw of you, wouldn't I."

An honest enough affidavit, under the circumstances. I returned her caress pat for pat. If I could trust anyone in Butte, it was Grace.

If I could trust anyone in Butte.

"SANDY, HOW ARE WE TO DO THIS?" Stumbling along before dawn in Sandison's wake, I dubiously approached the depot platform. "If I am not mistaken, those are ore cars." The line of heaped railcars stretched off as far as I could see in the dim light.

"Keep walking, don't be a nervous Nellie." Sandison strode along recklessly enough himself that I wished the pair of depot goons would pop around a corner and be steamrollered by him. No such justice, however, at that early hour. Only a yawning conductor, beside what I perceived to be one lone Pullman car behind the train engine, stood in our line of march.

I followed Sandison aboard, feeling tipped to one side by the unaccustomed gun in my coat pocket, even if it was the most decorous of firearms. He and I were the only passengers at that hour. As the train lurched into motion, I could contain the question no longer. "West is a long direction—where exactly do we get off?"

My traveling companion grumpily pawed at his whiskers as if herding the word out.

"Anaconda."

"The company?"

"The town."

IT TURNED OUT TO BE BOTH. A company town, Anaconda was as orderly and contained as Butte was sprawling and unruly. The train pulled in past boxy workers' houses lined up in neat rows, along streets laid as straight as shelves. Sandison appeared to pay no heed to the town itself, gazing away into the valley beyond. At least, I thought as I looked out the window on that side of the train, it was a bright clear day for this. I happened to look out the other side, and the sky was clothed in heavy gray.

When the two of us climbed off at the trim crenellated depot, another chess piece of municipal order, the division in the sky over Anaconda was made plain. On a slope above the murky side of town could be seen the immense smelter for copper ore such as had accompanied us from Butte, and dominant over the smelting works stood a skyscraping smokestack, thickly built and hundreds of feet tall. The scene leapt from every accusatory line ever written about dark satanic mills—the smokestack like the devil's forefinger, black fume trailing evilly as it pointed its challenge to heaven.

Dumbstruck as I was by this sight, only slowly did I register the other product of the smelter besides copper and smoke, a series of slag heaps surrounding the town like barren hills.

"That's Anaconda for you," Sandison growled. "Let's get a move on." So saying, he stalked off toward a livery stable across the tracks.

Now I was alarmed. A saddle horse is not my preferred mode of transportation. Of necessity, I had spent some time on horseback during my prairie teaching career, but no more than I had to. Sandison brayed to the stableman that we wanted genuine riding stock, not nags, and shortly I found myself holding the reins of a restless black horse with a bald face, named Midnight. When a rangy steel-gray steed was brought out for Sandison, he looked in disgust at the stirrups on the rented saddle and lengthened them six inches to account for his height. That done, despite his bulk he swung up onto the horse as easily as a boy and waited impatiently for me to hoist onto mine.

"Going to be a blisterer out in the valley. Here." He tossed me a canvas water bag to tie to my saddle and spurred his horse into motion, leaving Midnight and me to catch up.

We managed to do so at the edge of town, past one last ugly dark slag heap where children ran up and down. With the cries of their playing fading behind us, the horseback pair of us cantered into another existence entirely, a sudden savannah-like landscape that seemed to exhale in relief at leaving the pall of Anaconda behind.

The valley extending before us was a classic oval of geography, broad and perfect as a French painting. Rimmed by mountains substantial enough to shoulder snow year-round, the valley floor was uninterrupted except for a few distant settlements strung out near a willowed river like memory beads on a thong. Gazing wide-eyed at the breadth of landscape—truly, here a person was a fleck on the sea of ground—I said something about this startling amount of open country so near the industrial confines of Butte and Anaconda.

Unexpectedly Sandison reined to a halt, and I pulled up beside him. He massively shifted in his saddle to turn in my direction. "Take a good look, Morgan. I owned it all."

At first I thought he meant the plot of land we were riding across. Then I realized he meant the entire valley.

I cannot forget that moment. Picture it if you will. A woolsack of a man, surely two hundred and fifty pounds, nearly twice of me, sitting on his horse, looking down on me like a wild-bearded mad king.

Suddenly he raised a meaty hand and swiped it toward me, his action so swift I had no time to grab for the pistol.

Paralyzed, I felt the swish of air as the thick palm passed my face and descended to mash a horsefly on the neck of my mount.

Flicking away the fly carcass, he rumbled, "Don't just sit there with your face hanging out, we've got a ways to go."

He put his horse into a trot, and mine followed suit. I rode holding tightly to the reins and my Stetson. In Montana, it is a good idea to keep your hat on your head so the wind doesn't blow your hair off. Besides, it gave me something to concentrate on, other than the thought that I might have shot a man for swatting a fly. But Sandison's behavior still unnerved me. Keen as a tracker, he stood in his stirrups every so often to peer ahead at the print of ruts we were following; it might once have been a road but looked long unused.

Leading to where? There were wide open spaces around us to all the horizons, but no arithmetic of logic that I could find in the destination Sandison had set for us. I knew from my time among the homesteads of Marias Coulee that land is surveyed into townships of thirty-six sections, each section a square mile. The numbering starts over at each township. Where, then—and for that matter, *what*—was Section 37? Was I going to survive to find out?

After an eternity of joggling along, we came to a plot of land boxed by a barbwire fence. We—rather, I—opened the treacherously barbed gate, and the horses stepped through, skittish enough about it that they had to be reined hard.

It could be said they were showing horse sense. The ground changed here. The soil, to call it that, had an unhealthy grayish hue, like the pallor of a very sick person. The sudden change was puzzling to me. I did not know thing one about the raising of cattle, but what was beneath our horses' hooves would not pasture any creature, I was quite sure.

My riding companion now simply sat in his saddle, lost in contemplation of the expanse of valley. I resorted to my water bag. The day was warming to an extreme, and I could see sweat running down Sandison's cheeks into his beard, although he paid it no heed.

"Back then," he all at once spoke in the voice of a man possessed, "this was a paradise of grass. And I bought up homestead claims and mining claims and every other kind of land until every square foot of it was Triple S range. I tell you, there never was a better ranch nor a prettier one." His words cast a spell. What a picture it made in the mind, the green valley filled with red cattle with that sinuous brand on their hips.

The bearded head swung in my direction. His voice dropped ominously.

"Then it got to be the old story. The snake into Eden." The meaty hand swept around again and, past my ineffectual flinch toward the Lady's Special, pointed over my shoulder.

"That thing."

He had taken dead aim at the smelter stack. Even at this distance, the giant chimney dwarfed all of nature around it, clouding that half of the horizon like a permanent storm. Staring at that ashen plume along with Sandison, I felt something more oppressive creep over me than the heat of the day.

With a great grunt he climbed down from his horse, stooped low, and scooped a handful of dirt. Holding the dull-colored stuff up to me, he uttered:

"Here. Have some arsenic."

Choosing to consider that rhetorical, I cleared my throat and managed to respond.

"Sandy, am I to understand we are camped on a patch of poison?"

"That's what it comes down to," he said, letting the unhealthy soil sift from his fist. Each word bitter, he recited to me that the furnaces of the smelting process released arsenic and sulphur, and the Anaconda stack piped those into the air like a ceaseless spout.

Wiping his hand on his pantleg, he went on: "It kills cattle like picking them off with a rifle. The first year after the smokestack came in, we lost a thousand head. Hell, it wasn't ranching anymore. All we were doing was burning carcasses." He shook his head violently at the memory. "We sued the mining company every way there is. The Anaconda bunch had the big money for eastern lawyers, so they beat us. But that was later." His voice sharpened again. He gestured as if in dismissal toward the smokestack and its almighty smudge. "That isn't what you're here to see. Let's get to it." With cowboy agility, he again swung onto his horse and headed us toward a grove of trees along a slip of a stream not far ahead. Damp as I was with sweat from the unrelenting sun—and just as relentless, Sandison—I welcomed the notion of shade.

The trees, though, revealed themselves to be leafless as we approached. What had been a thicket was now a stand of lifeless trunks and limbs, graying above the soil that had sickened them. In the midst of the witchy trees stood eight or ten huge old cottonwoods, dying more slowly than the rest.

Sandison dismounted and walked his horse over to the nearest great wrinkled trunk. I gingerly did likewise. Under a big overhanging limb, he turned to me with that unsettling royal glint in his eyes again.

"Welcome to the grove of justice, Morgan."

At first I did not take his meaning.

"It was before copper was on everyone's mind," he began. "This valley was just sitting here, best place on the face of the earth to raise cattle. My backers put up most of the money and I built the herd, cows from here to breakfast. Until one branding time when the count was way off. There weren't dead cows lying around from winterkill or some disease, so you didn't need to be a genius to figure out the malady was rustlers." The fixed intensity of that blue gaze was hypnotic as he told it all. "The money men threw a fit, said if it happened again they'd sell the place out from under me. They were town men, they didn't have a fig of a notion about how you have to let the good years carry you through the bad ones in the livestock business. I had to do something to keep the herd count up or lose the ranch." Trickles of sweat from under his hat into his beard retraced that predicament of long ago. "My riders told me they'd seen some of the squatters up in those hills"—he indicated across the valley to coulees that must have held shanties at that time—"acting funny around our stock. And there were always drifters riding through, you could bet they'd about as soon rustle your cattle as look at them. Try tell that to a sheriff who'd rather sit with his boots up on his desk

than chase after rustlers with a couple of days' head start, though."
His gaze at me never wavered. "Now, you know what my answer to
that was, don't you?"

I was afraid I did. The Montana necktie had a reputation to the
far ends of the world, ever since frontier times when vigilantes in the
untamed gold camps took the law, along with a noose, into their own
hands.

"My riders knew how to handle a rope in more ways than one,"
he was saying in that voice terrible to hear. "Anybody they caught
in the vicinity of a cow or calf with a Triple S brand on it had some
hard answering to do." The man who had been lord of this valley
turned ponderously, broad back to me now, toward the line of sturdy
cottonwoods. "We hung them like butchered meat. Right here." Facing around to me again, he lifted those thick hands. "Many a time
I tied the noose myself."

The old saying could not have been more right: my blood ran
cold.

Had I gambled wrong, in coming with him to this desolate patch
of earth? Was I about to be murdered, for knowing too much? The
pistol stayed glued to me where it rode in my pocket; I realized,
for once and all, that I could not bring myself to use it. Sandison's
stare had my fate in it, but I could not read those icy eyes. I tried
to speak and couldn't.

He stared at me that way long moments more, then his words
came slowly.

"What gets into a man, Morgan, to set himself up as an execu-
tioner? I made those dim-witted rustlers pay far too high a price." He
shook his head. "Cows are just cows." Turning from me, he gazed
at the gray old trees as if looking a long way back. His shoulders
slumped. As I watched, the Earl of Hell was deposed, by himself.

After some moments, I found words.

"Section 37 is off the face of the earth."

"That's where I sent them, on a length of rope," Sandison was speaking huskily. "Now you know why I brought you here, eh?"

I thought so, but said nothing, watching the same shrewd expression come over him as when he found a bargain in a rare books catalogue. "You're a learned man," he said in that husky tone, "you know a little something about how to read a life. But there's always more. I know what they say about me behind my back, but they miss half the story." One more time he shook his head. "'The music of men's lives' isn't as easy to recognize as the average fool thinks, you were right about that. Back then"—he pointed his beard to the cottonwood grove—"I let the money men call the tune on me and did more than any man should, to hold on to the best ranch in Montana. And then poison came out of the air and I lost the Triple S anyway."

Now he looked hard at me, nodding as if making sure to himself. "It takes a collector to know a collector, even if you do stack your treasures in your head instead of out on a shelf. You'll remember this, fair and square, there's that about you. Not like the ones who only gossip, which is almost everybody." He set his face as if into a prevailing wind. "I goddamn well know I could turn Butte into a city of gold, and still the one thing I'll take with me to my grave is the reputation for stringing people up."

Monumental and weary, Samuel Sandison cast a last glance at the hanging tree, then turned away to where our horses stood. Over his shoulder, he said, as if we were back in the library:

"Add it all to your brainbox, Morgan."

ight was coming on, with the streetlights of downtown Butte starting to glow golden and the mines of the Hill already lit like the mineral earth's own constellation, when Sandison and I left the train.

He had said next to nothing during our journey back from Section 37. As ever, the beard masked more than just his jawline. Accordingly, there on the depot platform he turned to me and dispensed the day in the shortest manner possible: "That takes care of that." His boot heels resounded on the planks as he traipsed off, leaving me with the parting sentiment: "Don't be late for work in the morning, it's a bad habit."

I stood there for an extended moment, inhaling the chill air, simply to breathe free.

"*Hsst!* Over here, you!"

My nerves shot back up to high alarm, the threat of goons never absent. Fumbling for the pistol in my side pocket, I stopped when I got a full look at the figure speeding toward me from the depot waiting room. "Grace!"

In a sensible woolly wrap against the early October night, she still shivered as she drew up to me and stared after the monumental form of Sandison receding into the dusk. "If you hadn't been on this train, I'd have gone to the police yelling bloody murder. Where on earth did that creature haul you off to?"

"It is not exactly on the map."

Setting off together up the sloping street, I recounted the day to her as best I could, on edge as I was, and she listened the same way as we navigated the noisy neighborhood and reached the boarding-house. The shared time of the previous night was still with us, but so was too much else and we were uncertain and awkward with each other. It didn't help matters that Venus Alley, a mere block away, was filling the night with lusty laughter and more.

Paused at the door of our lodging, I glanced aside at Grace and could only come up with: "Thank you for watching out for me."

"You seem to need it," she replied with a small smile, shyly pock-eting the pearl-handled gun I had handed back to her. "Besides, I hate to lose a boarder."

"You'll have this one again in the morning." I gestured in the general direction of the library. "For now, though, I'm too wound up to go to bed—there's something waiting for me I must tend to."

"Good night, then, Morrie. Don't let the bad dreams bite," she said soberly.

I SWITCHED ON the mezzanine lights. The Reading Room below was as dark and hushed as the audience portion of a theater. Up onstage, so to speak, the books waited in titled ranks, and in their reassuring company I moved idly along the laden shelves, running the tips of my fingers over the exquisite spines, taking down an old loved volume every so often and opening it to the stored glory of words. Around me was the wealth of minds down through all of recorded time. The dramatic capacities of Shakespeare, as all-seeing in his foolscap scripts as in the sagacious portrait above the doorway to reading. The gallant confabulations of Cervantes, showing us the universal meaning of quixotic. The Russian army of impossible geniuses, Turgenev, Tolstoy, Dostoevsky, Chekhov. Mark Twain, as fresh on the page as a comet inscribing the dark. Robert Louis Stevenson, master of tales goldenly told. (The twofold nature of Dr. Jekyll and Mr. Hyde seemed a lot more convincing after being around Samuel Sandison.) And my ever-familiar exemplar of classic Latin and daring generalship, Caesar, in tanned leather and impeccable threading. These and the hundreds upon hundreds of others Rabrab and I had evaluated, insofar as mortals can, into the inventory. Valued treasures, in more ways than one.

In such company, you wonder about your own tale in the long book of life. What would they have made of me, these grandmasters of storytelling? Arriving out of nowhere to the richest of hills with the intention of filling my pockets from it, and all this time later, finding that the only thing that had paid off was the railroad, for my own trunk. Thrown together for a second time in life with an appealing widow, and for a second time gaining no ground there, either. Casting my lot with an unpredictable bibliophile who also turned out to be Montana's leading vigilante. No matter how I looked at it, my story lacked conclusion.

Suddenly I knew what to do. Can inspiration come off on the fingers? I rubbed my hands together appreciatively, there among the literary classics. It was as if the risk-taking lifetimes of composition, the reckless romances with language, the tricky business of plots stealing onto pages, all the wiles of Samuel Sandison's glorious books answered to my touch. There was no mistaking their message: sometimes you must set sail on the winds of chance.

Stroking a last row of embossed titles as I went, I turned off the mezzanine lights and made my way out of the darkened library. What I was about to attempt was a gamble, but that was nothing new in human experience. The first thing it required was a messenger who was not Russian Famine. I headed directly to the cigar store where Skinner hung out.

DISCORDANT AS IT WAS by nature, the song session the next night came as something of a relief after Section 37. At least, up there onstage I did not have to fear for my neck when one rough-hewn miner or another climbed up with me and sang off-key, although my ears were another matter.

The songwriting efforts unveiled at this tryout were all over the map, in more ways than one. The only thing the musical penchants of the neighborhoods of the Hill had in common was strenuous exercise of the vocal cords. As diplomatically as I could, I touched up rhyme and word rhythm here and there, and the concertina tuned things up a little, but in the end the attempted songs were pretty much the same rough creatures as at the start of the evening.

Well, no one in his right mind could expect to turn the basement auditorium of the Butte Public Library into Tin Pan Alley, I had to tell myself afterward. But Jared and Rab and I were a somber trio when we adjourned to the Purity.

"What do you think, Professor," Jared asked directly over pie and coffee, "is the work song we want hiding in any of those?"

"You heard the same performances I did," I sidestepped. "The groups still have almost a week to work on things, perhaps something"—I almost said *miraculous*—"unforgettable will find its way in." We both looked to Rab for a boost in our spirits.

"I'll stick with my sixth-graders," she passed judgment ruthlessly now that she was back to teaching. "They only get into fistfights at recess." At the height of the song session Jared had needed to jump in and separate a Finn and an Italian who came to blows over a question of tempo.

He conceded that was a case of somewhat too much enthusiasm, but maintained strong feelings of that sort could be a good sign. "The men are fired up against Anaconda, and the right song will catch that," he insisted, as if insistence would do the job. I could see what was coming next as he looked over at me: in his checklist way he would want to know how I was going to handle the big night when two hundred people had to materialize in the library basement without anyone noticing. Omitting to say it was the brainstorm of Griff and Hoop, I brightly volunteered that our salvation was an eisteddfod.

Jared turned his unscathed ear toward me as if that would help with the word. "Run that by me again?"

I did so in as much detail as I could think up. The dubious expression on Jared kept growing until Rab, at her conspiratorial best, poked him insistently. "Mr. Morgan has the knack of doing what can't be done," she said, canny as an abbess. "You either have to let him or think up something better, sweetheart."

That decided him. "Well, hell, if none of us can savvy it, maybe the cops and goons can't either." As we rose to go, though, he gave me the Butte salute, a whap on the shoulder, and warned, "Just remember, Professor, plenty of people are going to want your hide if this doesn't work out right."

Out into the night he and Rab went, with me brooding behind, when the bow-tied impresario at the cash register called after me: "Hey, you with the pie in you, don't run off!"

Just the ending the evening needed, I thought to myself balefully, Jared sticking me with the bill.

That proved not to be the case, however. Hopping down from his stool and coming up close to me, the Purity proprietor dropped his usual repartee. "Haven't I seen you with that messenger kid who goes around like his pants are on fire? What is he, your nephew?"

"Second cousin," I answered negotiably; Russian Famine barely had a shirttail, let alone a shirttail relative, but imaginary kinship might be better than none. "Why?"

"I need someone to run errands and so on," he said as if that ought to be perfectly obvious. "Tell the kid he's got a job after school if he wants it. I'll give him a fair wage."

"He needs more than that," I interjected. "His is the, um, lean side of the family line. He very nearly lives hand to mouth."

The cafeteria owner swayed back from me, frowning. "What are you, his union?" Observing the rules of the game, he hemmed and hawed for a minute before grandly offering: "Oh, all right, I'll throw in his meals, how's that?"

"Allow me." I squared his bow tie for him; tonight's was royal purple. "All he can eat, I trust that means?"

"Sure. How much can that be, a runt like him?"

IN THE BOOK OF LIFE we are chapters in one another's stories, and with Russian Famine given a place at the feast, so to speak, I felt like an author drawing a scene to a successful close. That was only the first episode to be resolved, however, while more than I wanted to count waited in line.

A crisp expectancy was in the air of Butte those next days and nights. The season turned as if October was a signpost for the weather: the first snow, dazzling and spotless, appeared in the mountain heights above Columbia Gardens, while downtown blocks at midday echoed with the loudspeaker version of anklet baseball— *"Flash! The Redlegs win again, they lead the White Sox in the Series three games to two!"*—and in the dusk, fresh war cries whooped from the Hill as boys played football on barren patches between mine heaps. The change in climate could be measured any number of ways. More than once I noticed women and daughters trooping past the boardinghouse with gunnysacks, and I asked Grace about it. "Coal," she said simply. The thought of it pulled the skin tight around her eyes. "They go down to the tracks and pick up what's spilled from the trains. I did it myself when I was a girl and a strike was coming. Anything to get ready for the worst."

I knew the feeling. As a precautionary measure, I resumed my habit of keeping watch into the shadows for the darker presence of goons; Eel Eyes and Typhoon now had no reason to pack me off to Chicago, but if it ever entered their thick heads that I had turned the library into a choir loft of the miners' union, they were bound to be renewed trouble. Nor were they the only concern. In the back of my mind the Welsh minister kept preaching his "unlawful assembly" sermon (*"Butte's finest, to call them that, will pick you off like ripe apples"*). And there was always Sandison. The man had wrung out his soul for me to see, there beneath the hanging tree, but he still was impossible to predict. Which was I going to encounter at the crucial time, the merely gruff city librarian or the Earl of Hell?

When I at last told him, as I had to, that the Lyre Club would be honoring an old bardic tradition by holding an eisteddfod and braced for a volley from him about the library turning into a madhouse, he merely grunted and said, "What's your next field of knowledge, Morgan, druidic chants?"

All the while, Hoop and Griff assured me at every meal that there was nothing to worry about.

READY OR NOT, the night of nights arrived to us.

"Remember, Professor, when you step out there, this isn't some lilies-of-the-valley crowd. These men have been through everything Anaconda could do to them and they're about to be on strike for hell knows how long. They're not here to fool around. Don't get carried away, just run the songs through and have them vote, savvy?"

"I am not aware that I ever get carried—"

"Oh, don't forget the hat, Mr. Morgan. I stirred the slips of paper around, so when they draw it'll be perfectly fair. Just don't drop it or spill it or—"

"Actually, Rab, I have handled a hat before, thank you very—"

"Another thing. Don't let Quinlan hog the stage when he gets up to sing whatever his bunch has come up with. This is serious business, not some Irish wake, got that?"

"Jared, I promise I shall muzzle Quin if necessary. Now do you suppose the two of you could possibly give me a minute to get myself ready for this?"

Not that there was any proven way of doing that, given what awaited me out beyond the stage curtain. The buzzing auditorium was filled with men hardened by the copper in their blood, and beside them, doubtful wives brought along for protective coloration. A couple at a time, they had filtered past Hoop and Griff and other Welsh-speaking venerables out there in front of the library acting as doormen beneath the drooping banner that read, like a much magnified eye chart, EISTEDDFOD! Passersby and other curious types asking about it were answered with such a spate of baffling syllables that they went away as if fleeing from banshees. Thus, only the mine families whom Jared counted on to be the heart of the union during the strike made up this gathering. Unanimity stopped at that, however. The neighborhoods were mapped in this restless audience as they were on the Hill: the Finns in sturdy rows, the Irish in a looser, louder group centered on Quinlan, the Cornish in chapel-like conclave, the Serbs and Italians across an aisle from each other as though the Adriatic lapped between them. Perched on tables at the back of the hall, Griff and Hoop and the Welsh cronies were like a rebel tribe grinning madly at the edge of the plantation.

My mind raced, but in a circle. As thronged as the place was, I kept feeling the absence of Grace. When I had gingerly asked if she might be on hand to lend moral support to the three of us from the boardinghouse, she just looked at me as if I had taken leave of common sense. "Morrie, I very nearly broke out in hives when you went off with Sandison, and I can't risk it again. Besides, somebody should be on the outside if the lot of you get locked up, or worse." Wise woman. I took one last peek past the curtain and drew the deepest breath I could. It was time to face the music, in every sense of that saying.

Stepping out to the front of the stage with a music stand in one hand and the hat held upside down in the other, I cleared my throat and spoke into the general hubbub.

"Good evening. Welcome to an evening of magic."

Naturally that brought hoots to pull a rabbit out of that hat. Down in the front row I saw Jared cover his face with his hand, while Rab mouthed something like *The songs, get to the songs!*

"Ah, but there are more kinds of magic than the furry sort that a

262 · IVAN DOIG

stage conjuror plucks up by the ears," I said, carefully setting the hat aside so as not to spill the slips of paper. "The more lasting sort is not really visible. And that is the variety we hope to produce tonight. Something that will sing on and on in us like a fondest memory."

"It better be a doozy, mister," a skeptic in the middle of the crowd yelled out, "to beat what the Wobs have got."

"I take it you refer to that celestial pastry, 'pie in the sky,'" I replied, more cordially than I felt. "You are quite right, that is indeed a clever musical couplet. Yet it is not on the same footing with the classic musical compositions your fellow miners are striving to emulate here."

"Like what?" came back like a shot.

That snared me. A couple of hundred unconvinced faces were waiting for my response, which had better not be a stuttering one.

The lesson of the old tale-tellers whispered itself again: sometimes you must set sail on the wind of chance. I whipped off my suitcoat and tossed it over the music stand. Rabrab nudged Jared forcefully, recognizing the signs in me. I stepped to the lip of the stage, snapping my sleeve garters like a sideshow barker. "You leave me no choice," I announced, "this is the kind of thing I mean." In music-hall style, I shuffled some soft-shoe and twanged out at the top of my voice:

> In a cavern, in a canyon,
> Excavating for a mine,
> Dwelt a miner, a Forty-niner,
> And his daughter Clementine.

As catchy as any song ever written, that ditty caught up this audience to the fullest extent, a roomful of voices lustily joining in with me by the end. After raucous applause and my brief bow, I slipped into my suitcoat again and stepped back in favor of the song contestants. "Just as darling Clementine is unforgettable to us all," I told the readied crowd, "now we shall choose the song that works a similar wonder for the union." Or not. I hoped with everything in me that the efforts of the neighborhoods had improved spectacularly since the last Lyre Club session. There was one way to find out. "The representatives will now come up to draw for order of presentation, please."

The burly half dozen of them crowded around me as I held out the hat with the numbered slips in it. Quin winked at me; the others were as serious as novitiates into some mystical ritual. At my signal, work-callused hands dipped into the hat crown and drew out.

"It be we!" The man at my left happily brandished the slip with a big penciled "1" on it, while the other five studied their lesser positions.

"The luck of the Cornish has prevailed," I announced. "Our Centerville friends will sing first." I retired to the side of the stage, the concertina made its pneumatic presence known, and the song competition was under way.

It was a contest, I realized with a sinking feeling, in which the participants felt bound by no particular rules but their own.

The miners from Cornwall in their practical manner sang from a standard recipe: a verse about the iniquities of the mine owners, then a verse about the travails of working in the mines, followed by a verse about the toll on miners' families, capped by a verse about standing solidly together and defeating the villainous mining overlords.

The Irish entry, as rendered by Quinlan, sounded suspiciously like a borrowing from a drinking song.

The Welsh nomination was so grave and bass in register that only the Welsh could sing it.

And so on down the line. By the time Finntown and the Italian contingent from Meaderville had been heard from, I had to generate a good deal more gusto in my remarks than I really felt. The plainly mandatory smile on Jared and Rab's overenthusiastic clapping told me they had reached the same conclusion; even Hoop and Griff looked a little worried. One by one and all in all, the songs were at that level which causes a person to say, "Oh well, it could have been worse." Which always implies that it could have been much better.

The audience members were muttering among themselves, not a good sign, when I reclaimed center stage after the last song.

"There we have it"—I swung my arms as if pumping enthusiasm into the room—"somewhere among those is the anthem that will carry the union to victory. Now, Jared, if you would come up and conduct the vote, and I'll do the tallying."

As Jared was getting to his feet, I searched through my coat pockets for the tally sheet I had tucked away. When I looked up again, something like a shock wave from the audience met me. A roomwide gulp might be the closest description. Whatever had materialized in back of me, it had caused two hundred people to swallow their Adam's apples and Jared to angle his arms out to protect Rab.

With a sense of doom, I turned around expecting to be face-to-face with Eel Eyes, Typhoon, or some walrus-mustached policeman.

It was worse than that. It was Sandison.

An Aztec god could not have loomed any more ominously than that massive white-bearded figure. For a long, long moment, he just stood there, looking stonily around at the crowd as if counting up the total of trespassers to be dealt with. His sudden appearance from the back of the stage changed the equilibrium of the room, tilted the will in us all. There were men here who had done things beyond reckoning in the mineshaft or on the battlefield, but none with the reputation of having sent other men off the face of the earth with their bare hands.

As for me, I wanted to dissolve into the floorboards.

The crowd began to stir, with Quinlan and other hard-faced miners looking around for the best route to fight their way out through the police, the Anaconda goons, whatever phalanx of enforcement the lord of the library had brought with him.

"Sit down, nitwits," Sandison thundered at them.

They sat.

He caught sight of Rab in the front row and gave her a gaze that said what a pity it was she was associated with riffraff like us. Inevitable as fate, his attention shifted to me.

"Stay where you are, Morgan, you've caused enough trouble." Now he scowled at the silent audience. "Who's the head fool here?"

Jared drew himself up. "I happen to be president of the mineworkers' union, and we've been having a social evening of musical—"

"'Social,' my hind leg," Sandison overrode him. "A person would have to be deaf not to know that you and your gussied-up inside accomplice"—that initial adjective I found unfair; I was merely wearing my blue serge suit with a dove-gray vest added—"are using the Butte Public Library for a purpose the powers that be say is against the law."

I must say, he summarized the situation beyond dispute. Standing nervously on one foot and then the other as he glowered around, I wished I was elsewhere, such as Tasmania. From the sound of it, the audience was witnessing more of a show than it had anticipated; someone now shouted out from the back in jittery defiance, "Are you going to string us up, or what?"

Shaking his head and beard at Jared and me in turn, Sandison said, with final disgust, "Let's get this over with." He lumbered to the very edge of the stage and thrust a sheet of paper in Jared's face.

Handling it as if it were the warrant that would put the whole crowd of us away, Jared scanned the single page. Then studied it with more deliberation. He sent Sandison a measuring look. Strangely, he had that fixed gleam toward the next objective when he passed the sheet up to me. "Better do what the man wants, Professor. We'll sit tight until you get done."

Apprehensively I read the piece of paper. I saw why Jared had done so twice. Once for the handprinted words, then for the dotted lines of musical notes.

"I shall need help," I announced at once; this was too important for me to flub alone. "Quin, would you come up, please?" Next I singled out the Cornish leader: "And Jack? And, mmm, Griff?"

With no great willingness they joined me onstage and we huddled around the music sheet. The Cornishman's eyebrows drew down in concentration, while Quinlan's lifted as if liking what he saw. Griff ceremoniously cleared his throat. At my signal, the concertina wheezed a note for us. Somewhat ragged at first, our impromptu quartet gained harmony as we sang.

> Drill, drill, drill,
> That's the music of the Hill.
> The Richest Hill on Earth
> We work for all it's worth.

> Those who mine are all one race,
> Born and bred 'neath a tunnel brace;
> Down there deep we're all one kind,
> All one blood, all of one mind.
> I back you and you back me.
> All one song in unity.

Drill, drill, drill,
That's the music of the Hill . . .

It was homely, it was distinctly old-fashioned, it was not particularly profound, but most of all, it was infectious. You could jig to it, march to it, swing a pick and chip out ore to it, hum it, whistle it, sing it in your sleep—it was as catchy as "Camptown Races," what more can I say? The atmosphere in the auditorium changed for the better with every line we sang of that lucky combination of unifying words and bouncy tune, Sandison's song working its magic like the proverbial charm. When we were done, the audience came out of its reverent spell and jumped to its feet, clapping and cheering.

Leaping to the stage, Jared seized the moment, raising his arms for attention. "Are we agreed? 'The Song of the Hill,' is it?" Unanimity answered him.

AFTERWARD, as Hoop and Griff and the cronies craftily discharged people into the street in imitation of whatever an eisteddfod is like when it winds down, I tended to last things, such as chairs, with Jared helping. At the back of the auditorium Rab was in one-way conversation with Sandison, enthusing about the evening's outcome while he stood there like a totem.

"Well done, Professor." Grinning keenly, Jared gave me credit I was not sure I entirely deserved. "It's a dandy," he was saying of the song. "It'll help pull us through any strike. The Wobs can't outsing us anymore. They can keep their pie in the sky, we've got hold of the Hill in one sweet damn tune. And the Anaconda bosses will hear it in their sleep before we're done. They might bend us, but they can't break us now," he vowed. He stopped to whack my shoulder in appreciation.

Buoyant with relief, I admitted: "Now I can tell you, I half-expected that pair of goons and forty others to burst in on us tonight."

He tugged his ear thoughtfully. "I guess you haven't heard. Butte has seen the last of those two."

Stunned, I visualized the two of them meeting the fate that had been hinted at for me, at the bottom of a glory hole.

I must have gasped, because Jared lifted his hands in clean denial. "None of it was our doing, and they're still among the living. The word is"—I understood he was alluding to gossip on the Hill—"the Wobblies were pretty badly annoyed about that noose and decided to return the hint. So, when the goons went to turn in the other night, there was a dynamite fuse on each pillow and a note saying next time it would be the dynamite." He grinned in admiration of a maneuver neatly done. "The last anyone saw, the pair of them were piling onto a train with their suitcases."

Alas, then, for Eel Eyes and Typhoon, their part in the story flickered out as Rab surged over to us. "See? I knew the two of you could bring this off." She linked arms with Jared and invited triumphantly, "Come celebrate with us at the Purity, Mr. Morgan."

"You'll manage nicely without me. I have one last thing to do here."

I waved them on their way, and as they went out, Jared did an about-face in the doorway and snapped me a salute, while Rabrab blew me a kiss.

WHEN THE AUDITORIUM WAS CLEARED, I took a final look around and went upstairs in search of Sandison.

His desk lamp was on, an open catalogue of rare books in the pool of light, but the big chair was empty.

When Samuel Sandison was in a room, however, you could feel it. Over at the window, the stained glass muted in the darkness, he was peering steadily at the Hill through a whorl peephole. With the starry host of night lights at the mines, it was a rare Butte quietude to remember. Hearing me come in, he glanced in my direction and away again. "What are you doing here? You know we don't pay overtime."

"I came to say what a wonder 'The Song of the Hill' is, Sandy. Written with a pen of iron and the point of a diamond."

Sandison grunted.

"And cleverly adapted," I said the rest to his back, "from when the unheralded pastoral poet Jonathan Cartwright put it to paper as 'The Song of the Mill' a century ago."

He stood deathly still, long enough that my heartbeats grew loud in my ears. At last the slope-shaped man swung around to me, the dim light making it hard to read the face that had taken other men off the earth. *Clomp, clomp,* the boots advanced toward me, the beard and summit of hair growing whiter as the lord of the library came looming into the lamplight. Just when I began to fear for my neck, he stopped short, an armlength away. "Morgan," he sighed heavily, "you're the only one in Butte who's enough of an educated fool to know that. Sit down, nuisance."

Relieved, I took to my chair while Sandison squashed into his. "All right, just between us, I helped myself to old Cartwright's work where it seemed to fit."

I could not resist: "Rustled it, might one say?"

Another gusty sigh. "That's fair, I suppose. Who the hell ever knows what you end up doing in this life?" He rested his folded hands on his belly. "Anyhow, Dora touched up the tune a little," he blandly shared the credit and guilt. "She's musical, you know."

"How did you know about the songwriting sessions?"

"Hah. Don't you savvy anything yet about running an outfit? First rule is to keep track of what's going on in the bunkhouse."

"You sided with the union."

He brushed away virtue, redemption, whatever it was, with a rough hand. "Anybody who puts a hornet up Anaconda's nose, I'm with."

"If I may say so, Sandy, you've given the miners one of those anthems authored into the mind beyond forgetting."

"They'll need it, won't they."

For a minute we sat in silence, in tribute to the workers' battle ahead for a fair share of the yield of the Hill. Sandison stirred before I could. Gruff as a grindstone, at least trying to be, he appraised me. "You didn't come by just to say nighty-night. Am I going to see that milk face of yours from now on?"

"I fear you won't, Sandy. I have another chore to tend to, and the library is best left out of it." Goodbye was not easy to say, no matter how I tried to dress it. "I must draw my wages and—what is the ranch phrase?—ride the grub line for a while."

Sandison frowned sadly and reached for the cashbox. "Now I'll have to hire a pack of flunkies to do whatever you've been doing."

We both stood, and shook hands the way people do when they know it is for the last time. "One good thing about you, Morgan," he looked down his beard at me. "You don't stick around long enough for a person to get sick of you."

FOR THE NEXT MATTER I needed the satchel, which I had brought with me and stowed in the sorting room. A full moon carpeted the library steps with silver as I departed the citadel of books, and there was a promise of frost in the air. Butte slept as much as it ever does. The main activity in the downtown streets was out front of the *Daily Post* building, where the night janitor was dismantling the scoreboard, and I tipped my hat to it as I strode by. Like everything else, baseball was over with the passing of its season.

A few blocks farther on, I turned in at the well-lit cigar store. The regulars telling stories at the counter fell silent and met me with stares, all except the messenger, Skinner, who jerked his head toward the back room.

When we were alone there, Skinner jittered from one foot to the other in agitation. "How'd you know?" he asked sourly. "The World Series stinks. The Sox should of won."

"Rightly or wrongly, Cincinnati did," I chided. With the kindness that can be afforded from picking a winner, I elaborated: "Use your noggin. If you were any of the White Sox being paid Maxwell Street wages, would you play your heart out for Cheap Charlie Comiskey?"

"It beats me," he surrendered, and got down to business. "Like I told you, we had to lay your bet off with the big-city boys to cover it. The bookies back east in Chicago ain't happy with this, but we pay off honest in Butte."

"I was counting on that." I opened the satchel. Sorrowfully, Skinner began dumping in the bundles of cash.

GRACE WAS WAITING UP.

"I heard." Apronless there in the dining room, she nonetheless appeared to be laboring over something. She tried a smile that she couldn't make stick. "Hoop and Griff came home to spruce up before they spend the night celebrating in a speakeasy. They went out of here singing the thing at the top of their lungs."

"The union has its work song," I concurred, "and its work cut out for it, as always." I halted near one end of the dining table as she had stopped at the other. From her eyes, I could tell that a question was tugging hard at her. "What is it, Grace? You seem on edge."

The catch in her breath audible, she made a flustered motion in my direction. "I wasn't sure you would be back. I don't know why, I just had a feeling—I peeked in your room and saw your satchel was gone."

"I needed it for an errand." Setting the satchel on the table, I opened it as wide as it would go. "Come and see."

Bringing her quizzical expression, she looked inside, and looked again.

"Morrie," she gasped, "did you hold up a bank?"

"Not at all. An honest wager on a sporting event paid off."

Before she could tell me again what she thought of betting, I hastened to add: "It was very nearly a sure thing." Still, it seemed only fair to give myself a bit of credit. "Although perhaps not everyone would have recognized it as the kind of chance that comes along only once in a lifetime." History soon enough confirmed me in that, as several White Sox players were found to have been bribed and made miscues that let the Red Stockings win. So much for the 1919 Anklet Series.

Unable to resist, Grace peeked into the satchel for the third time. "There's an absolute fortune in there!"

"Mmm, an adequate fortune, I'd call it."

"I'm still in the dark." She gestured helplessly at the trove on the table. "To win this much, didn't you have to put up a whopping stake? Where did you get that?"

Her eyes widened with every word as I told her.

"You"—she had trouble finding her voice—"you bet the library books?"

"Sandison's, let us say." I explained that the inventory with the accompanying assessment made a highly impressive asset, and Butte bookies had seen stranger things put up as a stake. "They don't ask too many questions."

Grace still fumbled for adequate words.

"But—then—what if you had lost?"

"Ah, that. Sandison would have told the gamblers in no uncertain terms the books belonged to him and not some minor functionary of the library, I felt quite certain."

With an incredulous laugh Grace sank into a chair at the table and sat looking up at me as if I had grown wings. "You're rich. How does that feel?"

"Better than most other choices," honesty compelled me to say. I gestured to the satchel. "There's enough to go around. Take what's needed to put the boardinghouse on easy street, why don't you. And the union strike fund will get a share. So will a certain pair of young lovers, as a wedding gift. Then another sum for them to help Russian Famine along in life and keep the copper collar off him." I knew myself well enough to admit: "As for the rest, I'll see how fast it wrinkles."

I paused. The time had come. Sitting down across from Grace, I reached over and took her hand, patting it as she so recently had caressed mine before I set forth with Sam Sandison to Section 37. "There is a complicating circumstance, unhappily." If I knew any-thing in this world, it was that the Chicago gambling mob was going to be angrily curious about the major betting loss in some outpost of the Rockies. So it had to be said, and pats of the hand did not really soften it: "I must move on."

A goodbye to a good woman costs a piece of the soul, and having already paid once when I departed from Rose in that earlier time, not much was left in me after I spoke this one. The old feeling of leaving love behind came back like a terrible ache; pernicious bachelorhood was no joking matter. With regret I watched Grace's face, so near and yet so far, for the effect of my news. I hoped she was not going to cry, because that affliction is catching. But there was a glisten as her eyes met mine. Her chin came up an inch in the Butte way, and I was bracing myself for a landlady-like farewell when she uttered instead:

"Morrie? I've never seen any of the world except Butte. I—I want to go with you."

Something like a galvanic shock went through me. Could I have heard right? Her tremulous look took the question away. Mutely I gestured to the two vacant spots at the table.

Those she took care of with boardinghouse dispatch. "Griff and Hoop could scrape by on their own. They pretty much run the place anyway."

Still wordless, I touched a finger to skin.

"No sign of hives whatsoever," she reported bravely, "yet."

"Ah," I recovered my voice. "This is most serious, Grace. We must examine this matter before we do anything rash. Let us say you board the train with me tomorrow—"

She nodded tensely.

"—in full sight of this town and everyone you have ever known—"

She could not help sending a lip-biting glance toward the wedding photograph of Arthur Faraday, on duty at the sideboard.

"—in which case," I finished, "we should perhaps do it as man and wife."

Grace blinked.

"Or, if you prefer," I spread my hands in offer, "woman and husband."

My proposal took full effect. She covered her mouth with her hand as if a hiccup wanted out. When the hand came away, there was a rosy glow of anticipation on her face, dimple and all. "You mean it?"

"I do. As you shall hear me repeat at an altar, if you so wish."

"Grace *Morgan?*" she tested out with a lilt very close to music. "I'll need to make a clean start on the name."

I gave her a smile that went back to the beginning before this one. "You wouldn't be the first."

Acknowledgments

My imagined Butte and its Richest Hill and Morrie's beloved library could not have taken shape in these pages without the unflinching help of librarians in the right places: Rich Aarstad, Ellie Arguimbau, Karen Bjork, Jodie Foley, Lory Morrow, Barbara Pepper-Rotness, Brian Shovers, and Zoe Ann Stoltz of the Montana Historical Society; Anne M. Mattioli and Christine Call of the Butte–Silver Bow Public Library; and Sandra Kroupa, Rare Book Curator of the University of Washington Libraries. My heartfelt thanks to them all.

I'm similarly indebted to the cadre of talented souls who vitally aided in one way or another in the making of this book: Liz Darhansoff, Charles Hulin, Marshall J. Nelson, Becky Saletan, Elaine Trevorrow, Marcella Walter, Mark Wyman; and Carol Doig, this lucky thirteenth time.